A HEART OF SALT & SILVER

ELEXIS BELL

A Heart of Salt & Silver

By Elexis Bell

This is a work of fiction. Resemblance to actual persons, living or dead, is purely coincidental.

Copyright 2019

ISBN: 978-1-951335-10-6

Eager to stay up to date on the latest dark fiction from Elexis Bell?

Sign up for her newsletter at: www.elexisbell.com

HARTA
N
W
E
S
GLOWFLY MIGRATION
RETTLAND
IOR
ROARN
BAMON
NESS CABIN
The Forest of Immortals
EVERSON
EVAYLA

Table of Contents

Chapter 1
Ness

I lay back in the grass, spreading my red hair out around my shoulders. But I keep my true form concealed. My eyes are a simple blue, not their natural, conspicuous gold. My skin is merely pale, and no horns protrude from my skull. For all intents and purposes, I appear human.

Birds flit from branch to branch above me, and the setting sun shines bright beyond my closed eyelids. I consider revealing my true form, knowing the sense of freedom it would bring, but the birds would scatter in the thunderous cacophony that follows.

They sound so nice… Chirping and singing freely…

I drag my hand through the long blades of grass and open my eyes to peer at the branches which crisscross overhead. Light picks its way through the leaves to dapple the ground. To my right, the earth rises, and the forest holds fast against gravity, climbing up Mount Surm. But here, the ground is level. This perfect little clearing seems to have been made just to while away the hours.

A seldom-reached sense of peace spreads through me.

My hand goes to my necklace, as it so often does, and *his* eyes appear in my mind. Dark and smoldering, surrounded by long lashes. They send waves of warmth through me. I can still see the way he used to smile at me, lopsided, always as if we were sharing some inside joke.

Only... We don't really smile at each other anymore. Not for almost an entire season, now.

My damned heart just can't forget him, though. I see him in my dreams, hear his name whispering through my thoughts. A twinge of pain twists my heart.

Nolan…

I still think of how we felt together, the heat that bloomed over my skin when he touched me, when he kissed me. Even now, I crave him.

My fingers caress the little knob on the side of the disk of my necklace, raising and lowering the sundial to release the excess tension building within me. But it does no good.

I drop the necklace he made me, and it falls heavily upon my skin. I slide my hand down, gently, slowly, over my breast. I pretend that the touch is his, and for a moment, a thrill of pleasure slips down my spine.

But without his weight on me, the illusion soon falls flat, leaving me wanting.

Voices stir in the distance, coming closer, and my hand falls away. It lands with a thud at my side. Frustration boils to the surface, never far from reach considering what I am. My skin tingles, and my jaw clenches.

Growing louder as they draw near, three men shout. Bursting through a wall of underbrush, one man tumbles into the clearing. Seething, I prop myself up on bare elbows and stare at him.

Instinct begs me to reveal my true self, to eviscerate him for disturbing me. My hands clench. But I restrain myself.

Scrambling to his feet, the man tries to flee his pursuers. His light brown hair does its best to flutter in the wind, but it's far too short. Vivid green eyes sparkle with urgency, even as his fear turns the air in the clearing acrid.

My blood quickens.

Two more men explode from the brush, and one of them slams into their prey. Tumbling to the ground, they tussle, each reaching for weapons as they fight.

The overly crisp scent of the undying wafts through the air, meandering over to my nose. No mortal could discern it. Yet, the reek of bourbon tells me that one of the men is a vampire, namely the one driving a dagger into the stomach of the green-eyed man.

Gaining tentative control of my anger, I deny myself the visual of their fight. With a single motion, I take control of their weapons. Two daggers and a sword lift into midair, one dagger pulling itself from the flesh of Green Eyes as it flies upward.

But the pursuers hold fast to their weapons, and I lift them into the air with their blades, merely raising my arm. Rising to my feet, skirts tickling my legs as they slip over my skin, I watch as one man, the vampire's pledge, releases his sword. He falls only a short distance.

In an instant and with no more than a single, sweeping motion, I use my other hand to push the compliant men to the edge of the clearing. Green Eyes and the pledge skid across the ground until their backs find bark. With a twirling motion, I use one finger to call forth sufficient Nether to tie them to the tree trunks they rest against.

In the center of the clearing, floating far above their heads, the vampire still clings to his dagger. The blood of the green-eyed man drips from the blade to the vampire's head, soaking into short, blonde hair.

Lifting my arm just a touch higher, I say, "I'd let go if I were you."

Dropping my arm, I watch the vampire nearly collide with the earth before I jerk my hand back up into the air. The hilt of the dagger slips free of his grasp, and he falls, landing with a thud.

I don't even bother pretending I don't enjoy the look of terror on his face. A smile lights up my pale face, and I breathe deeply of his fear. He gets to his feet quickly, but I secure him to a tree with no trouble. Silence fills the clearing, but only for a moment.

Reclining against a tree trunk behind me, held up only by the Nether which binds him, Green Eyes coughs. I spin, and my eyes focus on his black shirt. A dark, shining stain spreads slowly across the fabric, leaking from his stomach.

My heart races, and I inhale deeply. The sharp metallic scent of life mingles with undercurrents of cedar and sap.

Unusual for a mortal…

My eyes narrow, and he has the sense to drop his gaze to the ground.

His chest rises and falls unsteadily, too quickly. His heart beats shakily in his chest, resonating with the Nether and stammering in my ears. He apparently knows enough to realize he's outmatched.

I tear my eyes from the blood. Normally, my kind would have no problem with violence among mortals. Not that I'm at all like most of my kind, and not that these are mere mortals squabbling over trivial matters.

But a perfectly relaxing day has been ruined, a thing which mustn't go unpunished.

My hands clench. I take a deep breath, reminding myself of Kirk, the Knight who raised me, and all his lessons in morality.

What would he think of this?

"Unhand us, witch!" the vampire shouts.

The mortals, apparently far smarter than this vampire, remain silent. Even the vampire's own pledge seals his lips shut. A wave of Nether wafts off him, marking him as a Nether witch.

But fury sparks within me, and a dark grin overtakes me. I lower my arm, setting the blades down gently in the middle of the clearing.

"What was that?" I ask, daring the vampire to repeat himself.

Stupidly enough, he does. "I said, 'unhand us, witch!' Let us go quickly, and I might not kill you."

Arrogant fool.

I laugh quietly, and all the birds fly away, deserting their treetop perches. A dangerous glint shines in my eyes as I saunter within arm's reach.

"Witch? You think me a witch?"

"How else could a pitiful, puny little woman like *you* do all this?" He jerks his head at the other two men, unable to move his arms. Cheeks flushed with anger, he draws back and spits in my face, dark eyes flashing, all the while.

Nearby animals sense my anger reverberating on the Nether, and the woods fall completely silent. Fury roils within me, and visions of blood fill my mind. Everything in me demands his evisceration.

Or perhaps the removal of some limbs…

With eyes narrowed, I lift one hand. He flinches, and I smile, baring my teeth. His spit floats into the air, leaping happily from my skin. My spine shivers with disgust and hatred as I force the spit to smear itself over the vampire's face, over his eyes.

Slowly twirling one finger, I tighten his bonds. Air rushes from his lungs, and his soft face goes red as he struggles to breathe.

"You underestimate me. I don't know a single witch who can do everything I've done without at least three days of spell and potion preparation. Not to mention the difficulty of lugging all those ingredients out here."

Lifting one average looking fingernail to his face, I trace one of his cheekbones, then the other, splitting the skin wide. A line drawn down the center of his nose, from bridge to tip, releases still more blood.

My eyes flutter as the darkest parts of me savor the sight.

"As for spitting on me," I whisper, knowing my voice will carry to the others, echoing in their bones despite its low volume, "that was a grave mistake. Most of my kind would have killed you on the spot, simply for the disturbance."

Voice suddenly a hiss, I say, "You're lucky I've learned patience."

My soul riots for revenge, and my blood boils in my veins. I fight the damnable words, hating my own weakness before my rage, but still, I say, "But ignorance must not go to seed. Your family line will end with you. You will never again create, or prolong, life."

And I shift the Nether to make it so.

"Your kind? What are you talking about? What makes you think *you* can curse *me*?" All bluff and bluster, the vampire tries to appear brave and defiant.

But I feel the fear leaking off him. I smell it in his blood, acrid and spoiled. I hear it in his sputtering heartbeat, slightly more erratic than those of the others.

Again, I say nothing. Drawing a deep breath, I close my eyes slowly.

Thunder roars through the clearing, rumbling in all our chests. I open my eyes, glittering gold sending light reflecting back at the vampire, and my skin grows paler. Fingernails become golden talons, embedded in black skin which reveals hues of purple as it fades to white just above my wrist. My eyelids are colored similarly, pulsing with the Nether that reaches out through my skin.

Black horns burst from my skull, sticking through locks of deepest red. My horns twist as they taper off, curling back over the top of my head.

The color drains from the vampire's face, concealed as it is by his blood. Sick glee spikes through me.

"Did you know you would *feel* my revelation in your blood? Did you know the very air would tremble with it?" I ask, knowing the answer to be a resounding "no."

"You're a..." he trails off, unable to speak for lack of air.

"Demi-demon is, I believe, the word you're looking for," I say, smiling malevolently. "Now, I'm going to untether you, and you're going to run. Before I change my mind."

He nods, still gasping for air. Blood drips from his drawn face, landing on the grass beneath him. I keep my eyes from following its progress or tracing how it spreads over the leaves of the clovers at his feet. Shivering with suppressed rage, I stare through his brown eyes, right into his damned soul. He shrinks from my gaze, and I lift my chin, lips curling into a satisfied smile.

Stepping back, I stand near the pile of confiscated weapons. My hands itch to do more. My heart cries out for vengeance for such a slight.

I lift one hand, and all three men flinch. My smile spreads wider, revealing fangs far sharper than those of the vampire. Though I know I'll hate myself for it later, for the moment, I delight in their fear.

Twirling my finger in the opposite direction, I release the vampire and his pledge from their bonds. Gulping air, they run for their lives.

"We're just going to run?" the pledge asks, though with more curiosity than fear.

The vampire hisses through rivers of blood, "For now."

Awesome. That sounds promising.

Behind me, the wounded man waits.

Turning to face him, I take in his appearance. A bit of scruff decorates his jaw. Dark eyebrows and tan skin frame shining green eyes. Simple clothes stretch tight over a well-honed physique.

Not that his muscles did much good to ward off a dagger.

No words cross his lips. He stares up at me, part fear and part awe. It's a strange mixture, but not one I've never seen before.

Again, I twirl my finger in the air, releasing his Nether binding, and he slumps against the tree.

Several deep breaths quell the desire to finish him off. Still more chase away the vastly different images of him beneath me, positioned between my legs to drive Nolan from my mind, just for a while.

I blink once more and conceal my true form so that nearby animals may feel at ease. For all the world, I appear to be a normal human woman.

Jaw dropping, he presses a hand to his side and leans his head back against the tree.

"Can you walk?" I ask.

"I'll manage," he answers, deep voice coarse with pain.

"And your name?"

"Elias." His voice comes out strained.

A small part of me wants to heal him. Whether it's my half-human heart, the morals instilled in me by the Knight who raised me, or the years I've spent working at self-control, I can't be sure. Perhaps it's my stupid, overly emotional, half-demon heart sympathizing with him. Regardless of the cause, I want to take away his pain.

And yet, another, darker part of me wonders what the ground beneath him would look like dyed red with his blood.

"I'm Ness," I say, concealing my dilemma carefully. "How about some tea?"

Chapter 2
Nolan

The sea rushes against the bow of the ship, and Ness' hand tightens around mine. She's never crossed the sea before, never been aboard a boat, at all.

Lucky, 'tis no more than a two-day trip.

Rettland isn't quite so far as it feels, most of the time. Excitement builds within me, and not just because I'm returning to my homeland.

She's goin' wit me.

That makes it far more exciting than any of my previous trips, spreading my lips in a wide smile.

Ness grins as she watches the dolphins swimming alongside the boat, and her shining red hair whips about her face. Her blue eyes are alight with joy.

If only they could shine liquid gold... But no' here.

She looks up at me, pushing the hair from her face.

"I told yeh, 'tis bett'r ta tie it back," I say, teasing.

She reaches up, and unties my long hair, letting the wind take the ribbon. Dark waves fly madly about my face.

"I don't seem to remember such a warning," she says.

Stepping closer, Ness puts her hands on my chest. My heart skips far too many beats, and I know she can hear it. The devilish glint in her eyes is evidence enough that she listens for it.

My hands find her waist, pulling her against me, and the world falls away. The boat, the call of the birds flying overhead, the splash of the dolphins leaping from the water… They all disappear.

She pushes the hair back from my face, knotting her fingers in my unruly curls.

Inching forward, my eyes fall shut. I brush my lips over hers, moving from side to side and loving the way her chest rises and falls, pressing against mine. Our lips part and her breath is hot. We crash together, amidst the wind and the spray of the sea.

The sight of her blurs, and the feel of her against me is ripped from my mind. My hands ache to feel her, to pull her tight against me. My soul yearns for her eyes, gazing into mine.

Spinning through blackness, I'm torn from one memory and tossed into another.

I lie with Ness on a blanket in the grass, staring up at the trees. The ocean wind blows through birch trees, struggling to reach us. Their trunks and branches huddle together, sparing us the worst of the cold night breeze. Waves break upon the base of the cliff beyond the trees. The coming night chases rays of orange and pink from the sky, and anticipation builds within me.

A glance at Ness finds her staring at me, all amber eyes and dark horns in this secluded spot, mostly at my urging. It will keep the animals at bay, preventing them from disturbing the glowflies.

At least, that's the practical reason I gave her, the one that brooks no argument. Really, I just love to see her like this, the way she's meant to be. Not ashamed or hiding.

Her fingers lace into mine, and my thumb caresses her skin. Fire dances through my veins, surging up my arm and spreading through the rest of my body. I ache to kiss her but know I must wait. I've got the whole thing planned.

It wouldna do ta get impatient, an' mess the whole thin' up.

So, I wait.

My eyes find hers, and we smile at each other. The purest happiness I've ever seen sparkles in her liquid gold eyes, putting even the stars above, just now winking into existence, to shame. My breath catches in my throat.

I hope she likes this… 'Tis one o' my favorite mem'ries o' Rettland, my favorite mem'ry o' my whole childhood.

My insides a tangle of nerves, I chuckle silently, recalling the danger I once put myself in to see this. After Harta invaded Rettland, after one of the soldiers enslaved my entire family, I still snuck out to come here.

'Twas rather foolish. Not that I'd trade the mem'ry ta avoid the beatin' I got. Dinna get ta see this again fer years, after that.

Swallowing nervously, my eyes flicker between her eyes and her lips. A single lock of red hair falls across her face, and I reach over with my free hand to push it back behind her ear. My hand lingers on the side of her face, thumb moving gently over her cheek. I trace her jaw, and the corners of my mouth lift into a smile.

"Thank you, for bringing me here," she says, voice wistful. "It's so beautiful…"

"Yeh've no' seen a thin' yet."

A small flash of vivid blue stirs above us, catching our attention. On another branch, a male glowfly answers the female's quick burst of light. His own wings, much larger than those of the female, nearly the size of my palm, slowly come to life. They hold the brightest blue I've ever seen for several seconds before gently fading out.

Gradually, the birch trees come to life, with bursts and slow fades of arctic blue decorating their limbs. In time, the males desert their perches, seeking females, their softly glowing wings looking like so many shooting stars brought to earth.

Ness gasps, her hand tightening on mine.

I pull my gaze from the sky which has fallen around us and watch her, instead. Wonder and joy shine brilliantly in her eyes. Her mouth hangs open, black lips parted beautifully. She draws a deep breath and turns to look at me.

Smiling wide, eyes beaming, Ness scoots closer and nestles into my side. I move my arm to wrap around her, and her head fits perfectly on my shoulder. Her hand traces burning patterns on my chest, chasing my heart into my throat.

For a long time, we just lay there, watching the mesmerizing glowflies floating above us. I know I've got to speak. The glowflies will all be partnered soon. This display only lasts half an hour.

I canna miss my chance…

But my heart lodges itself in my throat, choking back the words. It flutters nervously, and I know she hears it. Even if her head weren't resting on my chest, she'd hear it.

Tipping her head up, she meets my gaze. A smile brightens her face, and her eyes practically glow with it, set as they are against the black and purple skin of her eyelids.

My breath catches, yet again.

She props herself up on one elbow, looking down at me, and suddenly the stars beyond the canopy and the twinkling glowflies frame her. I swallow hard, and my hand finds the soft skin of her neck. Her heart beats strong beneath my palm.

Jus' say it.

"I love you," I whisper, voice husky.

Her jaw drops, but she closes it quickly. Though she smiles deeply, sadness moves behind her eyes.

I smooth back a few locks of hair which have fallen forward, waiting. Time stands still. Yet, when she speaks, it is not the response I wish for.

"How?" She shakes her head, brows furrowing. Her voice breaks as she asks, "Why? I'm just…"

Her eyes fall to her hand, now motionless on my chest. She pulls back.

Pain lances through my chest, and I rise onto one elbow. With our faces just inches apart, I touch her neck. Resting my forehead against hers, my eyes flutter between her eyes and lips.

"Because yeh're stronger than anyone I've ever met."

Her eyes are nearly closed, unable to meet mine.

I slide my hand to rest just beneath her collarbone. "Because yer heart is more pow'rful than any magic."

Letting my hand rise so that my thumb may trace her lips, I say, "Because yer soul is kinder and more passionate than I could've ev'r expected."

Finally, she meets my gaze, and gold swims behind a sheen of tears. "But I'm… me…" she gulps painfully.

"Tha's the point," I say, inching closer. "I wouldna have yeh any oth'r way."

She brushes her nose against mine, softly, and slides her hand up my chest. Shivers course through me, and my lips part. Taking a deep breath, I relish the scent of wood smoke, the scent of her.

"Are you… sure?" she asks, voice still broken by unshed tears.

"I've nev'r been more sure." My lips whisper over hers as I speak.

The fire that always pulls us together in a writhing tangle of passion now burns deeper, churning in my belly. I brush my lips over hers, and she parts them.

When we finally come together, mouths melding, the usual cataclysmic intensity rumbles at a softer pace. Our bodies yearn to join, and our hearts ache for it.

But we move slowly.

I lean her back onto the blanket and kiss her neck gently. Her hand slides down over my back, nails trailing over my spine, and my body quakes.

Flowing like molten rock, we move together without the usual power struggle. This time, Ness lets me show her just how much I truly do love her. Gentle touches and achingly sweet kisses guide us.

Her hand quests over my stomach and slips around to the small of my back. Our mouths move together, and she tugs at my bottom lip with her teeth, careful not to bite too hard. A moan escapes me, and I grasp her thigh tightly.

Flushed with desire, she wraps her legs around me as I move deep inside her. She arches her back, pressing her chest against mine. Hearts racing, our breath comes in short bursts.

Voice low and breathy, she gasps, "Nolan…" Her eyes hold mine, heavy-lidded.

I kiss her neck, so softly that I ache. My arm slips beneath her, wrapping around her waist, and I pull her against me. Bracing myself on my other arm, I ease myself deeper.

She arches, tipping her head back and crying out. Her nails dig into my back, sending luscious waves of pain and pleasure through me.

And suddenly, I can't help myself. My teeth find the flesh at the base of her neck, and I bite down, groaning all the while.

She digs her nails in deeper and shudders against me, giving herself over to the collapse.

And I follow her down.

She pants every bit as much as I do, breathless with all that we've done and all that we've become. I fall onto my side, utterly exhausted, and she turns to face me. After planting a tender kiss on my lips, then my neck, she brushes her lips over my ear.

Finally, she whispers, "I love you too, Nolan."

Her breath is hot on my skin, and her eyes glow with warmth when she pulls back to meet my gaze.

Yet, somehow, my heart is breaking.

The night sky, suddenly starless, falls upon me, shoving me from the dream, the partial memory.

My eyes open to my dark bedroom, only to find my hand searching the other side of the bed for Ness. Agony fills me when I realize she isn't there, hasn't been there in months, and my heart lurches. Fresh anguish pricks at the corners of my eyes as I recall the only part of the dream that never happened.

Ness never told me she loved me.

Chapter 3
Ness

After an exceedingly painstaking trek east, my small cabin appears in the distance, built in yet another level plot of land.

Elias is lucky I'm half-demon. Without the powers I got from my mother, there's no way I would've gotten him back here. Carrying him all that way would've been impossible. Floating him here, not so bad.

I suppress a shrug.

The door opens with a flick of my hand, and I pass him through ahead of me. I lower him onto the bench by the biggest window in the place, and he reclines on the pillows. Lush curtains hang in front of the bench, pulled to one side to allow for seating, though now they conceal his face as I bustle about my cabin.

A few hand gestures, and logs fly into the fireplace. A snap of my fingers, and they ignite, as do the candles spread around my home. Another set of gestures replaces a burnt stick of incense with a new one and ignites it.

A gift from Nolan to help me remember his scent in his absence, incense always comforts me, though I'm running low. I can't exactly ask him for more. I'll have to make a trip to Rettland to get them myself.

Not that they'll be the same...

Meanwhile, Elias stares on in shock. He still bleeds, though not as much.

I combine marigold and lavender blossoms with Echinacea roots and shredded broadleaf plantain leaves in a mortar. Before grinding them up, I use a few flicks of my hands to get a simple chamomile and lavender tea going on the hearth.

"What are you doing?" Elias asks, pushing the red curtains back further and craning his head around to see me. His black tunic shines wetly in the firelight, and I forbid myself from looking directly at the blood.

Glancing over my shoulder at him, I say, "Making a poultice for your side and a tea to help you sleep. If you'd rather condemn your soul to the Netherrealm, I can just heal you with Nether." My lips quirk into a smile before I turn back to my work. "I just assumed you'd prefer this."

A small chuckle, low and musical, escapes his lips, followed quickly by a moan of pain. "Probably for the best to do it this way."

A few moments pass as I work, adding water as necessary and grinding the ingredients to a fine pulp. The tea comes to a boil, and I pour it into two cups. It won't have as much of an effect on me as it will on him.

It'll still be nice, though.

"Why are you helping me?" Elias asks.

I glance at him again, only to realize he's been staring at me for a while. I inhale deeply, feeling the blood rush through me just knowing his eyes have been drawn to me. Then, a deeper, shameful blush colors me. Because he isn't Nolan.

Not that Nolan wants me, anymore. I messed that up.

Just like I mess up everything…

"Because I'm only half demon," I say, keeping my thoughts to myself. My voice dips in volume, as I continue, "I do have a conscience."

He seems to consider this and falls silent.

Elias surely doubts this since I cursed a man with sterility today after cutting his face open. But he did spit on me. And it's far better than what I thought of doing…

If Kirk were alive to have seen it, would he have been proud? Or disappointed?

He was typically kind and extremely patient. He's the only reason I didn't fall to the mercy of my strengthened instincts and desires, the only reason I built up my impulse control. If he hadn't been the one around when I was young, I'd be a very different person, today.

As usual, thoughts of him bring me low, and I'm suddenly glad I thought to pour two cups of tea. It'll ease a bit of the sadness, smooth the edge, so to speak.

Gathering everything on a tray, I meander to the table, purposefully within arm's reach of the bench seat Elias rests upon. I set the tray down and drag a chair next to him.

Handing one cup to Elias, I prompt him to drink. His hands catch my attention, and my eyes linger on long fingers, tracing the scars which adorn his skin. He drinks deeply, trusting that what I've offered will be no worse than the wound in his side, though I could certainly put him through the wringer.

When he meets my gaze, I find myself transfixed. Long lashes surround piercing green, lustrous and smoldering, all at the same time. Granted, the smoldering bit could just be tightness from pain, rather than lust. I deftly avoid breathing in the scent of his blood to determine which, knowing either answer will leave me wanting.

Forcing myself to the task at hand, I glance at the things I've arranged upon the table for him and realize that, of course, I forgot to bring a bowl of water and a rag. A few hand motions bring them forth from the kitchen, and they land easily in my hands.

"I bet that comes in handy," Elias says awkwardly.

I smile. I hear that line every time I take someone in. Somehow, the pun isn't amusing, anymore.

"Let me see your side."

Nodding, he places his cup on the window ledge and tries to sit forward to lift his shirt. Several grimaces twist his face, and his cheeks redden with the effort.

I stuff down the sick glee of watching a human struggle, along with the guilt that comes swiftly on its heels. Instead, I listen to the part of me that Kirk helped bring to the forefront, so many years ago.

After setting the bowl and rag on the table, I lean over Elias and lift his shirt for him. My fingers graze his skin, feeling the tense muscle beneath it. His breath quickens, and I hear his heartbeat pounding, hard and fast.

His eyes seek mine, burning with intensity. Again, I tell myself not to seek the reason, be it fear or lust.

In my mind though, I see myself atop him in a quick glance of what we could be.

Then, I blink the image away, knowing it can never happen. An act such as that would damn his soul faster than healing him, and I've caused more than enough trouble in my life already.

Rushing in to fill the gap, memories of my times with Nolan surge through me. The power struggle and the heat, the sweetness of his touch and the delicacy of his breath, hot on my skin. His dark eyes peering into me, really seeing me and never shying away from what I am.

I can still feel Nolan's hand clutching my naked hip and sliding around to grasp my buttock. In my mind, I see my hands in his long, dark hair, pulling his lips to my chest as I tip my head back. For a split second, I watch as we move together in my memories, lips finding each other to melt into one as our bodies merge.

My heart skips a few beats, and my breath catches. I roll my shoulders to work out the tension.

Elias sees my reaction but can't possibly know the real cause. A shy smile spreads over his face.

No good can come of that...

Ready to move on, I help him lean back and drape his shirt over the back of my chair.

Wetting the rag, I dab at his side, cleaning away the blood to see the wound better. The feel of his skin beneath my hands, broken or not, brings a rush of heat to my face. As I administer the poultice, I busy myself with talk, hoping it will be distraction enough to force my unruly body into submission.

"So, what're you doing out here, anyway?"

"Well, my sister is getting married…" Elias trails off.

"So, naturally, you headed for the hills, as anyone would." I offer a sarcastic smile. "Is she a demanding bride?"

"No, no. Nothing like that." A nervous laugh punctuates his words. "You see, our mom told us our dad died when we were little, just two and three years old. But a few days ago, I found a letter she was going to send him about the wedding, and she found me reading it. He's not dead."

Bitterness creeps into his words as he continues, "He just left us. So now, I'm on my way to talk to him."

"And he lives in *this* forest?" I say, skeptical. "This isn't exactly a safe place for mortals. He may actually be dead."

My hands still on his side. "Hard to believe *that's* the silver lining here," I scoff.

Our eyes meet for a moment before I resume my work, plopping dollops of poultice onto his wound and smudging it around to make sure it covers well.

"The two bandits that ran me down seem to be managing just fine out here," he says. He winces as I pull the skin to the side so the thick salve can make its way inward.

"They weren't exactly mortal, and they certainly weren't just trying to rob you." Not for the first time, I wonder how mortals survive, as oblivious as they are.

"Really?"

"One was a vampire, the one that spit on me," I say, pursing my lips. "The other was his pledge, a vampire-to-be. He *reeked* of Nether magic, too."

"And the vampire stabbed me because…?"

"I guess I shouldn't be surprised you don't know this since most mortals don't survive meetings with them, but vampires are vain creatures. They play with their victims, just because they can."

Then, for a frame of reference, I add, "Sort of like cats."

A small chuckle escapes Elias' lips, and I smile.

He lifts his cup from the ledge and takes another long pull of the soothing tea. His shoulders rise and fall with a deep breath, puffing out his chest. He grimaces at the stab of pain when his wound is pulled apart, but not as much as he would have moments ago.

The tea and salve are working. Again, my lips lift into a smile.

Kirk would definitely be proud of this.

Silly as it is, my spirits always lift when I do something I know he'd approve of. I'm not sure if it's the intrinsic value of doing something good or knowing that I'm strong enough to overcome what I am. Regardless, it's a strong motivator.

"Well," Elias says, voice slow and drowsy, "either way, dear old dad is probably alive. He isn't quite mortal, either. He's part of the Pack."

I nod, finally understanding the scent in his blood. "Makes sense, now," I mutter.

"What does?"

"You smell just a bit like a werewolf."

Elias shakes his head, confused. "What do they smell like?"

"Like the woods," I say, dabbing a bit more of the poultice onto his side. "They all smell like different parts of it, but you," I glance at his eyes for a second, "smell like cedar and sap. But only faintly. Vampires, if you were curious, tend to smell like types of alcohol."

He purses his lips, considering this strange revelation, and we fall silent for a moment.

"Anyway, walking out on family doesn't exactly fit with the Pack," I say, setting the mortar on the table. Cleaning the salve from my fingers, I go on. "Loyalty and blood are big deals to them. He probably died. You'd be better off going home."

Then, I say, "You know, before *you* die out here."

He laughs, deeper and more wistful. Silence descends on us yet again, and I use the time to wrap his stomach, helping him to sit forward as I do. He only groans a bit.

Shaking his head, he says, "I have to find out for sure. I've got to see them. If it were you, if you were in my shoes, would you go?"

I try desperately not to think of a certain night in my past, one filled with terrible mistakes, disappointment, and far too much blood. My voice eludes me, choked by the regret of having summoned my own mother, once. It all flashes before my eyes, but I blink it away as quickly as I can.

Pain stabs my heart, twisting my insides into knots.

I merely nod, grateful that my hands are no longer on him. They shake, ever so slightly, resting on my lap. I'd rather not have to relive that evening to tell him about it, and I get the feeling he'd ask if he noticed my trembling fingers.

When I finally compose myself, thankful that the tea has made him groggy enough not to notice my lapse, I say, "I'll escort you, then. It's about time I pay Nolan and Liam a visit anyway. I haven't seen them in a while. Catching up will be nice."

I notice my tea-induced slip too late, and his name, spoken aloud, stings me.

Elias breathes deeply, chest rising and falling gently as he nods.

"Thank you," he whispers.

"Get some sleep," I say, rising to clear away the mess.

Chapter 4
Elias

The world blinks in and out of focus, and it takes me a moment to realize it's only my eyes blinking.

Whatever was in that tea was strong.

Then, it all hits me, and I open my eyes completely. Lush red curtains hang to my left, brushing against my face as a gentle breeze catches them, and light streams through the window to my right. Birds chirp happily in the trees outside. The mountain rises sharply beyond Ness' garden.

The smell of wood smoke drifts from the hearth to fill the cabin, lazily mingling with the smell of various herbs, hung in bundles throughout the place to dry. My eyes search for the demi-demon who saved my life just yesterday, but I find only a house that perfectly embodies what I've seen of her so far.

Beautiful red curtains of crushed velvet adorn every window, and candles rest on most surfaces. Exotic sticks of incense burn here and there, expensive imports from Rettland. A few burned out long ago, but two burn, now. Swirls of fragrant smoke twirl from them, dancing in the sunlight streaming through open windows.

A few tomes perch on shelves in the sitting room, and still more sit on a countertop in the kitchen, eagerly awaiting page-turning fingers. Pressed leaves and flowers stick out between their pages, lending themselves to the assumption that these books taught Ness how to make potions and salves.

My sister, Alva, would love to see those. They're not the same ones she used to learn the trade, and likely contain a few things her books do not.

Jewelry hangs from bottlenecks, spilling over the shelves they rest upon to dangle in the air below them. I recognize some of the pendants' designs as belonging to the Knights of Evayla, Harta, and Rettland, while others are tokens for various Gods.

A few beg the wearer to summon the demon they symbolize.

The cabin breathes with a life of its own, softened by fabrics which hang loosely from window frames and doorways. The wood feels old, grounding the place in a way that freshly built homes can only hope to achieve much later in their lives.

It feels genuine. Earthy and heavy in its significance, the place sets me at ease, despite its exceedingly dangerous occupant.

Though, she isn't at all what I expected of a demi-demon.

Speak of the devil.

Steaming mug of tea in hand, she enters the main room, sauntering out of what I assume to be her bedroom. Her emerald green nightgown dips low, scooping well below her collar bones. The front of the hem doesn't reach her knees, but it sweeps down to drag the stone floor behind her. Pale legs draw the eye, pulling my attention from the shining satin with ease.

Beautiful blue eyes hold my gaze when my own eyes drift away from her legs. Her face glows with a mischievous smile.

My chest fills with a deep breath, and it catches there. My side aches where the vampire's blade split my skin, but not so bad as expected. Eventually, I remember to exhale, pushing air past my heart, which has firmly lodged itself in my throat.

For a moment, I wonder why she's chosen this form. For a few moments longer, I find myself wishing she wouldn't, longing for the lustrous, exotic gold her eyes could be.

Should be.

Swallowing, I say, "Good morning."

"Don't you mean good afternoon?" she quips, breezing past me to the kitchen.

I spare a glance for the woods outside, trying to glean the time from the sun's position, but the trees make it difficult.

"I suppose so," I say.

In seconds, she's back at my side, offering me a mug of warm tea. "Don't worry," she says. "This one won't knock you out. It's just normal tea."

I take it without question, assuming she would have killed me by now if that were her aim. I shuffle from reclining to sitting with a great deal less agony than should be present and take a long drink. The hot liquid soothes and gentles as it flows through me.

Ness busies herself in the kitchen, hidden from view by the curtains beside my head. The sounds of cabinets opening and closing and the clatter of dishes and knives being taken out and placed upon the counter fill the place. She soon returns to my side with a tray of food. A few slices of bread, an assortment of jams, and a small jar of butter sit atop it.

"I'd offer you more, but I'd rather not upset your stomach. Your body's been through a lot. Better take it easy for a bit," she apologizes.

I happily slather a few slices with elderberry jam. I open my mouth to assure her that apologies aren't necessary, but she goes on.

"The salve will make quick work of that wound, though. A few days, maybe?" Bustling about, gathering up the poultice and more linen, she adds, "After that, we can get you to the Pack."

I take a bite, and she comes to sit in the chair she pulled near me last night.

"Then, you can be their problem," she says, voice light and teasing.

Despite the bite of jelly laden bread, I chuckle, careful to keep my mouth closed in the process. Easy conversation compliments my meal, and she waits patiently for me to finish eating. Her eyes dip occasionally to my bare chest, sending heat rushing through me despite the placid expression on her face.

After all, she's looking, isn't she?

The feel of her hands on my stomach, unwrapping the bandages from last night, makes my skin tingle. Her hands are gentle, cleaning the wound efficiently and applying more of the poultice.

Struggling to get myself under control lest I make an ass of myself, I ask, "Are we close to the Pack?"

Laughing, she says, "Nowhere near them. You must have gotten turned around. That, or you started out *very* far from them."

She leans close to wrap me up again, and her luscious red hair spills over her shoulders to tickle my chest. She passes the linen behind my back, bringing our faces close, and my eyes fall to her lips.

"You'll be stuck with me for a while," she says, voice low. "Unless you'd rather go it alone."

I shake my head, dislodging my gaze from her lips.

Rationally, I know I should go on alone. Traveling with her… I'm bound to slip up. At some point, I know I'll make her angry. I may not be so lucky as the vampire. Sure, he got his face cut up and was smacked with a pretty hefty curse. But she could've killed him.

She could easily kill me.

And I know that.

Of course, that's saying nothing of the pull of her, the magnetism.

I have to wonder if she's drawing me in intentionally. But there's her assumption that I'd rather be in pain for a few days, suffering through traditional healing rather than letting her simply heal me, all for the sake of my soul…

If she cares about damning me to the Netherrealm, she wouldn't be using the call on me. Which means this reaction is all me.

An even more frightening prospect, somehow. I swallow hard.

The words fall from my lips without my permission, not that I would have stopped them, given the chance. "I'd rather have you along." To save a bit of face, I clear my throat and add, "You know, in case any more vampires come along."

Tying off the linen, Ness nods. Without another word, she's up and clearing away the dishes from my meal.

***

Sitting in the garden behind Ness' house, quite comfortable on a bed of pillows she arranged specifically for me, I watch her harvest a plethora of fruits and vegetables. She kneels in the dirt, caring naught for the smudges it leaves on her dark trousers or the dust collecting on the hem of her long tunic.

Birds sing freely in the trees all around this oasis, and the sun shines bright through the canopy. Bits of light flicker over my skin, alternately chasing shadows and receding from them. For a moment, I close my eyes, at peace in the warmest place I could have found within this forest.

Immortal beings have made this place their home for centuries, taking advantage of the sanctuary provided by trees and mountain alike. By and large, they seek company with each other more often than with mortals. The more malicious of them, vampires and demi-demons being rather high on that list, come out when they wish to inflict a bit of pain.

I glance at Ness, her pale hands plucking a plump strawberry from the vine.

What made her so… forgiving? So patient?

So well-contained?

I suppress a chuckle, realizing the irony of my descriptors. To describe a demi-demon as such is tantamount to idiocy.

And yet, anything else would fall short of the mark. She's been kinder to me than most humans likely would be. She took me in, fed me, treated my wounds. All without question.

For a moment, my mind recalls the feel of her hands on my bare skin as she dressed my side. The heat which flowed freely through my body comes back to soothe my muscles. Again, I see her eyes, so close to mine, her lips even closer.

Clearing my mind, I shift on the pillows. I reroute my thoughts, but only slightly. Still, I wonder at her, just not in the same way.

After all, she's offered to escort me through an exceedingly dangerous forest for the sake of saving my life. With no mention of compensation. At least, no mention, as of yet. The trill of fear that pricked my spine through most of yesterday returns now, nipping at my skin and pulling up goosebumps.

Surely, she would have killed me by now if that were her aim. She's gone to great lengths to help me in ways that won't damn my soul. What could she ask of me in return for her aid that would spare me a chance at the Etherrealm?

No possibilities which offer salvation present themselves, so a few, more damning, scenarios flood my mind. I imagine leaning in a bit closer when she dresses my wound later, brushing my lips to hers. I picture myself pulling her atop my lap, staring into those wonderful amber eyes…

Clearing my throat, I shift again on the pillows.

Opting for a distraction, I ask her how she learned to make potions.

"Believe it or not," she begins, "you're not the first person to come traipsing through these woods, only to get themselves in trouble."

Plopping a juicy looking berry into her basket, she adds, teasingly, "There are a lot of idiots in the world, after all." Her lips quirk up into a smirk, and one eyebrow lifts.

A hearty laugh bursts from my lips. "Isn't that the truth."

"I was tired of offering ultimatums. You know, healing at the risk of damnation. Plus, I needed a steady way to get some coin. A woman in the Pack taught me a bit, enough to start making basic salves," she says, rising to her full height with a wistful look on her face.

She moves to a different part of the garden and kneels beside a bushy tomato plant. "I used to go into town, just like this," she gestures to her face and hands, "and sell my salves. When I had enough coin, I bought some books to learn more, and it grew from that."

She takes a plump tomato in hand, and it leaps from the vine at her touch. I know, rationally, that it's just nature, that ripe tomatoes fall from the vine easily. But it feels more like that little fruit wants to be in her hand.

Or perhaps, that's just projection.

"Of course, back then, it was a little more nerve-racking to go into town. The Knights were more… vigorous, then," she says.

Suddenly, it strikes me that I have no idea when "back then" really was. She looks young, perhaps younger than I am. But she's immortal. Unless someone kills her, not exactly an easy feat, she'll look exactly like this for the rest of time. Who knows how long it's been since she stopped aging.

For all I know, her "back then" could mean forty or fifty years ago, when the Hartan Empire ruled these lands with iron fists, aggressively tracking and killing Netherspawn. She could mean thirty years ago, when Evaylan citizens rose up, declaring independence.

Or she could mean 100 years ago when Harta first sent soldiers over to conquer Evayla. Perhaps even further back, to the time of the plague.

How much has she seen?

Piercing blue eyes dart upward, meeting mine. My silent reverie was apparently unexpected and conspicuous.

"What is it?" she asks.

"It's just… so easy to forget. That you're not mortal, I mean."

"I suppose," she says, picking a few more tomatoes. "Would you rather I looked like this?" she dares.

She closes her eyes slowly, and thunder rolls through the air. My chest rumbles with the sound, filling and shaking. The trees around us rustle, deserted by birds in their canopies and rabbits and squirrels in the underbrush.

When she opens her eyes, they shine a brilliant gold, and black reaches out over her eyelids, fading to purple, then alabaster at her eyebrows and cheekbones. Horns appear, sprouting from her skull and parting her magnificent red hair as they curve back over her head.

When she raises a hand to pick more fruit, her nails are long and pointed, glittering the same gold as her eyes. Skin as black as ink covers her fingers and fades through the same purple hues as the skin around her eyes. Just past her wrists, it becomes as white as perfect snow.

My breath deserts me. Words fail me completely, and my jaw hangs agape. Blood quickening with fearful desire, I stare.

In this instant, I realize that I like her better this way.

Not that that makes any damn sense.

Suddenly aware of my silence, I bumble out, "Whatever's more comfortable for you." My words are uneven, at best. Quiet and way too husky. Closing my mouth, I swallow back any and all of the stupidity threatening to overflow.

"Well, the animals prefer the more human form. They hate when I switch," she says. "They settle back in eventually, but it unnerves them. So, normally, I just hide."

And with that, she closes and opens her eyes again, shifting back seamlessly.

I find myself longing for her golden eyes. For the horns and the blackened, purple skin. It calls to something deep in my veins.

Perhaps, that's the bit of werewolf blood?

Or, maybe it's because she's a demi-demon. She can use the call. She can bewitch people, almost as easily as her demonic ancestors can.

Chapter 5
Ness

Determined to cut off whatever words may follow Elias' tone, I go on, deftly altering the subject. "The main difference, as far as temperament is concerned," I say, "is that my impulse control is considerably weaker naturally, and my desires are… stronger."

By a long shot.

Leisurely picking fruits and vegetables, I explain.

"Anger always demands revenge. My blood boils for it," I say, consciously pushing away the sight of the vampire's blood dripping over his pale face. I close myself to the scent of it, wafting through my memories.

"Happiness practically *requires* celebration. Lust…" I take a deep breath, letting it hang in the air.

A million images of Nolan float before my eyes. The shadows which trace the muscles honed through hard work, the smolder of his dark eyes so close to mine…

The feel of his hand in my hair, his lips on my skin…

Pointedly, I focus on the plants before me. My skin flushes with a wave of heat, and I do my level best to ignore it.

New images rise to assault my senses, now. I see him smile at me as he wakes, hair a tousled mess. He winks at me, a hundred times over, and my heart melts each time. I watch him run with our friend Liam, playing with Liam's kids, chasing them on the grass between their houses.

Now, I shove away the ache of knowing that nothing will happen with Nolan, again. My heart clenches, and my stomach plummets.

I flinch before the pain, reliving far too many arguments in the course of a second.

But I need to say something.

Where was I?

Nolan always seems to distract me.

Searching through my thoughts, I come up with the thread I'd been following.

Pulling in a long breath through gritted teeth, I say, "With time, and the will to do so, self-control can be learned."

With an arm draped casually over his face, Elias says, "Must be hard to raise a demi-demon."

His tone is idle, clueless to the wound he's just ripped open.

"Very," I answer, gritting my teeth. "Kirk was a good man, though. As patient as I could've hoped for."

Lowering his arm from his face, Elias sits up abruptly, wincing as he does. "Man? Were you raised by a human?"

"Of course," I answer. "All demi-demons are raised by humans. Demons and demonesses aren't exactly interested in being parents. Demons desert their conquests, leaving them to die during the pregnancy. Demonesses bewitch someone to raise their child for them. They're usually banished by the person they bewitch."

Staring at me, openmouthed, Elias asks, "But… How could a human ever survive raising a *demi-demon*?"

"They don't," I say. Regret seeps into my voice, and my face falls. I stare at my hands, motionless on the handle of my basket. Pale skin, once vibrant, appears drawn. Drained of life, I close my eyes. "Kirk *almost* did."

All the air rushes out of me. Someone may as well have punched me in the gut. My heart aches, and I feel it in my bones.

Before Elias can ask what happened, I'm on my feet, basket in hand.

Lifting my other hand, I pull him up into the air with ease. Agony erases the small thrill I would normally experience watching a mortal struggle with the sensation of floating. His limbs flail for just a moment, but this time, no twisted joy seeps into me.

No joy exists within me, at all, twisted or otherwise.

After settling Elias on the window seat and arranging the pillows to his comfort, I set about making tea. I haven't cleaned his wound or redressed it, yet. We haven't even eaten dinner.

But my hands…

Oh, how they shake.

I gather up herbs, little leaves falling between my fingers, and put the water near the fire. My chest constricts, suffocating my heart even as it claws at me.

I see it all, playing out in my mind, again.

My eyes close, and I feel myself startling awake to the sound of a door closing. Twelve years old, I clamor from my bed and wander into the living room of our cottage way up on the mountain. I see the note Kirk left behind, messy handwriting scrawled hurriedly across the page.

He couldn't take it anymore, had to leave.

While he could.

Only the week before, I almost killed him, completely by accident. He bled a lot, but wouldn't let me heal him. We just waited to see whether he'd pull through.

I can still see his blood dripping from his forehead, down over his eyes. It all flashes through my mind, as clearly as if he were here, right now, bleeding in front of me. It mats his dark brown hair to his face in clumps.

I still hear my voice when I sang, calling him back when he tried to abandon me. The lower notes kick in, soft and subtle, almost inaudible beneath the human notes…

My hands still on the cups I was about to pull from the cabinet, and I lean my forehead against the wooden shelf. My heart twists guiltily, for even now, I see him run back through the door, anguished tears streaming over his face, cascading from eyes the warmest brown I've ever seen.

I watch him fall to his knees before a younger me, begging, "Please, let me go. Please!"

But I was selfish, then.

"What's wrong?" Elias asks from the bench, jarring me from my tragic reverie. He's swung his legs over the edge, letting his feet rest on the floor, at some cost to himself. His face scrunches with discomfort. Concern laces his words and pulls his lips downward.

"I was just…"

For a moment, I consider lying, making something up.

But for some reason, the truth comes out. Maybe it's the way his eyes shine in the waning sunlight, looking a whole lot like sympathy. Maybe it's the frown I've put on his face, and now the conscience I've worked so hard to build merely wants me to make that look go away.

Either way, I find myself explaining.

"I was thinking about Kirk."

Closing my eyes, I breathe deeply, damning my demon half. Were it not for that part of me, the emotion of all this would have faded years ago.

Then again, were it not for the demon blood in my veins, Kirk would still be alive.

"He tried to leave when I was twelve, but I didn't want to be alone." My hands desert the cups, and I lean one hip against the counter. Slowly, I turn to face Elias. I can only hold his gaze for a second before I find myself shying away from it.

"I used the call, and he came back. I knew he would, even though he didn't want to. The call doesn't allow for choice, but I didn't care. I just… I didn't want to be alone." My voice breaks.

Staring out the kitchen window of my little cabin, I say, "I've only used the call twice, and I regret both times…"

Again, my eyes fall shut, and I watch the grisly scene play out.

"We were eating dinner a couple of weeks after he tried to leave," I say. "We were laughing at a drawing I made, and for a split second, I thought he might be glad he'd come back. I hadn't hurt him, accidentally or otherwise, since I brought him back. I was careful."

I still hear the footsteps outside, deliberately quiet. I still see the Knights bursting through the door, armed with all the proper tools for my destruction.

"The Knights came for me. I... I should've known they would. And they saw Kirk there... His Knight gear still hung in the corner, though he hadn't worn it since the first year with me. He wasn't even going to take it with him when he tried to leave."

In my mind, I watch them shout at Kirk, calling him a traitor and spitting on him. I watch one of them shove a blade deep into his stomach before I can even move a finger.

"I still dream about it," I whisper. "I still see his blood dripping from their dagger... I still hear him, shouting out, 'Run!'"

For a second, it seemed like he meant it for them.

"But I was angry."

Before my eyes, heads roll. Blood splatters the walls of the cottage high up on the mountain, and bodies fall. They never opened their bags of salt. They never drew their silver blades, none save the one which stabbed Kirk.

The fury of that night boils in my veins to this day.

"When I dream about it, I still hear their bodies hit the floor. I still see their eyes, staring at nothing. I see the blood..."

Strong arms wrap around me, pulling me against a muscled chest. I didn't even hear Elias stand up, but now, here he is, folding me up against him. Hesitantly, I slide my arms around him and feel him tense when I accidentally bump his side. I rest my head on his shoulder, giving myself over to the momentary pleasure of his embrace.

Warmth seeps into me everywhere we touch, trying desperately to chase away the ache coiled in my belly.

"When it happened, it felt so good to hurt them. But even then, I knew better. Kirk taught me to care. Then, I saw him… lying in the floor…"

Just as I see him now.

In my mind, Kirk pulls himself up, propping himself against the leg of our humble table. Blood gushes from his stomach, and he presses a hand to it, instinctively trying to stop the flow. I kneel beside him, blood soaking into the knees of my dress, and wipe away the drops which trickle from his lips.

But more come to take their place.

My chest aches, and tears pour down my face. Silence rules the forest outside. The air quakes with my sobs and his labored, gurgling breaths. I try to heal him, but he shouts, "Ness, it's time! Stop! Just let me go."

He watches, waiting for me to wipe my tears away, even puts one hand on my face. "*This* is where we part ways."

When I open my eyes, I see a dagger gleaming in his hands. Confusion makes me hesitate, unsure of his intentions.

Would he kill me?

The blade is silver. Salt is spilled all around the cabin. I feel it weakening me. It isn't a perfect circle, but a mangled ring still has an effect.

Could he kill me?

My insides clench with the potential betrayal, and my eyebrows knit themselves together.

A smile tugs at his lips, but his eyes are pulled tight by emotion or pain or both. In an instant, he plunges the blade into his own gut and twists. Blood gushes, and I scream until my throat goes raw. My voice becomes harsh, breaking into a million tiny pieces as I gather Kirk into my arms.

He dies swiftly, cradled against me. No amount of healing could ever bring him back from the Etherrealm.

If he made it there.

The thought of him in the Netherrealm pierces my heart.

It'd be my fault if he ended up there.

I double over in agony and guilt, face dipping into the blood which drips from his chin to pool on his chest.

And the only person who ever cared for me... dies.

Because of me.

Sure, he was forced to care for me initially by my mother, but I always thought he became fond of me, despite what I am.

Whispering against Elias' shoulder, I tell him what happened. My tears wet his shirt, and my insides ache with the confession. "I should've just let him go. I shouldn't have called him."

My fingers clutch at the back of Elias' shirt. "I ended up alone, anyway."

Elias tightens his arms around me.

And I let him.

For a long time, I stand there, head against his chest and arms around his waist. At some point, one of his hands moves to the back of my head, moving in my hair. He leans his head against mine, and I start to wonder about him.

The warmth of his touch eases the ache in my heart, slowly undoing the knots in my back. When my tears have run dry, I pull back, and he gazes into my eyes.

Then, I realize something. The real reason I just bawled my eyes out in his arms. The reason I let myself open up to him.

The one thing that makes him like Nolan.

He isn't afraid of me.

His eyes probe mine, looking for something, but only he and the Gods know what.

Heat builds between us, and I feel my body aching to move into him. His eyes smolder and dip toward my lips.

But this can't happen.

Nolan flashes before my eyes. His dark, unruly curls hang loose about his face, reaching well past his shoulders.

Stop.

I can't think of him, either.

He doesn't want me, and it's just going to hurt, again.

But my body is already wishing for the tickle of his hair against my skin as he rolls me onto my back, as he moves over me.

I force myself to swallow it all down.

To break the tension, I tell Elias, "You're either very brave, very trusting, or very stupid."

Chuckling, voice low and smooth, he says, "A little of all three?"

Giggling, despite everything, I reach up to wipe the tears from my face. Again, I bump his side, and he grimaces. Guilt wraps cold hands around my heart, reluctant to let me go.

"Lay back down," I urge him.

"Yeah yeah," he shushes, but shuffles away. He moves with more ease than yesterday, a true testament to the potency of the salve. Casting a glance over his shoulder, he tosses back, "So bossy…"

My eyes threaten to roll out of their sockets.

But again, I laugh.

***

Pushing down on the knife, I cut up chunks of venison and scoop them into a pot. Elias bustles about behind me, occasionally reaching around me to add water and torn herbs. His sleeve brushes the top of my hands as he does so. The addition of a few vegetables and some water sees the stew prepared, and I escort it to the hearth with a wave of my hand.

Elias sets to work clearing things away, moving easily despite having been stabbed only days ago. It makes me wonder if perhaps, while sleeping, I didn't unintentionally heal him. To keep my uncertainty from making me insane, I tell myself that some god smiled upon him and blessed the salve.

He steps past me, one hand landing comfortably on the small of my back. My body ignites at the touch, the air around me suddenly hot and stifling. Yet, deep down, I know he's getting too close, too comfortable.

As the stew cooks, he salts the remainder of the venison for me and settles it into the pot I use for curing. I can do it, but my skin tingles when I touch the salt. So, he volunteers.

"Can't have my savior growing weak," he quips, eyes alight with a teasing grin.

I can only smile in return, throat constricted by glee. Grabbing from the nearest jar, I toss a handful of mint leaves at him. I even stick my tongue out. My own jubilance surprises me.

"So wasteful. Tsk, tsk."

Rolling my eyes, I lift one finger, and the mint leaves rise from their various resting places on his shirt and the floor. A simple swish, and they fly to their jar.

Elias begins to lug the brine pot to the cellar, pushing himself much harder than he should.

"Not so fast," I say. "I'll take that."

A few gestures, and it floats gently through the air. The cellar door opens, and the pot disappears within its depths. Lowering one hand, I close the door.

Shaking his head, Elias leans back against the counter. "You've certainly got *that* down to an art."

"What can I say? I've had time to practice."

Having no one around to help with chores certainly made this little ability very useful.

He tips his head to the side thoughtfully and asks, "How long?"

"Well, as immortals go, I'm still pretty young. I'm only 42."

"I'd love to see how skilled you are with those hands after a few centuries," he says, one eyebrow quirking upward with curiosity.

I inhale deeply, and a light blush warms my skin.

When the realization of his wording settles onto his shoulders, he buckles beneath it, rather awkwardly. His eyes fall to the floor, unable to hold mine.

For a second, I delight in the heat which radiates from him, the quickening of his pulse which shakes the air. Breathing deeply of the warm, earthy scent of lust pouring off him, I revel in images of us moving together in my bed. His hands explore my body, tracing and grasping. I watch as my golden nails scratch his back, pulling him down against me.

Then, I blink it all away, forcing my mind to clear.

Nothing can happen.

I certainly couldn't ever dig my nails into his back. They'd drive straight through his flesh, cleaving muscle from bone. Not exactly romantic.

He could never withstand it.

Not like Nolan did.

A deep sadness wells within me, and I ache to see him, again. But he doesn't want me, anymore.

Not since I broke his heart.

Chapter 6
Ness

Dinner finds us reserved, each content to hold our thoughts prisoner for the time being. I've already dressed for bed, and the cool night air whispers against my bare legs. I sit at the table, acutely aware of Elias' eyes on my calves, my thighs.

I shy away from his gaze, for many reasons, reminding myself of each one in turn.

He isn't Nolan.

He's mortal.

It wouldn't be fair to use him.

Of course, I know all these things. Using him to forget Nolan would be wrong. *Deeply* wrong.

But that doesn't stop my skin from warming when I see appreciation and longing in his gaze. It certainly doesn't stop my mind from wandering. My eyes dart to his hand for just a second, and I can almost feel it, touching me.

Stop this.

My whirlwind emotions take the twinge of guilt that sweeps through me and run with it, hammering me with reminders of the man I actually want. The man that I… miss.

Closing my eyes, I hate that even here, in the sanctity of my mind, I can't own how I feel for him. Even now, knowing that the very thing I always feared the most has already happened. The paralyzing dread that always held my lips still when he uttered those precious, unbelievable, insane words… actually caused the pain I hid from.

I've already lost him.

I beg my mind to let up, to leave me in peace. I plead with my heart for some sort of reprieve.

Thankfully, I'm not left to suffer long. Elias speaks, shattering my thoughts and the silence that rested between us.

"So, when you brought me here, were you worried I'd run and tell the Knights you were out here?"

It's such a stupid question, and so unexpected, that I chuckle. "Well, no one I've ever done this for before now has turned me in. Most people are just glad to be alive."

Their faces flash before my eyes in a parade of fear, mistrust, and reluctant gratitude. The only thing I asked for in return for their care was their word that they would never tell a soul that I was anything other than a witch.

"Besides," I say, swallowing down a spoonful of stew, "I'd just do what I've done every time the Knights found me before. Defend myself and leave. I've never been in one place so long, though."

Glancing around, I take in my home. The floorboards are worn with my footsteps and those of the previous tenants, a family cleared out by vampires before

I found the place. A bear rug near the fireplace covers the stain from their blood.

Candles, herbs, and talismans rest on every available surface. Red velvet curtains adorn every window, smelling so much of sandalwood incense that I can feel it in the air even when I haven't burned any in days.

Which is just as well. I'm running low, and if I can savor the scent of Nolan just a bit longer, I'll take it any way I can.

I can't imagine going somewhere new, having to leave all of this behind.

Could I go somewhere Nolan's never been? Where he's never leaned over my shoulder as I mixed potions or wrapped his arms around my waist as I listened to the birds.

It doesn't seem right to breathe air that's never known the sound of his voice, be it his rugged accent or his miraculously smooth song. Or Nether take me, the moans that escape his lips as we join together...

Heaving a deep sigh, I shove the pain of those thoughts away.

"I've been here for 25 years. It'd be a shame to leave. Ever since Evayla won independence from Harta, the Knights here have been a lot more relaxed. The balance sought in the original precepts is more important than pure extermination of all of us Netherspawn. Especially to the Knights in Everson."

After all, leaving a few Netherspawn sprinkled through the mortal realm is pretty genius. It shows people the tortures that await them in the Netherrealm if they stray too far from the teachings of the gods.

Basically, it makes this place ideal.

Granted, they'd still kill me *on sight. But if they don't know I'm here… and I don't make a spectacle of myself… I'm relatively safe.*

"I imagine that's why my parents settled in Everson then, once they realized my sister and I weren't born werewolves," Elias says.

Silence descends on us again, and this time, I'm glad for it. Occasionally, when I look up idly, I find him staring at me. He drops his gaze quickly, each time.

Eventually, he speaks, again, apparently not content to sit quiet for long. "So, why here?" he asks. "If you know the Pack, why live out here, alone?"

He emphasizes the word *alone,* and a quiver of dread slips off him, filling my nose with an unpleasant scent. His heartbeat stutters.

Does he think I have a suitor or a husband that just hasn't been around for a few days?

Dismissing the notion as daft and ignoring the stab of loneliness which pierces my chest, I answer his question with a question. "How much do you know of Netherspawn?"

His brows furrow. Apparently startled, he hesitates. "Enough? I mean, enough to get by in Everson. Out here, I guess that isn't the case."

Eyes alight with a devilish glow, I say, "Not exactly."

Setting down my spoon, I pat a napkin against my lips and take a drink. A deep breath prepares me for a much longer conversation than I'd intended to have tonight. "You know that werewolves, vampires, sirens, all the human-based immortals were originally created by demons or demi-demons, right?"

He nods, and I go on.

"Well, since they're descended from demons and demi-demons, if I heal one of them, they're bound to me, sort-of like the bond of a werewolf and their alphas or a vampire and their Coven Master."

Elias' crisp green eyes drink me in, sparkling in the light of the hearth. He hangs on my every word, though I'm not sure why. He should have known all of this long before setting foot in these woods.

"I've healed a few of the members of the Pack since I met them. Needless to say, that causes a bit of a… conflict of interests when I'm around. I don't exert my influence over them, but it still distresses them if we're all in the same room, like they could be pulled in two different directions at any moment if I disagree with their alphas."

Picking up my spoon once more, I slurp up another bit of stew.

"So, you just stay away most of the time?" Elias asks.

Nodding, I swallow. "It doesn't help that one of the alphas can't stand the smell of me."

"What?" Elias sputters, suppressing a laugh. "Why wouldn't he like how you smell?"

"Kirk spent so much time with me that my scent clung to him. A few years before he died, he killed a very specific werewolf," I say. "Orwen's mother."

I still remember Kirk coming home, battered from the fight. He was covered in blood, and certainly not just his own.

"He'd gone into town for something. We were living much closer to Tor, then. The Pack was out hunting, and Kirk ran into Melida. She recognized the mark of the Knights on his hand and cornered him. But she didn't see it clearly. She thought he was Hartan, and since that was back when Hartan Knights pretty much killed any Netherspawn they came across, she attacked him. Kirk killed her and ran."

"His scent was all over her when Orwen found her. And since Kirk smelled like me, my scent was on her, too. Now, every time I'm near, he gets a little sad. I guess the sight of her, bloody and gasping for air, comes back to him."

"So, it's best that I stay away." I meet Elias' eyes for a moment, then resume my meal.

Then, there's Orwen and Nissa's daughter…

I shake my head and hold my tongue, unwilling to get into that, at the moment. The memory of her, bleeding on my table, quakes through me, but I blink it away.

Elias nods, and for a foolish moment, I think I'll be able to eat in peace. But of course, that can't be. I stifle a groan of frustration as he opens his mouth to speak, again.

"Do you know *all* the members of the Pack?"

My heart drops. I knew it was coming, obviously. That it took him this long to get around to it is all that surprises me. That doesn't mean I've been looking forward to it, though.

"No, not quite," I say, steeling myself for the name of whoever may have left his family.

"I was just wondering… if you know my dad. I probably should've asked when you first brought me here," he says. Nervous laughter bubbles up from his chest. "Granted, I wasn't quite thinking straight." His hand goes to his side.

"What's his name?"

I scoop up another spoonful of stew to give myself something to do.

"Everett Kalir."

My hand stills mid-air, spoon poised halfway to my mouth, and I stare at him. Waves of anguish wash through me, and my mouth hangs open.

Of course.

I should've seen it. The resemblance is clear, now that I'm looking for it.

Fate's cruel hand squeezes my heart, and my chest sucks in on itself.

But... Why did it have to be him?

"I met him, once," I say.

I pull in a deep breath, then fill my mouth with stew, lest I say something stupid. Yet, as soon as I swallow, something stupid finds its way out.

"It's been so long, though," I say.

"How long?"

"Just before I moved here, actually."

It isn't a lie. I did only technically meet him once. The fact that his face has haunted my dreams ever since doesn't really count as seeing him.

My stomach ties itself in knots.

I have to tell him. I can't not tell him what happened.

Yet, when he looks at me, I can't meet his gaze. Shame burns my cheeks. Though I mean to explain, what comes out when I finally pry my mouth open is anything but what needs to be said.

"You seem healthy enough, now. We'll set out tomorrow. I'll arrange our provisions before bed."

Chapter 7
Elias

Ness says nothing else, mind clearly elsewhere.

My teeth gnash at my food, and I barely taste it. My imagination runs wild, yet I can't figure out what could be bad enough to make her clam up like this.

She told me about Kirk. How much worse can this be?

I still feel her in my arms, crying against my shoulder. I'd thought, stupidly, that we were growing closer. I'm not sure how I thought anything would work between us, but it felt like… Maybe…

A deep breath lifts my shoulders, flowing out on a sigh. Apparently, this specific topic is closed for discussion, so much so that she simply wants to be rid of me.

The Pack is my only option, my only chance at answers.

Before I realize she's eaten her food, she's up and gathering what we'll need for the trek.

"It'll be several days before we get there," she says, mostly to herself.

Her hands flicker, gesturing wildly, and things fly from shelves. Jerky and dried fruits explode from the cellar, stuffing themselves neatly into a couple of knapsacks. Blankets fold themselves, and drinking gourds appear from a trunk in the living room.

"I'd offer to help," I say, "but clearly you've got it well under control."

She casts me a sideways glance as if to say, "Oh, no, don't trouble yourself."

I can *feel* the sarcasm.

Reluctantly, I smile.

Yet, sadness lurks within her eyes. As she finishes packing, doing so far quicker than I could have imagined possible, I find myself wishing to make her feel better.

Angry as I am that Ness won't just tell me, it clearly hurts her.

Did my dad... do something to her? Did he try to kill her?

She goes to the hearth, stacking a few more sticks upon the fire. Solemnly, she stares into its depths. The wood crackles and hisses. Her face falls further as yet another memory or emotion overtakes her.

Despite all my better judgment, I rise from my chair. My feet carry me toward her, pulling me up behind her. My arms wrap around her waist.

Unlike last time, when she wept over Kirk, she doesn't relax. She doesn't lean against me. Instead, she goes rigid in my arms. I lean my head against hers, meaning to show her she doesn't have to hold back.

"We should get some sleep," she says, abruptly.

Taking a deep breath, nose filling with the scent of wood smoke, I release her. She doesn't turn to face me, merely bids me goodnight as she walks away.

I nod slowly, then meander to the bench. I dress my side, missing her touch, all the while. But there's no need for her to do this. I'm more than healthy enough to manage. Blood loss no longer makes me dizzy or weak, as it did the first day.

And apparently, the tension between us no longer pulls her to my side.

I settle in for the night, but my mind keeps me awake, lying there, staring at the ceiling. The red curtains flutter uneasily beside me as a restless wind blows in through the window. Light rain pitter-patters on the roof of the cottage and shakes the foliage outside.

Staring out the slightly open window at Ness' garden, darkened by nightfall, my mother's cottage comes to me, and I wonder what she's doing. A bit of guilt claws at my heart, and I hope she isn't too worried over me. She certainly has reason to be, but I hope I haven't caused her too much trouble.

Somehow, I always do, though.

Dropping my head back against the wall, I do something rare for me. I look back on my life. Scrutiny reveals a pattern of jumping into things too quickly, and my impulsiveness always brings my mother stress.

Whether it's ten-year-old me getting into a fight because some boy teased my sister, Alva, only to come home with a bloody nose, or rushing off into the woods to hunt down the father I thought was dead, I've been a never-ending source of problems my entire life.

At least the fight with Tristen ended well. Sure, my nose was broken, and my shirt was stained up. But he and I ended up talking while we waited for our irate mothers to come get us. I got a new best friend out of it, and now, all these years later, Alva is marrying him.

What will come of this, though?

Luck or some easily amused god seems to be smiling over me, keeping me alive, so far. But I can't exactly count on that.

Can I count on Ness?

So far, it seems that I can.

Now that I think of it, acting on instinct, going with my gut and my heart, has always served me well, in the end.

Outside, a bolt of lightning flashes through the sky, and thunder follows closely on its heels. Turning my eyes from the window, I look over the home I've been brought to. Even in the night, it breathes with a life of its own. But right now, those breaths heave, racking the bones of this place.

For mine is not the only restless night.

From Ness' bedroom, I hear stifled sobs. I strain to hear them over the rain, hoping I've just imagined them. But this is no figment of my imagination.

For a moment, I consider going to her door, but I hold myself still. She kept it in for a while, probably waiting until she thought I was asleep. She obviously wants no comfort from the likes of me.

Again, I feel her tense in my arms, and I wonder what my father could have done to her.

The rain picks up, battering the poor little cottage, and covering the sounds of Ness' agony. I turn over uneasily and struggle to fall asleep.

****

When Ness emerges from her room for the day, she no longer hides what she is. Black horns out and eyes glittering gold, she mutters, "Good morning."

"Morning," I answer.

Though the silence between us makes breakfast an uncomfortable affair, I struggle to keep my eyes off her. Drawn like a moth to the flame, my gaze seeks her out. Remorse holds my tongue still as I notice the streaks of red around her irises, a remnant of the tears she shed last night.

The anger of her not talking about my dad has passed. Now, I merely want her to smile. To laugh. So, when a bit of jam leaks off her toast, streaking down her chin, I seize my opportunity.

"What a slob," I tease, careful to keep my tone light. "Don't you realize you have company?"

She fights it at first, but a smile tugs at her lips. "I can afford to be sloppy when my guest is an absolute wreck."

"What are you talking about?" I ask, narrowing my eyes.

A swirl of her finger brings a fallen hunk of jam up from my plate, and it smears itself across my face.

And just like that, we're laughing, again. She fights it, but joyous sounds bubble from her lips as she stares at the mess she's made of me.

I wipe the jam away and smile at her, eyes alight.

Content to eat with my clumsy left hand, I reach out and wrap my right hand around hers.

She goes still, and her hand is lifeless in mine. When she pulls it away, silence descends on us. I struggle for words for a moment, then withdraw my hand. It rests uncomfortably in my lap as I finish eating, not even bothering to switch back to my dominant hand. Then, we set off westward to find the Pack.

Chapter 8
Ness

He's Everett's son...

My heart twists in my chest, trying desperately to get away from that fact. I can barely stand to hold it in my thoughts for more than a minute or two. Yet, I'm leading him through the woods, all the way to the Pack… Despite everything I know.

I could just tell him. Break him and get it over with. But then, what excuse would I have to see Nolan, again?

A whisper of pain floats through me, and I know I have to go to Tor. One way or another. No matter how helpless it makes me feel dragging myself back to check in with my ex.

Besides, Elias needs to meet the rest of his family. I've only seen his dad's face in my dreams, hollow and lifeless, countless nights since… I owe both of them this much.

My mind slaps me with a fresh bout of guilt, and I run a weary hand over my face.

Disgusted with myself, I blow out a long breath. For a moment, I close my eyes as I walk, thankful that we've made it out of the underbrush and onto a mostly level, if a little muddy, path. The woods are still and silent, all animals hiding from me, but I can't afford to hide what I am around Elias. He has to see what I am, to be reminded every second.

He has to know.

Not that it stopped him from trying to hold my hand at breakfast.

Not that it's stopping him from smiling into my eyes, despite the gold surrounded by blackened purple, every time I look back at him to make sure he isn't falling behind.

I glance over my shoulder, and there he is, smiling like an idiot. Light brown hair darkens at his temples with a few beads of sweat. Vivid green eyes sparkle in the warm, amber light which filters through the canopy. Yet, they seem to shine with a light of their own.

And they shine for me.

I've only ever seen that particular look, outside the bedroom, in one other set of eyes before.

Nolan's.

He was there the night I first met the Pack, when I met Elias' father. The night I summoned my mother. Nolan helped me deal with a lot of the baggage from that night. At least… when he wasn't fighting in the revolution.

He gave me that same look so many times in the years after Harta retreated.

How many times did Nolan hold me as I cried? How often did he slip away from his home and sprint through the woods, just because he felt like something might be wrong, or just because he wanted to see me?

How many times did he smile at me with his thumb caressing my cheekbone where the purple becomes white?

We didn't work, though.

It feels like I've reminded myself millions of times. He was too serious, and I wasn't serious enough. Everything always had a deeper meaning with him, and nothing could ever just be a joke, made for the sake of a laugh.

We fought… so much.

And that's to say nothing of how impossible it all was to begin with. For him to love me… There's really no way.

For me to tell him that I…

I sigh deeply, unable to finish the thought.

Clearing my head, I refocus on the more practical reasons for Nolan and I to be apart. The fights over what needed done for Evayla and whether it was our responsibility. The arguments over my inability to see a future for myself at all, let alone… *with* anyone.

With him.

I drill it into my head, determined to force my heart to move on and hating how easily my mind slips back to him.

But now, a future, one with Nolan, is maybe… all I want.

STOP IT!

I plead, begging my mind for mercy, and my own cries reverberate through me. I wince before their ferocity, their desperation.

Because, honestly, what am I doing to myself? Why am I torturing myself? It doesn't matter what I want.

Kicking at the dirt as I walk, I pick at a little chip in my nail. I pull at it until it splinters, running up alongside the nail. The pain of it centers me. A tiny drop of blood appears, and I suck on it until it stops bleeding.

Finally, focusing on the world around me, I cast my eyes around. My pace slowed during my internal struggle, and Elias walks easily beside me. He smiles openly, and there's that look again, glittering in his eyes.

And I have to drive it away.

I'm just not sure I'll be strong enough to do it.

So many parts of me want to turn and throw my arms around him, if only to forget Nolan.

It's been nearly a full season, after all. I should move on, right?

I want so badly to do just that, to kiss those full lips, to feel Elias' strong chest beneath my hands. I want to know what he tastes like, what he feels like beneath me, how he moves over me.

Maybe just to ease the loneliness...

How seductive that line of thinking is. My skin warms, and I swallow, trying desperately to staunch the desire burning my flesh.

Because my heart won't have it. Guilt washes over me at the thought of being with anyone else. Especially with stakes so high as eternal damnation.

My steps falter as my feet try to obey my body. They want to spin me around, but I can't be with him instead of Nolan. I can't ruin him in the eyes of the gods. I have to turn him away.

And it's not like I don't know how.

Turning to face the path ahead, I stare up at the branches. Arched above us, they reach for each other, touching and twining like fingers. Widening my eyes, I marvel at myself, making even the tree branches sensual.

I shake my arms out, trying to loosen my muscles. It does nothing to lessen the sweet ache building within me.

Or the dread.

Ahead, a log lies across the path between two rock formations, wrapped with vines of honeysuckle. The scent of it reaches for me, and I try to focus on that rather than the faint scent of cedar and sap emanating from Elias.

The earthy aroma of him pulls at me, and I have to wonder if he knows I smell like wood smoke. I've never been around a mortal sired by a werewolf.

Did he inherit the acute sense of smell his father was gifted with?

Maybe then, he'd sense it in my scent. I even smell like the death of him.

Sighing, I step over the fallen log. The toe of my boot catches in the vines, and I nearly trip. My stomach jumps into my throat as I fall forward.

But Elias is close.

Strong hands grab my waist, holding me up. Propping himself up with one knee on the log for balance, his legs press against mine. My hip presses into his.

Turning my head to the side, I stare into those beautiful eyes, so close. Our noses almost touch.

Reflected in his eyes, I see us crashing together. I see him push me against the rock wall to our right, moving against me. The feel of his hands on me is electrifying, nearly irresistible. The sound of my own blood rushes through me, trying its damnedest to drown out my thoughts and trying even harder to push past my heart.

And there's that look again, that delicate yearning sparkling brilliantly in his eyes.

Clenching my jaw to steel myself, I drop my eyes, unable to hold his gaze much longer while still maintaining my fragile grip on self-control.

Now, I hurt myself, for his sake.

Conjuring up a thousand images of Nolan, I cut Elias' tentative hold on me. I think of the way Nolan's mass of curls falls about his face, framing his sultry eyes, dark and sweet, all at the same time.

I think of the first time he touched my hand. Liam had fetched me from my cottage, keen on having me present for the newest transformation attempt. It went well, proving my presence unnecessary.

But I didn't end up minding so much. Nolan and I hadn't seen each other in several months, and we spent every evening for a week and a half walking the shore of the river. We stayed out until morning a few times, neither of us wanting to say goodbye.

His dark eyes held mine so fiercely in the moonlight, flickering to my lips occasionally. But he's always been one for the long game. He didn't kiss me at all until the day I planned to leave, and though we both clearly ached for far more than that, it stopped with a kiss.

And the first time he held my hand…

Five nights into my visit, we sat by the river, just listening. When the sun said goodnight, we laid back on the shore, staring up at the stars. We sat there long enough for the animals to settle back into their normal routines despite my presence, and they sounded magnificent.

I closed my eyes, letting the hoots of the owls and the chirping of the crickets soak into my bones.

Nolan reached over, and softly stroked my wrist with the tips of his fingers. I opened my eyes, and he was propped up on one elbow, looking down at me. Eyes warm and heavy-lidded, he traced indecipherable patterns on my skin.

Agonizingly gentle, his fingers caressed my wrist, moving slowly to my elbow, then back down, again.

My heart lit up that night, far brighter than it ever could for Elias.

And suddenly, I don't want Elias' hands on me, anymore. My heart splinters beneath the weight of grief.

"Thank you," I say, forcing my voice to maintain some hint of normalcy.

Elias does no such thing. His voice comes out husky and quiet as he says, "Anytime."

Swallowing down whatever words were about to erupt, I put one hand on the log and use the other to disentangle my boot from the honeysuckle.

Reluctantly, Elias releases me, taking a step back. "Need a hand?" he offers hopefully.

"I think I'll be alright," I say. Then, dipping my head to the side to concede my own clumsiness, I add, "This time."

He laughs and clears his throat. "I must say, I expected a demi-demon to be less accident-prone. With this and your messy eating habits, you're just far too normal."

He means it in jest, clearly, but has no idea the weight those words carry.

"Yes, well," I say, stepping over the log successfully, "powerful doesn't always mean graceful."

"Certainly not," he laughs, stepping onto the tree trunk without a problem. Jumping down with ease, ever sure of foot, he mocks, "I mean, how hard was that? Really?"

I roll my eyes and turn away from him, trying desperately to wipe that look from my memory. Walking away, I listen to his laugh, rumbling through my veins. His footsteps crash through the undergrowth as he jogs to catch up to me.

Still, I sense it there, shining in his eyes, radiating from him.

Nether take me, I can smell it on him, sweet like pure sugar.

He's getting too close and far *too comfortable.*

My breath catches in my chest because I know what I have to do. I just don't know how. Or when.

Or how much it'll hurt me to do it.

But he has to know...

I'm the reason his dad is dead.

Chapter 9
Nolan

My stomach rumbles greedily as I enter the Golden Tankard. I breathe deeply, separating the cacophony of smells into categories. Which ones are the people filling the tavern, and which are from the food the Tankard has on offer tonight? Moving through the dimly lit tavern, pushing through the unusually large crowd, I let the smells of sweat and the emotions of far too many people fall away.

Goat, heavily seasoned with rosemary.

What is Terry's obsession wit' rosemary?

Then, the scent of apple pie finds me, and my mouth waters in anticipation. Terry may over season a lot of things, but she makes a mean apple pie.

No wond'r the place is packed.

Finally making it to the bar, squashed between a few men who somehow beat me here from the foundry, I wait. When Alina sees me, a too-bright smile shines in her eyes. The scent of sugar wafts over to me, though only for a second. She quickly reels it in, but not fast enough. She always catches it just a moment too late, unless she sees me first.

Since she obviously thinks she's hiding it, I let it go. I'm in no position to do anything about her feelings for me, so it's better to let it lie.

Not that Alina is unattractive.

I survey her curvy form, her long dark hair. The scent of honeysuckle pours off her. She's one of few werewolves who smell like a woodland flower rather than a tree.

She smiles wide, approaching me. Her dark eyes glow beautifully even in the low light of the tavern.

But she's no' Ness…

I groan, internally.

Don't.

Don't do this ta yerself. Ness couldna ev'r see a future, couldna want more…

My heart twists painfully, but I keep it inside. I do a far better job of hiding my feelings than Alina.

The worst part o' it all… I always thought she loved me. Tha's the part that makes it so damn hard to move on…

"Hungry?" Alina asks jovially.

"As always."

A man beside me bumps my arm, leaning into the bar to leer at Alina.

Good luck, lad. Though, it'd cert'nly make tings easier fer me if she went fer him.

"There's stew, as usual. Or goat roast," she says. Then, saving the best for last, she adds, "And some of Terry's apple pie, though there isn't much left."

"Stew an' some pie," I answer, fighting to keep from wrinkling my nose at the thought of the abundant rosemary on the goat.

"Coming right up."

Alina smiles at me again and assures the man next to me that she'll be with him in a moment. Before she even turns her back, a shiver runs through us both.

Less than a heartbeat later, an eerie, forlorn howl rattles my bones, resonating with the Nether inside me.

Gods, no…

My eyes meet Alina's, glazed over with dread. Her mouth falls. For once, she regains composure faster than I do, pulling it shut.

My own jaw hangs agape as three more painful wails pierce my mind and slither through my veins. Rising to my feet, I prepare to leave the tavern, ready to forsake my empty stomach. After all, we haven't seen these beasts since the revolution, and their creation can't bode well. We need to find them and dispatch them.

But worry creases Alina's brow.

"Please," she begs. "At least eat, first."

Her words echo in Ness' voice, reverberating in my mind, and for a second, I'm not in the dark, musty tavern. I'm in Ness' cottage, just about to eat. My bones shiver, and I rise to the call. I don't know if Orwen and Nissa will need me, specifically, but I can't shrug off the possibility.

I didn't know at the time that one of our commuter members had nearly been killed in Roarn. I didn't know that it was part of a bigger tension between Roarn and another city-state. I just knew trouble was brewing, and I needed to help.

For me, not for anyone else. *I* needed to help.

"Please," I can still hear Ness say, voice so small I could barely hear it. "At least eat, first."

But I left.

Her face, downtrodden and misty-eyed as I held her close, kissing her goodbye, pierces my heart.

Now, in this little tavern, many years too late to fix the hurt in Ness' heart as I rushed off to play hero for the hundredth time, I sit back down.

"Thank you," Alina says.

But this isn't for her.

If I'm ev'r goin' ta get Ness back, I have ta learn ta be… present.

My eyes close, shutting out the shaking in my bones as the howls roll through me. I grit my teeth against the pain gnawing at my heart.

As if I'll ev'r get her back…

Chapter 10
Ness

Chills run down my spine, and an eerie wail floats through my heart, resonating from afar. Three more times, the unnatural sound shakes my bones. The campfire does nothing to loosen the frigid hands which grip my soul.

That damnable vampire couldn't just leave it be. He couldn't count himself lucky and move on. The marks, inflicted with a curse, will scar. Sure, that's terrible for such a vain creature… Sure, he'll never have another pledge bowing to his every whim in an attempt to earn immortality…

But he yet breathes, and that's a far cry better than the fate any other demi-demon would've allowed.

"Loopholes," I mutter under my breath, admonishing myself inwardly.

I should've been more specific when I cursed him. I could have prevented this, had I just thought about the potential for such imbecilic revenge attempts. But I didn't think they'd go so far as to create Howlers. I should have. They're the perfect combination for it, a vampire and a Nether witch.

Shaking my head, I hold my hands out toward the fire. My gold talon-like nails shimmer in the flickering light. The moon above us waxes, only a week shy of a full moon, but little of its light reaches us through the trees.

The fire crackles as a log topples over, sending a shower of sparks curling upward, yet the warmth barely penetrates my skin. Pulling my hands back, I rest my elbows on my knees and bury my face in my palms.

Another chorus of wails erupts, vibrating through me. Goosebumps prick my skin.

"What's wrong?" Elias asks.

"Things are going to get... interesting. That's all."

Concern creeps in at the edge of his words, peeking out at me through his eyes. "Is everything okay?"

"For now," I answer, shivering even in the warm air of a summer night.

Dread fills me. Four Howlers. I can hear them, paws pounding the ground, shaking the Nether, as they hunt us. Each footfall, each and every howl, rattles my bones.

Elias scoots closer and wraps an arm around me. The lull of his warmth tugs at me, trying desperately to fight off the dread and loneliness which fill me. The scent of cedar fills my nose, pulling my head down onto his shoulder, even as I ache for sandalwood, instead.

But with my head and heart swarming with unearthly shrieks, there's little room for my conscience. The fear of one of those beasts catching him up in their rotting mouths expands within me, crushing my heart.

Because I brought them down upon him.

I shiver harder, and his arm tightens around me. He even wraps his other arm around me, tucking me neatly against him. But the sickening fear only grows.

I do what I can to block the sound, the feel, of the approaching Howlers, withdrawing from the Nether. But I won't have that luxury when they get here.

Elias nuzzles his face into my hair, and with the Howlers blocked for the time being, fear makes room for guilt.

Chapter 11
Elias

Walking beside Ness after a late lunch, I glance at her for what feels like the millionth time. She's barely spoken a word all day. She has yet to laugh, even once. Her golden eyes are tight with worry when they leave the ground.

We walk on, crunching twigs underfoot as we go. Small plants wrap themselves around our legs, reaching out to us from the edges of the narrow path. A scattering of rocks lies in our way, tumbled down in some long-ago rockslide. Moss coats their shadowed underbellies.

This path must not see much use. Surely, they would've been cleared away, otherwise.

My eyes dart uphill, searching for any boulders which could roll down toward us, but all I see is green. Far ahead of us, the undergrowth shakes with the sounds of small animals fleeing before Ness' true form. They scatter, some going high up into the trees, others fleeing downhill.

She hasn't hidden since the morning after she learned my dad's name. But why?

Maybe it's a defense mechanism. She seemed ready to go to great lengths to keep the animals comfortable before, but now she doesn't spare them a thought.

The animals before us move beyond earshot, counting themselves beyond Ness' reach. Silence rules the woods around us, ringing loudly in my ears.

Having tried comforting her, as well as employing humor, I resort to giving her space.

She clearly doesn't want to talk to me about… whatever it is that has her so worried.

For the first time in hours, she meets my eyes. Her face is drawn, and a deep frown etches itself into her skin. She looks like she's lost something she holds dear. I can't help but wonder if it has to do with my father and whatever he may have done when they met.

I break beneath the intensity of her gaze, wavering before the thought that I could be spawned from someone who hurt her.

Whatever happened between them, whatever he did, I'll see to it that things are made right.

I nod, confirming my own resolution.

He's got a lot to make up for.

He owes Ness some sort of apology, clearly. He owes a hell of a lot to Alva and me.

And then, there's Mom. He just left her. Not a word, no explanation. He just walked out and left her with two kids.

My hands clench at my sides, leaving little half-moon divots in my skin. I consciously keep my teeth from grinding together, moving my jaw from side to side to loosen it up.

What kind of man can do that?

When I meet him, I'll have to keep my wits about me, so I don't punch the bastard in the face.

I inhale slowly, expanding my chest to full capacity in a desperate attempt to calm myself. Pushing the breath out, I concentrate on the leaves around me, fluttering together in the gentle breeze. Taking another deep breath, I loosen the muscles which coiled tightly with rage just a moment ago.

Then, I hear it, way off in the distance. A blood-curdling howl. My head shoots up, staring up the mountain. My skin crawls as three answering wails ring through the air, and every muscle in my body tenses.

No animal I know makes a sound like that. Part wolf howl, part growl, and half scream, it raises the hairs on the back of my neck.

Eyes darting to Ness, I find her gaze fixed in the direction of that sound. The look on her face tells me *this* is what's been worrying her, at least for today.

And if *she's* worried, I *certainly* should be.

***

Through the afternoon, that sound haunts us. The creatures call out to each other at seemingly random intervals. When one wails, the others always answer.

And they're always just a little bit closer, a little bit louder. Their painful keening makes my blood run cold.

Every.

Single.

Time.

Ness fares no better.

Clearly on edge, she keeps herself between me and the beasts. The shimmering gold of her eyes intensifies, and every so often, her fingers arch like claws.

And all we can do is keep walking.

The unlevel ground now seems a tremendous disadvantage. The beasts, creatures Ness calls Howlers, perverse products of Nether magic and a post-mortem bite from a vampire, have the high ground.

Nervously, my eyes jerk downhill. Countless tree trunks await, ready to crush my ribs as I roll toward them, thrown from the path by one of these beasts. I kick a rock over the edge and watch it bounce off a stone here, a tree trunk there, until it comes to rest in a tuft of grass about fifty feet down.

Staring up the mountain, Ness calculates distance. "There's a clearing up ahead. We'll stop there," she says, piecing things together.

"How far?" I ask, but I really mean, "Will we get there before those things catch us?"

"An hour," she answers. "If we hurry."

"How long do we have?"

"About three hours. Unless *they* hurry."

Another round of sorrowful howls fills the air, and my head jerks toward it. A ruckus of wings erupts as birds throughout the forest take to the air, fleeing the monsters barreling toward us.

***

Night falls early in the forest. Our fire burns bright in the darkness of our clearing but does little to fend off the chill in my bones.

Ness insisted that going without a fire would do nothing to put them off. "They smell us, feel us on the Nether," she told me as we made camp. "They'll find us with or without a fire. This way, we can see what they're doing."

But now, with their sinister howls growing near, the fire makes me feel vulnerable. All I have with me is a knife, certainly nothing good enough to kill things which don't technically live.

They did at one point. Yesterday, perhaps.

Now, they shamble along, bodies moving through sheer force of will. The men who made them push them along, partially controlling them from afar, tormenting the poor beasts. The pain of death pervades every second, for their hearts don't beat, their lungs don't breathe.

Their voices cry out in agony, one of the only scraps of control the poor animals have left, rasping through throats that shouldn't move.

According to Ness, we only have two means of killing them. Sever their spines or damage their brains. Eventually, their bodies decay, bringing about a slow, immensely painful, final death. But it takes weeks. And they would haunt us, dogging our heels as long as they could manage it.

Staring at the knife in my hand, nothing more than a dagger, I know it will do little against such creatures. Not before they do far more damage to me.

A chorus of shrieking howls rises from the undergrowth, just up the path we took to get here, and the stench of decay slithers through the leaves. I rise to my feet, knife in hand. But Ness steps in front of me. She holds nothing, but I suppose she doesn't need to.

Massive paws pound the earth, running toward us at top speed. They fan out as they near our clearing, and agonized howls fill the air. My chest shakes with them, and my bones ache with chills. Circling us, the beasts scream as they draw closer and closer.

Yellow eyes reflect the firelight, glowing as the Howlers pace through the brush. One second, those burning eyes are visible, the next, they disappear behind a tree or into a thicket.

Pain pervades their every movement, but that seems only to enrage them. Snarling, they move closer, bringing with them the pungent aroma of death as they step free of the undergrowth for the first time.

Just a day ago, I would've called them wolves.

Now, with the flesh carved from around their eyes and blood dried in their fur, both on their faces and from wounds on their sides, they're anything but. A large patch of fur has fallen from each of their necks. Two fang marks rest in the center of their bald patches, charring the skin. Darkness spreads from the bite marks like tree roots.

Yet, their eyes grapple for my attention. They shine in the firelight, but agonized shadows move within. Every movement drags a whimper of pain from their throats. Every sound is labored, ripped across vocal cords pulled tight by death.

They snarl at us, but it comes out rougher and higher than normal. Torn between screams and barks, they assail us with noises that I know will haunt me for years to come.

If I survive the night.

My palms sweat as they circle us, heads low, looking for the weak spot. Countless keening wails reach for the sky as if they could call the Netherrealm down upon us. The cold ache in my bones half-convinces me they can do exactly that. Gripping my dagger, my hand trembles.

I'm in way over my head.

A glance at Ness reveals a face drawn tight with brows furrowed and eyes narrowed. She lifts a hand, and I prepare for carnage.

Before I can see what she intends to do, a tawny wolf moves toward me. I take a step forward, determined to meet my fate head-on, despite Ness' warnings that I stay out of this. Dagger in hand, I gaze into the pained eyes staring out at me from a scratched skull. Black blood encrusts the bone and the fur below.

The beast lunges, whimpering all the while, but it's found its prey. It knows that we're the reason it endures such pain, and fury rules it, now.

The Howler topples me over, landing atop my chest. My heart pounds, blood roaring in my ears. I shove one arm under the beast's throat, desperate to keep sharp teeth off my neck. Inches from my face, terrible, stinking jaws snap. Dark, bloody saliva drips onto my face as it growls and chomps.

Dagger held aloft, I plunge it into the wretched beast's skull, right at its temple. Brittle bone gives way to blade, and the beast goes still, collapsing on top of me. I struggle to free myself from its bulk, wriggling my arm free, then pushing it onto the grass. Shaking with adrenaline, I rise to my feet.

Affording me no opportunity to regain my balance, a great white Howler surges forward, leaping at me. Snapping and snarling, it flies through the air. Gnashing teeth inch closer and closer, and reflex takes over. My arm flies upward, driving the dagger into the beast's neck. Thick, black blood oozes out around the blade.

Spinning with its momentum, I pivot, and the Howler flies to the opposite edge of the clearing. Slick with old blood, my dagger slides from my grip. Firmly lodged in the Howler's throat, my only weapon leaves me.

"ELIAS!" Ness screams as the Howler comes back for me.

She raises a hand, and I fly upward, stomach dropping into my shoes. With the putrid stench of rot all around, it's nearly enough to make me sick. But the beast flies through the air beneath me, snapping as it goes.

Setting me gently on a tree branch, she shouts, "Gods, you're just as stubborn and impulsive as a werewolf, but you're still just a mortal! Let me do this!"

Tree bark digs into my skin, pressing at me through my clothes. Shuffling along the branch, I shimmy toward the trunk, determined to get back down there, to help her. I can't just sit here and watch those things tear her apart.

But she twirls a single finger, twining my legs to the branch.

"NO! Ness, let me down!"

She ignores me.

Three Howlers circle her, and she watches. She doesn't move, and I can't figure out why. Her hands are steady, despite being outnumbered. Our campfire burns low, and the shadows deepen. Golden eyes shine like stars in her black eye sockets. Panic wells within me.

The biggest of them all, a grey beast no less than 170 pounds, launches itself at her.

Time stops, halting my heart with it, and my blood runs cold.

What if I lose her?

Jaw dropping, I scream out, "NESS!"

Dropping to one knee, she drives one hand up, plunging gold talons into the stomach of the beast. Using its momentum, she rises beneath it and flings the massive creature against a tree trunk. Her nails slice it open, and gore rains down across our campsite.

It hits the tree, thankfully not the one I'm in, and the branches around me shiver with the impact. Leaves and sticks whip around me, slapping my face.

"Nether take me…"

How strong is she?

Chapter 12
Ness

It won't have died from that.

Torn between a deep bloodlust and an urge to put these poor beasts out of their misery, my mind writhes in chaos. Their anguished howls and pitiful whimpers drag tears from my eyes. But the pounding need for gore, now that the opportunity has presented itself, is tempting.

NO. Save it for the ones who made them. These poor wolves did nothing to deserve this. DON'T make it worse. Don't.

Save it. Bottle it. Put it away.

Kirk's face flashes in my mind, stained with blood.

Elias' father lies dead in my arms.

Rage burns in me, far hotter than any flame in this realm, but I strain against it. Lifting my hands as if holding something, I jerk them clockwise.

A Howler falls before me, neck snapped. No heartbeat stops as it finally dies, having stopped days ago. The once-beautiful white wolf with dark patches of old blood spilled across her coat can find peace, now. Elias' dagger still sticks out of her neck.

Behind me, the alpha struggles to gain its feet, slipping in its own gore over by the tree. I turn to show it mercy, but the remainder, a small black wolf, grabs my right thigh in its jaws. It shakes its head back and forth, pulling my leg out from under me.

The ground rushes up to meet me, and I feel my nose break with the impact. Pain explodes through my skull. Blood gushes out, pouring down over my lips when I roll onto my back. The Howler drags me toward its alpha, arching its back and jerking as it does.

Thrashing, I swipe a hand at its face, desperate to end the pain for the both of us. My slash falls short, merely catching the flesh of her muzzle with my nails. It tears away in a bloody hunk. The poor thing screams, and the sound is just a bit too human.

It pierces my soul, sending shivers through my body.

But she lets go of my leg.

Scrambling upward, pain exploding through me with every move, I pull the wolf's head to my chest. Holding her still against me, I take her head in both hands and snap her neck. She goes limp in my arms, and I set her gently on the ground.

Her eyes shine with nothing more than firelight, finally lifeless in death. As they should be. The bone around them glows against her black fur, matted down with dried blood.

Finally gaining its feet, the massive alpha charges, barreling into me as I wipe tears from my face. Its teeth find my left arm, sinking in deep. Lightning bursts of agony explode across every fiber of my being.

Pulling my hands apart, I pry the Howler's jaws from my arms without ever touching the beast. A single twirling finger secures its jaw with a Nether binding, a thing I probably should have done from the start.

Another thing I'll regret later…

Pulling the great grey beast against me, I hold it tight, despite its thrashing, finally finding a use for my unnatural strength. Staring into its eyes, I see pain.

And fear.

With one hand on the side of its face, I fill my own eyes with compassion, letting my emotions seep into the beast. Another seldom used ability. I'm much more likely to keep my feelings to myself.

But here, now, it soothes this poor creature. The beast lays down across my lap, staring up at me.

Snarls become whimpers, and howls morph into soft whines. I feel death in the poor thing. His body is cold, and thick blood drains from its gaping stomach. Eyes like caramel stare into my soul, aching for release.

Twirling one finger counterclockwise, I release Elias' legs from the tree and free the wolf's jaws. He won't bite me, now.

With tears streaming down my face, I place my right hand atop the wolf's head. My savaged left arm lies limp across the beast's side. Stroking gently and hiding a grimace of pain, I try to show this poor animal a bit of comfort.

Then, I place one nail over the top of his head. He whines softly, and I make gentle sounds of reassurance.

"Shhh… It's okay, now," I whisper, petting the poor animal slowly and driving my talon through his skull.

Black blood oozes out around it, but for a split second, before the life fades from his eyes, he finds peace. His muscles go limp, finally relaxing as they should have when he first died.

Heaving a great sob, I haul the massive wolf's head to my chest. My cries drown out the sounds of Elias climbing down from the tree. I hug the cold, dead wolf to me, weeping into matted fur.

My body shakes with sobs, and my chest aches. My world goes black, wiping the stars and the moon from the sky. My breath catches in my throat as my fingers tighten around dirty fur.

Then, strong arms tug at me, begging me to release the poor creature.

Elias whispers my name, and I lift my gaze to him. Short hair a mess with little bits of bark, he stares at me with tenderness in his eyes. When my lungs forget how to breathe, bordering on hyperventilation, he gathers me up in his arms and lifts me onto his lap.

"Are you okay?" he asks, voice urgent and sweet. The scent of sugar seeps from him, mixing with the stench of death all around us. "How bad is it?"

"I'll be fine," I answer, choking the words out. The pain in my limbs is nothing next to that which shrouds my soul in shadow.

These poor creatures…

Had I been more specific, had I chosen my words more carefully…

Had I not reacted so quickly and so angrily…

Had I revealed what I was sooner…

They wouldn't have insulted me. I wouldn't have cursed him. There would've been no reason for them to retaliate.

But I didn't.

Another round of sobs bursts forth, and Elias pulls me tightly against his chest. The ground falls from beneath me, and I feel myself begin to spiral. Light leaves me, and a chasm opens within me, swallowing all hope.

Kirk would be disappointed in me.

I clutch Elias' shirt, shredding the fabric in my talon encrusted grasp. My tears and the wolf blood which coats my face now stain his shirt.

I don't count the moments as we sit there, amidst old blood and fallen wolves, but they are many.

"Shhh…" he says. "It's okay, now."

I open my eyes, startled by the parallel his words find with the ones I uttered moments ago. Light finds me again, no longer blocked by eyelids. The moon perches high above us, nowhere near the last place I saw it.

"We need to get you cleaned up," Elias whispers, clearly concerned. "I don't even know how much of this blood is yours."

Nodding, determined not to fall prey to my own emotions again, I say, "There's a small stream, up ahead."

That stream is a big part of why I always stop in this clearing when I make the trip to see Nolan or Liam. Looking around at the blood which stains the ground, I'm not sure I'll stop here in the future.

"Can you help me up?" I ask.

It's only a short distance, after all. I don't need to wait. I can make it.

"I'll do one better," he says.

Elias lifts me as if I weigh nothing, and settles me on the ground beside him, careful to keep me away from the desecrated wolf. Pulling himself up to a crouch, he scoops me up into his arms and stands.

I gasp, but he doesn't notice.

"Just down the path?" he asks.

Staring into emerald eyes, I nod. I gaze at him, dumbfounded as he carries me away from the carnage. Each step bounces me against his chest, and my nose fills with cedar and sap. Breathing deeply, I let it soothe me, pretending that my arm and leg aren't on fire.

Pretending that this is okay.

When we reach the stream and the small rocks placed to allow easy passage, he skirts the path, moving uphill to step into the stream. Stooping, he settles onto his knees and lowers me directly into the cool water. Compared to the warm air, it's refreshing.

He tears away the remnants of my left sleeve and tosses it onto the bank. Scooping water into his palms, he pours it over my arm. The water runs over the gaping holes and slashes in my flesh, coming away dark. The stream runs black with my blood and that of the Howlers as it rinses from my dress.

Unbuttoning his shirt, Elias sheds it and rinses it clean in the stream. Weak as I am, I find my eyes drawn to him. With no tree branches over this portion of the stream, the moonlight dances on his skin, shimmering as his muscles ripple with the effort of wringing out his shirt. Lifting the soaked fabric to my face, he wipes away the blood, searching for any cuts or scrapes that it may have concealed.

None reveal themselves.

The Nether within me has already pieced my nose back together.

I search his face, desperate to find something, anything, that might explain away such care. Gratitude for saving his life, perhaps. Or maybe for taking him on this trek to find the Pack. But all I see is tenderness.

I falter before it, dropping my gaze.

I don't deserve such compassion.

With my good arm, I pull my leg up to bend the knee. Hiking the hem of my dress up, I reveal torn muscle and shredded skin. I wince as the fabric moves over it, tugging flaps of skin in directions they aren't meant to go.

Elias' hands set to work, scooping water up, and pouring it over my thigh. Each drop, gentle as the administration of them may be, pulls a moan of pain from my lips. Wrapping fingers tightly around a stone, I do what I can to bear the pain without making Elias feel worse.

The blood washes away, revealing the true devastation wrought by the dead wolf's jaws. My leg hangs open, dark muscle showing itself to the sky as it was never meant to do.

"Itand have mercy," he whispers, calling on the goddess of fortitude.

But she'll spare no blessings for the likes of me.

"What do I need to do?" he asks. His eyes roam over me, and one hand finds its way to my cheek. Brows knitted together, he clearly longs for something to do, some reassurance that I'll be ok.

Does he want me to be alright for the sake of spending more time together? Or merely for the sake of having an escort for the rest of the trek?

I hope for his sake that it's the latter. But the well of loneliness within me wishes for the former.

Either way, there's nothing he can do.

"My body will mend itself," I tell him. "It'll hurt, but it'll mend. It's already started."

His eyes drop to my arm, my leg. The bleeding has stopped, and the cuts aren't as deep as they were mere seconds ago. Had he seen it when the wounds were first inflicted, he likely would've been sick.

"I wish you would've let me help," he murmurs, sliding his hand along my jaw until his thumb finds my earlobe.

Exhaustion pulls my inhibitions low. Despite myself, despite the guilt churning within me, I lean into his caress.

Nolan won't want me back, anyway.

My heart shrinks from the thought, and I close my eyes, nuzzling my cheek into Elias' palm.

"Letting you help would've been a terrible idea. They could never kill me. They had no salt, no silver. They couldn't say any incantations."

I pause, squeezing my eyes tight against the horrid images which flash before them. I don't want to see the ways they could've hurt him. I don't want to watch them tear him to shreds. I don't want to see his blood on the ground.

"They could've killed *you*, though," I whisper.

Suddenly desperate to see him alive and healthy, to ease my conscience just a bit, I open my eyes. Sure enough, he's there, face inches from mine. The moonlight glows in his magnificent eyes, but the blood of the Howlers still adorns his face.

Reaching for his sodden shirt, I lift a corner of it to his face. Wiping away the dried blood, I memorize the strength in his jaw, the kindness in his eyes. I trace the small kink in his nose, a remnant from a previous fight.

From a distance, it's almost impossible to notice, but this close…

My eyes drop to his lips, full and soft. They part, but only to speak.

Confusion wrinkles his brow. "If they couldn't kill you, why were they sent after us? To maim you and kill me?"

"No," I say, shaking my head. I stifle a groan as my thigh stitches itself together. "They sent them to find us. They know where we are, now. They know which way we were headed. They'll find us."

Those words sew our lips shut, for we both know. This won't be the last of the vampire and his pledge. And if this was just the search party, what awaits us down the path?

Hearts heavy with all that's happened, we sit in taut silence. When the blood has rinsed from my dress and the stream no longer runs black, Elias lifts me free of the water. He carries me back to camp, and guilty as it makes me feel, I bury my head in his warm chest. Sodden shirt left unbuttoned, my face rests against bare skin.

It does wonders to ward off the chills my wet clothes could have otherwise inflicted.

But the bodies loom in our clearing.

Elias sits near the fire, keeping me tucked against him on his lap. Tears fall, but I lift my good arm. With a few hand motions, I sweep away a patch of undergrowth and scoop out a large grave.

One by one, I float the wolves across the clearing and lower them into the grave together. I take care to arrange the alphas together, the big grey male and the white female. I can't bring myself to retrieve Elias' dagger from her neck. I can't stomach the sound I know it'll make.

With rivers cascading over my cheeks, I sweep the dirt pile over them, trying to drown out the hollow sound it makes when it hits their bodies rather than the dirt below them. Choking down a sob, I sniffle.

Elias buries his face in my hair, inhaling deeply, and tightens his embrace.

My heart soars and plummets, simultaneously.

***

Morning comes too soon, and pain bursts through my arm and leg. The skin is patched, and the muscles are repaired. But bruises linger. I open my eyes, but the morning sun blinds me. I slam them shut, once more.

Strong arms tighten around me, pulling me closer, and my nose fills with cedar, a comforting scent amongst the blood of dead wolves. The bruise on my arm protests, rubbing against the ground as I scoot closer to Elias, but every other part of my body tells that pesky arm to mind its own business.

Sliding my hand up his chest, I revel in the feel of his skin. My mind, sluggish with half-sleep marvels at the sweet warmth pulsing through me.

Our legs tangle, pushing the skirt of my dress up. One of his hands slides down over my hip to find the bare flesh of my thigh, and his thumb caresses the once-mangled skin. The beating of my heart fills my head. Loud and thunderous, it roars at me.

Finally opening my eyes, I can do nothing but stare. Peace rules his sleeping face. Dark lashes fan across his cheeks. A deep breath pushes his chest out against my hand.

Shifting, I move closer and close my eyes once more, happy to return to sleep. Shrouded in the warmth of barely waking, my conscience mumbles groggily.

My movement wakes Elias. He pulls me against him, making soft, drowsy sounds of joy. His hand deserts my thigh, seeking my neck, instead. As his thumb caresses my jaw, I grant myself the wonder of his face.

Eyelids low and voice husky, he whispers, "Good morning."

My eyes drift over his face, taking in everything. The soft feeling of drowsiness holds back my inhibitions, so I don't move away from him. Rather, I nestle in closer.

Breaths coming faster, his eyes fall to my lips.

They part, invitingly, and my hand slips over his side to his back, all of its own accord.

Moving closer, he studies my eyes as he brushes his nose against mine. My skin tingles at the touch, and a delicious heat builds within me. My eyelids fall as his lips come close.

Softly, oh so softly, our lips meet. Elias moves his mouth against mine, devilishly tender, and a low sound escapes him.

I arch against him as my body betrays my heart, and our kiss becomes one of hunger. Mouths questing desperately, our lips part and melt together. My hands make fists in his short hair, pulling him against me.

As the hunger overtakes him, dragging him along, he pushes my shoulder back to the ground. With one hand on my hip, he slides one leg between mine, and immediately, I twine my leg around it.

But the adrenaline is waking me, dredging my conscience out from under the surge of desire which has risen to claim me. In the back of my mind, I hear it whispering about the Netherrealm taking Elias' soul.

My heart wakes and yearns for the scent of sandalwood. It begs for dark, smoldering eyes to look down at me, rejecting the crystalline green of Elias' eyes.

My hands loosen in his hair and slide forward to his jaw. My body begs for more, aches to rip away the shredded remnants of my dress and his shirt. I even move my hands to his chest, ready to push the fabric back over his shoulders.

This will damn him.

Thoughts of Elias falling prey to hordes of demons, a victim of humiliation and torture and bloodshed, flash before my eyes, and I grind to a halt. My hands still on his shoulders. My lips go motionless against his.

And I pull away.

Elias grips my hip, searching my gaze.

Closing my eyes, I suck in my lips. My body warms, wanting this.

I need him, if only because I can't have Nolan.

I flinch away from the thought of never being with Nolan again, unable to sustain its weight, and force myself to the task at hand.

My stomach clenches, and I say, "We can't."

Breath coming in short, shallow waves, we pant. I swallow hard, pushing away the fire burning inside me.

Dropping his head to my shoulder, Elias tries to calm himself. He plants a kiss on my neck, sending delicate shivers and crippling waves of guilt washing through me. He lays back down beside me, even as my heart screams.

His hand finds mine, and he laces our fingers together.

But I pull my hand free and sit up.

What have I done? He's surely damned, now.

A stray thought, one that shouldn't compare to the thought of damning someone's soul, creeps through me.

Will Nolan be able to forgive me for this?

Even now, even with someone's soul on the line, he's the one I think of.

He's the one I want.

Chapter 13
Elias

Ness releases my hand. Not roughly, not hurriedly. But she does. My skin goes cold in the absence of her touch, and my heart riots at the change. Sitting up, she draws her knees up to her chest and rests her arms on top of them.

She must feel this.

Why else would she have gone to such lengths yesterday to keep me safe? Why would she have allowed herself to lean on me so much after the fact?

She's been living alone for twenty-five years. Clearly, relying on others isn't something she does much of.

But she leaned on me last night.

It has to have been more than just… necessity.

Right?

Turning to look at her, I find her eyes shut to the world, to me. Her hand lifts to rub at her face, and she blows out a deep breath.

"Ness," I begin, tone deliberately gentle.

But before I can say another word, she shakes her head. "We should be going."

She springs to her feet and begins packing up camp, careful to give me no opportunity to damn myself further through either words or actions.

When we begin walking, she moves quickly over the unlevel ground, keeping me breathless if I hope to keep pace with her. A few times, she stumbles but recovers before I can reach out to help. Our pace makes conversation impossible, leaving me no way to ease her concerns.

Because… If having feelings for someone like her, someone kind and strong even when all the Netherrealm screams in her bones demanding otherwise, is enough to send me to the Netherrealm, then I'm already lost.

And I'm not even sure I care.

Chapter 14
Ness

After a tense, silent lunch, we kill the afternoon walking far too quickly to speak. I leave Elias no chance to frustrate me with confessions, though his scent gives him away. A pungent aroma of sugar mixes with the cedar, sweetening the air to a sickening degree.

With some effort, I convince him we should eat our dinner of dried rations on the move.

"The next clearing is still farther than I'd like it to be. We won't make it by nightfall otherwise," I say, justifying such extreme measures.

Let's see him argue with that…

"Too bad someone was so talkative at lunch," he quips, casting a wry smile my way. He pants with the effort of speaking while moving so quickly.

Reluctantly, I grin at his ridiculous comment, though only after a critical sidelong glance. With my self-control fully restored now that sleep no longer hangs over me, I wipe the smile from my face quickly.

Don't encourage him.

I scoff inwardly, furious as this morning flashes before my eyes.

Too late to worry about encouraging him…

"When we reach Tor in the morning, we need to find a witch."

"Why?" A smile splits his lips, and his eyes twinkle.

Pointedly, I avoid his gaze, saying, "One who communes with Roata would be best, but I'm sure any Ether witch could seek her blessing."

"Roata? Really?" He suppresses a laugh. "You want me to seek a blessing from the goddess of forgiveness?"

"Yes, I do," I say. My tone brooks no question, but I get the feeling that I'm in for a few, regardless. I watch my feet, tearing across an especially trodden down part of the path and kicking up whirls of dust.

"Why would I do that? It won't do any good. My feelings haven't changed since this morning."

For a moment, I stare at him open-mouthed. My hair flutters across my eyes, lifted from my shoulders by a light wind to conceal my view of his face.

How can he be so dumb as to openly admit this? Why doesn't he want saved? He can't be so lost as all that, not so soon. We only just *met.*

"They *will* change, though," I mutter and drop my gaze. My feet carry me forward, dreading the coming confession and desperate to move away from it.

"And how do you know that?" he asks, pursing his lips.

I open my mouth to tell him about his father, but my answer dies on my lips as we walk through a wall of hot air. The trees beyond are still. Not a leaf stirs, and no animals scurry away from me. The gentle breeze has vanished.

Everett lies forgotten in my memory, for the moment. My confession will have to wait.

Elias turns around to glance at the Nether wall we walked through, but he'll find nothing behind us but darkness. Overhead, no moon shines through the leaves. A dome encapsulates us, and everything just… stops.

Trees are cut off, and branches appear seemingly from nowhere. Leaves dip out of the blackness, halved or quartered by the wall, defying logic and gravity.

We can't skirt this damnable thing, not with any hope of Elias surviving the trek. The ground on either side of the path here is far too steep. Which, of course, is why they chose this spot…

I step in front of Elias and lead him a few steps further inside the barrier.

What will the vampire and his pledge have waiting for us in here?

My eyes search frantically for the threat. I try to listen for any footsteps, but Elias' heart gallops in my ears.

If only I could tell him to shut up…

Torchlight awaits us, burning brightly around a bend in the path. Shadows flicker over the trees around us, and voices whisper. We round the corner, and sure enough, the vampire and his pledge stand in a circle of torches, waiting for us.

But so do six other men and women.

Elias' heart stutters against my eardrums.

"Tivoli," I say, tone even, "It's been too long."

Chapter 15
Elias

Ness addresses a man before us, far too calmly.

The dark-skinned man inclines his head. Shadows nearly conceal the tattoos on his face. Three thin lines reach down from his bottom lip, terminating on his chin. A single line falls from each eye, reaching almost to his cheekbones. Several undone buttons reveal thick lines tattooed over his collar bones.

I've never seen their like. No one else in Evayla has tattoos like this, or *any* on their faces, for that matter.

His deep voice booms across the clearing, "A shame we do not meet under better circumstances," he says. The formality of his words suggest this might not be his native tongue, but I haven't the foggiest idea where he may hail from where face tattoos would be common practice.

"I disagree," Ness rebuts. "I'm glad to have the chance to get your little welp here under control."

Tivoli tilts his head, lifting a single brow. A smile plays in the shadows of his lips. The vampires assembled behind him, three men and two women, seem surprised.

One, a woman with black hair down to her bellybutton, spits, "It would seem your temper is what needs to be controlled."

I swallow a lump of fear, trying to ignore the beads of sweat rolling slowly down my spine as I take in the shining weapons at their sides and pouches dangling from their belts.

Are those… what I think they are?

"I controlled myself far better than he deserved," Ness says. She squares her shoulders. "Let's hear it, then. What did he tell you?"

"You really think you're going to try to defend yourself to us?" The same woman takes a step forward, and shadows caress her dark skin. "We can see for ourselves what you did to his face," she hisses.

"Althea," Tivoli says, voice low. He puts out a hand and casts a single glance at her.

Stepping back in line with her fellows, she bows her head. "Excuse me, Master," she concedes, but her gaze still bores into Ness.

Dark eyes drinking in the light, Tivoli speaks smoothly, "Alaric informed us that you robbed him of a meal and cursed him. His only trespass, apparently, was to have stumbled across you during his hunt. His pledge, Simen, confirmed this to be true."

"What?" I blurt out.

Ness laughs, and everyone but Tivoli and I shivers at the sound.

"They failed to mention a few rather important details," Ness says.

Tipping her head to the side, Ness stares at the accursed vampire.

"Alaric here seems to have forgotten that he called me a witch. True, I was concealing my form," she says, before dipping her words in disdain, "but surely he knows enough about Netherspawn to know that no mere witch can rival my power. His little assistant here is evidence enough of that, with all his potions and the sheer amount of ingredients and time necessary to cast even a single spell."

Turning her gaze upon Tivoli and dropping the condescension from her tone, she adds, "He seems to have left out the bit where he spit on my face, as well."

Alaric's throat tenses as he swallows back his regret. His and Simen's eyes go wide.

How did they expect this to go? Did they think they'd all just slaughter Ness on sight?

Turning to face his underling with hands clenched into fists, Tivoli whispers, "Alaric, is this true?"

"Of course not!" he insists, voice rising a tad higher than it should when addressing his Master.

Tivoli lifts his chin and squares his shoulders. Alaric dip his head in submission.

"Your pardon," he begs, though his tone says otherwise.

The torches around us burn freely, solid flames without wind to whip them about. Taking a step forward, Ness offers, "I can show you. If you'd like."

Tivoli inclines his head in a barely discernible nod and breaks from the ranks. He and Ness meet in the middle of the Nether dome, and I stand alone. My palms sweat as I survey the predators assembled before me, wondering which ones would kill me quickly for a drink and which would draw it out.

Alaric and Simen glare at Ness, then at me.

Ness reaches one hand out and places it on the side of Tivoli's face.

And here I thought my heart couldn't possibly beat any faster…

Jealousy digs its heels in, spurring my heart along, and the poor beast hammers my eardrums. Dropping my gaze to the dirt at my feet, I do what I can to avoid any foolish moves. I only just see Tivoli's eyes close, barely glimpsing their movements behind his eyelids.

By the time I manage three deep breaths, his voice rumbles from his chest, quiet despite the anger held within it. "I will not tolerate lies, Alaric."

I hear his footsteps and lift my gaze. Ness stands alone, and Tivoli towers over the sniveling blonde vampire.

"Have you anything to say for yourself?" he demands.

Eyes trained on his boots, Alaric whispers, "She can show you whatever she wants. Why would she not twist the scene in her favor? Who do you really believe?"

One massive hand wraps around Alaric's throat, "Still you try to manipulate me? How prideful can you *be*?"

Squeezing tighter, Tivoli lifts Alaric's chin so that their eyes meet.

"Several of us have crossed Ness in the past, and she's handled every instance with more grace than even I would have managed. Were we dealing with any other demi-demon, I'd take their word with a grain of *salt*. Her," he pauses, leaning down to stare deeper into Alaric's eyes, "I believe."

Releasing Alaric with a shove, Tivoli watches him stumble and fall. "Try to bend my will again, and you'll not take another breath."

Hands shaking with fury, he turns to face Ness, once more. "I'm sorry for any trouble these incompetent fools have caused you." As he gazes at her, his eyes soften.

Ness inclines her head, neither accepting nor rejecting the apology. Her eyes never falter before Tivoli's.

Glancing at a blonde vampire behind him, he says, "If you will, Marie."

She closes her eyes for a split second, whispers a few words, and the world beyond the little dome reappears. Wind saunters in to flicker the flames of the torches and rustle the leaves above us. The sound of animals in the distance greets my ears.

And I breathe a sigh of relief.

Tivoli and the others make their exit, but Alaric and Simen hang back, apparently unsatisfied. Simen extends a hand to help Alaric to his feet, then rounds on me. Stomping over, he gets within a few inches, staring right into my eyes.

"You knew she was there, didn't you? You led us right to her, thinking she'd save you." His eyes narrow, and his voice is low.

"You think I would've willingly run in the direction of a demi-demon? If I'd known she was there, I would've run the other way. I'm not stupid. Who, in their right mind, would knowingly run to a demi-demon? There's no way I could have known she'd react how she did. Honestly, I would've assumed the three of us would've been killed or tortured."

Of course, only after the words have left my lips do I realize the way they sound.

Ness leaves the path, meandering into the undergrowth. She doesn't look back.

"Are you sure you're not stupid?" Simen hisses and shoves me.

I stumble back a step but recover quickly. Hauling back a fist, I plant it right on Simen's nose. The pledge lands flat on his back, and strands of hair fall free of their tie to drape over his forehead. But still, he snickers.

"Go on, run after your master." A sneer curls his thin lips.

Tivoli's voice rumbles through the woods, calling Alaric and Simen after him, and I spit, "Run after *yours*."

They gather themselves and trail along in the Coven Master's wake.

Shaking my head, at Simen and at my own carelessness, I desert the path. Twigs and vines claw at my ankles as I run in the direction Ness went. The terrain rises slowly, and my breathing becomes uneven.

"Ness!" I call out.

No answer finds my ears, and the fading light of sunset does little to illuminate the land around me, not here in the thick of the forest.

Stumbling blindly through the undergrowth, I panic.

If I get lost in here, no one will come looking for me. No one will tell my sister or mother what became of me.

But if I don't look for Ness, I'll never be able to make this right.

So, my feet carry me further, leaping easily over fallen branches that my eyes barely register. Finally, completely out of breath, I come to a halt.

"Ness?" I ask of the near-darkness.

Again, I receive no answer.

But over the frantic beating of my heart and my ragged breathing, I hear a soft, feminine voice. Sweet and gentle, the voice forms no words, only sound, lilting and falling. Ebbing and flowing.

I follow it, knowing it can be only her.

The trees become scarce as they near a rocky precipice, jutting up into the sky, and tall grass fills the space between their trunks. Wandering through it, I come to the bottom of the cliff which edged the path at the Nether dome and look to my left.

Finally.

Ness stands near a sapling with one hand outstretched. Grey light filters through the trees to dapple her with shadow. Palm up, with all fingers curled in except her index finger, she stops singing and drags her nail along the underside of a small branch.

A low hum reverberates through the air, and death consumes the branch, following in the wake of her touch. The bark falls away, and the leaves wither. As she nears the tip of the branch, the process speeds up. The end of the branch rots before her nail ever reaches it.

Eyes dancing over the rest of the tree, I find several similarly wilted branches on the same sapling.

Taking a few steps toward her, I try to explain. "Ness, I didn't mean that the way it came out…"

But she doesn't let me finish.

"You should have. I can't be more to you, or to anyone, than a demi-demon."

"You are, though," I whisper. Approaching her, I reach out a hand to touch her arm. "You're so much more."

Before my hand reaches her, she spins around. Finally, those golden eyes are upon me, but they're far harder than the last time I saw them.

"No. I'm not," she says firmly. "And if you have any hopes of your soul ever seeing the Etherrealm when you die, you need to change your tone."

With that, she leaves me, trudging back toward the path. I stare at the dead branches of the sapling for a moment, before turning to follow her. My eyes drift back toward that little tree several times until the behemoths of the forest close ranks, shielding their young from my view.

Chapter 16
Ness

Leading Elias down the path feels a lot like leading a lamb to the slaughter.

The sun filters through the leaves, shining brilliantly, but this isn't a day for such things. Today is a day for loss. A day better suited to clouds and rain, but the weather rarely matches up with moods.

My heart aches with it, already. I force my lips to seal shut, lest I accidentally betray myself before we reach Tor.

Elias walks behind me, apparently content to give me space, or perhaps lost to his own thoughts. I reign in my abilities for deciphering such things, much like slipping my eyes out of focus. The information is there, but I refuse to process it.

The sound of his footsteps, snapping twigs on the path as he tromps along behind me, and the scent of cedar and sap filling my nose is more than enough of a distraction from what I know I must do. I can't afford to go sniffing around, trying to discern the subtler notes of his scent to suss out his emotions.

Don't complicate things. Don't get sympathetic.

Hurt him.

Of course, some small part of me delights in the prospect, and I can only sigh.

The sound of a horse whinnying in the distance tells me Tor isn't far, now. With a blink of my eyes, I conceal myself, hiding the black and gold of my nature.

Behind me, Elias makes a soft sound of… disappointment?

No. Don't read into it.

He was just startled.

Surely, he'll be glad to get back to his life, to his family. His world is about to expand to include the Pack. As it should.

Breaking him is just… a necessary step to get him there.

A dip in the ground catches me off guard, and the feeling of missing a step brings my mind back to the present. I stare at my feet for a while, watching the terrain as I propel us faster and faster toward tragedy.

My hands feel clammy, and my mood drags along the ground behind me. Each bump in the path bruises it just a little bit more.

But I have to do this.

As we draw nearer to Tor, the din of voices increases. Doubtless, the markets will have just opened for the day. Had I had the forethought to bring some salves and potions, I could've made this trip a bit more worthwhile, financially speaking.

I glance at Elias, and he meets my gaze with an open smile. His emerald green eyes sparkle in the sunlight.

But how will they look after I tell him?

I'm not so sure I'll be up to any sales after this, now that I think about it. I would've lugged the stuff all this way for no reason.

Sighing deeply, I lead him as close as I dare get to Tor. The bustle of the town awaits. Just a few turns of the path stand between us and the crowds.

Already, the town criers can be heard delivering the day's news, and a steady hum of haggling fills the space between their announcements. Horses neigh, and all manner of animals chatter at each other.

But I stop and lead Elias off the path. He follows, unquestioning. We meander to a great old oak. Its branches spread wide, stifling the saplings which struggle to take root beneath them and creating a beautiful little oasis.

For the first time in days, the birds chirp overhead, and squirrels scurry from limb to limb, happily flitting about. Yet, it doesn't bring me the joy it normally would. My stomach churns nervously, soured by anticipation.

"There's something you need to know before you meet the Pack," I begin, staring at the massive oak tree. Taking a deep breath, I turn around.

Elias stares down at me, brows furrowed and eyes intense.

He's really going to hate me. As he should, but… the thought of him hating me, the only person I'm sure holds any positive feelings for me right now suddenly hating me…

It's almost enough to seal my lips. Almost. My eyes fall to my hands, worrying uselessly at each other.

"You should go to them, regardless. They're still your family…"

One thumbnail picks at a hangnail on the other. I break it loose and grasp it, pulling until it runs up the side of the nail. I jerk it loose, and as the sting bites my flesh, I say, "Your dad is dead. And…"

A drop of blood pools beside my nail, far darker than normal human blood. Finally, I look up. I have to.

I can't hide from this.

Locking eyes with Elias, I confess, picking up where I left off, "…It's my fault."

I watch surprise transform into anger and confusion. Sadness overlays it all, pulling his mouth open and tipping the corners of his lips downward. The air fills with a violent maelstrom of scents as his emotions flood the little clearing.

He shakes his head. "No," he says. "That can't be."

"It is, Elias. I'm the reason your dad is dead." A weak attempt at a bright side slips through my lips before I can stop it. "But, hey, at least he didn't abandon you…"

I regret the words, instantly.

His eyes flutter with pain, and he stares over my shoulder at the oak tree. Snapping his mouth shut, he swallows a lump in his throat.

I open myself to his emotions, knowing I deserve that much. The scent of burnt sugar, sharp and acrid, swirls around me. Undercurrents of molten iron roil beneath the bitterness of heartache.

I hear his heart struggling with this revelation. It beats like the hooves of a newborn foal, unsteady and faltering beneath its own bulk.

My stomach fills with guilt until it's so heavy that I don't know how to hold myself up anymore. The knowledge that Elias deserves better than to have to comfort me when I've hurt him is the only thing that keeps me on my feet.

"Show me," he says, finally bringing his gaze to rest on me, once more.

"What?" I stare at him, brows furrowed.

His eyes burn into mine with intense sincerity. "Show me. Like you showed Tivoli what happened with Alaric. I want to see what happened."

"No, Elias. I promise, you don't."

"Maybe not…" he concedes. "But I *need* to."

I open my mouth to protest, but no words come out.

If this is what he wants, who am I to deny him? I already denied him a father and an easy childhood.

So, I nod.

Placing my hand on the side of his face, I fight the urge to let my thumb caress his cheek. I close my eyes and go back to that night. Everything in me hates the thought of seeing it, again. As it rushes to the forefront of my mind, my stomach sours and my poor heart braces for impact.

***

I kneel on the floor of the cave I've been living in for a couple of years and split my palm open with a knife. The skin starts to close as I pull the blade free, so I dig deeper, sending spikes of pain through my entire body.

But I bleed.

Smearing my broken palm across the dirty stones I call a floor, I make a circle. Within it, I draw the symbol of the Netherrealm. Three vertical lines with the center being the tallest. Then, an x which extends past the shorter lines but is not taller than the center line.

Bits of dirt become mud as my blood coats them, and a few pieces stick inside my hand. It stings, grating like sand, but I keep going.

When my blood stops flowing and the skin starts to close, I cut my palm, again. Dipping a finger into the gaping wound, gritting my teeth against the pain, I use my blood to write my mother's name, over and over, all around the outer edge of the circle. I draw her symbol, a downturned triangle with a diagonal line crossing the upper right corner. I smear my blood in that wretched shape, painting it on the stone between the repetitions of her name.

Before going any further, I raise my voice to the sky, singing softly. Allowing myself to use the call for the second time in my life, I let the deeper tones out, harmonizing with myself. For nearly half an hour, I call the nearest chapter of Knights. They'll have some distance to cover, but it should allow me time to get the answers I need about my father and his family.

Finally done, I snap my fingers to light yellow candles, arranged at the tips of the bloody x on the floor. Then, again, to light six black candles at the tips of the three vertical lines.

The wind outside changes, growing urgent and frantic as it whips past the entrance to my cave. It howls and cries desperately.

Stepping into the center of the circle, I lift the blade to my wrist and press it to my flesh. Living alone for three years made me desperate, but it didn't erase the conscience Kirk helped me to build.

I am my own offering. My blood is my tribute.

It drips from my wrist, and I dig the blade into my other arm, determined to get enough blood, desperate to get this right the first time. Little drops of crimson fall.

They splatter across the symbol at my feet, pulling forth a dark red glow.

Clenching my jaw against the pain, I clumsily maneuver through the hand motions necessary to float the requisite herbs toward me, despite the pain in my wrists and arms. I sprinkle them around the outer edge of the circle. The glow reaches out for them, and they ignite, wrapping me in a ring of fire.

I stare at the markings I've drawn on the walls with my own blood over the past few days, repetitions of the Netherrealm sigil and my mother's symbol. Forcing my jaw to loosen, I whisper my mother's name. The symbols on the walls of the cave begin to glow.

"Solvi," I repeat. "Child of the House of Strength."

The fire burns brighter with each syllable, leaping to heights those measly herbs should not afford it.

I chant my mother's name, over and over. The wind grows fierce beyond my cave, and the smoke of the fire fills the opening, blocking out the moon. But I no longer need its light, for the symbols around me burn with the red-hot intensity of the sun.

A great rumbling fills the air, shaking my chest.

Not for the first time, I reconsider this. I've second-guessed it many times over the past few days, but it's too late, now. I need to speak to her. I need to know where I came from.

A furtive glance finds the chest, protected from the heat of the summoning with a spell I paid an Ether witch dearly for. It contains all the things I need to banish my mother, once I know what I need to know. The process will cost me more than the spell, possibly even my life.

But I can't let her leave this cave.

"Solvi, Child of the House of Strength," I say, one last time, this time in the language of the Netherrealm. "Come to me."

The air vibrates angrily around me, and the wind screams. Before me, space is torn asunder, and black smoke seeps through the gap.

My heart beats wildly in my chest as I watch the gap widen. My lungs falter, and a chill runs down my spine.

And there's my mother, stepping through the chasm before me. Behind her, fires burn freely, and people run about in chaos across glowing orange stone. Somewhere far behind her, a few voices ring out in song, drawing my brows together in confusion, but my mother quickly wipes it from my mind.

She towers over me, and her massive black horns scrape the top of the cave. They curl back like those of a ram but split and curl upward, as well. Tines reach outward in many directions, and everywhere they touch stone, it liquefies, dripping to the ground around her.

Golden eyes alight with the fires of the Netherrealm, she stares down at me. The black around her eyes reaches down over her cheeks, and her black lips curl into a sneer. White fangs protrude, digging into her bottom lip. Blood drips over her chin, oozing freely over alabaster skin.

My eyes rake over her stark-naked form as I struggle to comprehend what I've done.

Rivers of raven black hair flow over her shoulders, partially concealing her breasts. Golden talons reach out from her fingers and toes, far longer than mine ever thought of being. The black skin reaches past her elbows and knees before it becomes purple, then fades to white at her shoulders and hips. A long scaly tail reaches out behind her and drags itself over my table, setting it aflame.

The air in the cave swelters, shimmering with the heat which radiates from her. Beads of sweat roll down my spine, and I gulp down my regrets. Bordering on hyperventilation, I stare up at the Demoness who birthed me, wondering at my own stupidity.

Words drip like acid from her black lips. "You've done well to bring me here," she purrs seductively.

Shivers course through me. Power rolls off her in waves, and the stench of bloodlust burns my nose. All the questions I wanted to ask seem insignificant, now.

Who cares who my father was, or why she seduced and killed him?

He's long dead.

What does it matter where his family lives? They'll want nothing to do with me, anyway.

I'd thought to ask her what would happen to my soul if I lived according to the gods' will, but now such a question seems ignorant.

This is what I'm born of.

And to this, I will return.

My mother's tail whips across the cave, slashing the side of the chest which holds the materials to banish her. The spell upon it freezes a couple of spines off her tail. They fall to the ground and shatter, sending pieces skittering across the stone floor.

She wails in pain and rage, throwing her head back as she screams with a thousand voices. Lifting one hand, she floats the chest, then launches it across the room. It splinters, and the contents spill everywhere.

Her eyes whirl about, landing on me.

Time stops, freezing my heart with it. My lungs struggle for air, and my chest feels as though it may implode with the slightest touch.

One black hand shoots outward, wrapping itself around my neck. My hair bursts into flames at her touch, and my skin melts. Blood trickles down over my shoulders, and I fight against my instinct to pull at her fingertips, knowing my hands will come away charred or melted.

Solvi lifts me from the ground, and my feet kick frantically. Instinct becomes too much to fight, and I pry at her fingers, trying desperately to loosen her grasp.

Already short on air, my lungs shrivel within me, and I panic. Tears stream down my face, sizzling and steaming when they meet my mother's skin.

"You thought you could banish me, again?" Tightening her grip, my mother hisses, "You sniveling, little bitch. You could never do it."

She throws me across the cave, and I slam into the wall. Ribs shatter, and my leg cracks, twisting at an odd angle. My body burns with the pain, and a scream bursts from my raw throat.

She cackles as the agony tearing me apart forces my dinner to come back up. Mania overtakes her, and she dismantles the paltry home I've built for myself. She throws my flaming table against another wall and burns my meager food stores.

This is my only chance.

Lifting my hands, I send bundles of rosemary and sage toward the flames. They catch fire immediately, and she wheels on me, screaming furiously. The smoke wafts into the air and gravitates toward her. As it circles her, she coughs, and I watch the tendrils force themselves down her throat.

The sound of heartbeats approaches the cave, all beating frantically, and for a moment, I think the Knights have arrived. The pungent aroma of fear and fury surges ahead of them, but it's carried on waves of woodland scents.

Werewolves.

Eyes bloodshot with the smoke she's inhaled, my mother pins her sights on the opening of the cave. Her black lips curl upward in a sneer, thinking she'll just leave. Sauntering forward, she spares a glower for me.

I lie there, neck still bleeding, leg barely straightened and beginning to stitch the bone back together. But I smile.

"What could you possibly have to smile about?" she snarls.

Weakly, I lift one arm and motion as if pulling a rope downward. At the mouth of the cave, a cloth unfurls, and a rain of salt begins. It makes a perfect line across the opening of the cave.

"You're not going anywhere," I say.

Neither of us can cross that line, so long as it remains undisturbed. That'll keep her here until the Knights or the werewolves arrive.

But Solvi won't let this go.

Clenching her hand in front of her, she takes hold of my leg and pulls me across the cave toward her. The bone, still struggling to mend, shatters, and pain rips through me anew. I scream out, and fresh tears pour over my face.

Turning onto my stomach, I claw at the ground. My golden nails dig into stone, but she's too strong. The nails rip free of my flesh, and I leave trails of blood in my wake.

Then, seven snarling wolves fly over the line of salt, smart enough not to disturb it. They set upon Solvi, tearing into her flesh despite singed fur and boiling gums.

Crawling out of the fray on my elbows, dragging my shattered leg behind me, I make for the splintered remnants of the chest. The emerald lies the closest, shining in the light of the fire. I snatch it up, coating it with my blood.

A few white candles lie scattered and half smashed near the wall, reminding me of another step I need to take. I stop moving, grateful for the moment of rest, and pinch thumb and forefinger together to extinguish the yellow and black candles. Flipping my hand over, I turn them upside down, so their wicks can't be reignited by the fire around them.

My head falls forward, stretching and compressing the poor melted skin of my neck, and I take a few ragged breaths. A shaky sob rattles my broken ribs.

Behind me, a yelp rings out, and a body smashes into the cave wall. The hearts beating feverishly around me convulse with pain, and my own heart resonates with them.

This is my fault. I should've just let it go. I shouldn't have done this. I'm so stupid, Stupid, STUPID!

Rivers cascade over my cheeks, and I begin to hyperventilate.

What have I done?

Heart shivering with panic, I struggle to catch myself as I fall into chasms of despair. The melted skin on my neck suddenly feels like a noose, tailored specifically for me. It presses in as my body heals itself, and a strange frenzy makes me yearn to rip it away.

Another yelp. A body slams into the ground, followed by the sound of flesh being torn from bone. A painful whimper shreds its way through lungs convulsing in terror.

More heartbeats gallop toward us.

The Knights. Finally. If I can weaken her, they can finish her off. I just have to get this started.

That centers me.

Using every bit of strength within my possession, I pull myself toward the white candles. I pant with the effort and fear my poor heart may fail me, despite how impossible that is.

Turning the white candles so they'll stand, I snap my fingers to light them. My poor, bloody digits threaten mutiny if I don't leave them alone, but I can't.

As werewolves howl and bite and thrash, as Solvi burns and tears them apart, I reach for the book which fell from the crate. Flipping through pages rapidly, staining pages with my blood, I find the one I've marked.

The Knights draw near, and I begin reading the ancient text. I stumble through the language of the Gods, maiming most of the words. But it's enough to draw her attention from the werewolves.

If only for a second.

One of them, a massive grey wolf with emerald green eyes, takes hold of Solvi's wrist. Chomping down, thrashing that great body, easily twice my puny size, he rips off her hand. Black blood rains down over him, and Solvi screams.

The haunting sound of a thousand voices pouring from one anguished mouth terrifies me to my core. Chills run down my spine, and I know this won't go unpunished.

I watch in horror as Solvi's other hand slashes the grey wolf's side. Five talons rip him open from hip to neck. His bright red blood soaks the stone as he falls.

The Knights burst through the entrance, careful of the salt barrier. Silver swords aloft, all but one rush into the fray. They slash at Solvi, letting the werewolves weaken her for the time being.

The Knight who hung back begins chanting, properly reciting the banishing spell. He's been taught the language of the Gods, likely from his first days in the Order. In one palm, he holds an emerald which glows as he speaks. From his belt, satchels of herbs and salt dangle, unused and unnecessary, given my preparations.

The words prick at my skin, but they're not the same as the ones necessary to kill me.

As my mother weakens, silver blades tasting her flesh and Godspeak withering her soul, the Knights gradually turn their blades on the werewolves.

Then, I see it.

On their armor the Hartan sigil shines, not that of the Evaylan revolution. My heart freezes in my chest as I realize the slaughter that's coming.

With Solvi sufficiently weakened, all save the chanter turn their blades to the wolves they fought alongside mere moments ago. But the werewolves are no easy targets.

They eliminate three Knights right off the bat, but five still fight.

The chanting continues, unfazed. The air tears open once more. A great wind rushes through the cave, pulling my mother's damaged form toward the doorway to the Netherrealm. She slashes golden talons at everyone she passes, and one cuts across my side. I bite back most of my scream, but enough escapes to alert the Chanter to my presence.

As Solvi disappears into the fires of the Netherrealm, the rip in the air closes. The chanter finishes the ritual and stows away his emerald. Sauntering toward me, he draws a silver dagger.

Hating the violence even as I do it, I hold my hands in front of me and twist them. His neck snaps, and he falls to the ground, silver dagger sliding toward me. The tip touches my ankle and burns a small triangle into my flesh, forever branding me with part of my mother's symbol.

Another Knight notices me and makes a dash for me, determined to take me out before the werewolves end him. His dark brown eyes burn behind his helmet, and his lips mouth the incantation to banish me.

I feel another wind reaching for me, feel a hole opening behind me. Heat seeps out of it, burning my back. But jaws close around his waist before he reaches me.

He falls silent, and the tear closes, leaving me in the mortal realm. I breathe a sigh of relief but get no time to rest.

Grabbing the air in front of me, I latch onto an ankle and jerk another Knight to the side just before his blade can slash open a massive black wolf. Slamming my hand down, I propel the man into the stone. His armor clanks, and his helmet flies away.

Hurriedly, he snatches some silver pellets from a pouch on his belt and drops them into the talon wounds of the great grey wolf. The black wolf rips the man's throat open, just a second too late to keep the silver out of his packmate's wounds.

Vastly outnumbered, the remaining Knights fall quickly, and the werewolves shift back into their human forms. Unaware of the bond it will form between us, I set to work healing the injured, immediately. They stare at their wounds, open-mouthed, as the Nether flows through them. They would have healed on their own, but my way is faster.

Only two escaped injury, a man with dark eyes and riotous curls and a blonde woman.

I groan as the skin around my neck grows back and the bone fragments in my leg realign. But I never stop working.

"Please, drag them to me," I whisper hoarsely. "I need to see what I'm doing."

Five naked men and women pull two fallen wolves toward me, still too weak to transform. Staring into the wounds, I pick the silver pellets from their bodies without ever touching them.

They can't heal or be healed with it still inside them.

One of the men present kneels and takes the head of the tawny wolf into his lap. "Trinny," he croons, and the smell of burnt sugar fills the cave.

She licks his face, whimpering all the while, and he buries his face in her fur.

Before I can find the last pellet of silver, she breathes her last breath and goes still. Her body transforms one last time, but no soul remains within it. Hunching over to kiss her lips, her lover weeps for her. Auburn hair tangles over his fingers as he pulls her empty body against his chest.

Tears cloud my vision as I search for the pellets within the wounds of the grey wolf. He whines all the while, bleeding profusely. His chest rises and falls, far too rapidly. His heartbeat drowns out all other sounds, speeding along far faster than any heart ever should.

The silver is taking him.

Working feverishly, sobbing so hard my shoulders shake, I remove pellet after pellet. But there's always one more hiding below the last.

Desperate, I try to heal him, despite the silver, hoping it will keep him alive until I can remove them all.

But it does no good.

The life fades from those emerald eyes, and his body goes still in my arms. His final transformation rocks his body, jerking limbs and arching his spine. Then, he rests.

Behind me, one of the other werewolves whispers his name softly, "Everett…"

Green eyes stare at nothing. The spark they held just seconds ago has vanished.

Pulling him against me, I sob into his dark hair, inhaling the scent of his death.

It smells a lot like me.

***

I open my eyes beneath the oak tree with tears staining my face. They track across Elias' skin, as well, pouring from eyes that look so much like his father's.

Voice thick with emotion, I say, "Go to Tor. Find an Ether witch and seek Roata's blessing. Find the rest

164

of your family. Nolan should be at the Golden Tankard later tonight. He usually is. He'll be the easiest to find."

I tell him which of the men in the memory was Nolan. I tell him to look for long, unruly curls and dark eyes. I tell him to listen for that signature Rettish accent.

I don't tell him that he's my messenger, my sign to Nolan that I don't want someone else. Because Nolan will know I was never with Elias. He knows me better than that.

Then, I walk away.

Elias doesn't call after me.

And I don't look back.

Chapter 17
Elias

My feet carry me to Tor, but only because I have nowhere else to go. I could try to find my way back to Ness' cabin, but the path doesn't lead straight to it. I'd certainly get lost after leaving it, if I survive that long.

The grim sight of my father, dead in Ness' arms, covered in both their blood and the blood of Ness' mother, haunts me. It follows along behind me, nipping at my heels. No matter how hard I try to shove it away, it bites at me, still.

Even with no memory of him, I would've known him. His eyes, his hair… They perfectly match mine.

And Ness…

So young, so broken. Even with her own body torn and splintered and melted, she tried to help him.

The sight of her holding my father, weeping into his hair, grabs hold of me, taking my mind hostage. A lump forms in my throat, and my world centers on a tragedy twenty-five years past.

Again, I try to force my thoughts away. Weeping openly as I meander through the busy streets of a town I've never visited is a good way to make people want nothing to do with me. I'm torn between continuing on this way or drying my face. I need to find the Pack, but I don't want to see anyone.

Pushing my way through the crowd, I rub my hand over my face and enter the first store I come across.

It's quieter in here than on the street, but people still mill about. Heading up to the counter, I buy the necessities to send a letter home.

Scratching out the things I've learned of my father, I try to keep my eyes from blotching the ink with tears. I leave out all mention of Ness. They don't need to know how I learned of his death.

After sending the letter off, I wander to the tavern Ness suggested. It's early, but I've nowhere else to go.

Early afternoon finds the place mostly empty, and I take a seat at the bar. Only the most dedicated drinkers are present, and they say little. The sound of mugs settling back onto wooden tables after leaving cracked lips takes the place of conversation. The din of the town square peeks in as a new customer arrives, then deserts us all the moment the door closes, letting us sit in our own travesties.

The barmaid saunters over and places a mug in front of me. Near-to-overflowing, it stares at me, begging me to drink the dark liquid.

Fumbling in my pockets, I search for coin for the drink I didn't request.

"I didn't ask for coin," the maid says. "You're the saddest, sorriest thing I've smelled in a long time. It's on me."

Her nose wrinkles, carving shadows in her tan skin. She turns away quickly, going to serve the patron who entered after me. Her dark braid sways behind her.

Her phrasing strikes me as strange, but I pay it little mind. Instead, I lift the mug to my lips and take a drink. The pungent alcohol burns my throat, but I gulp it down regardless, hoping it'll blur the sight of my dead father. Or the sight of Ness walking away from me.

When I've drained the mug, I cradle my head in my hands and stare into the bottom of it. At long last, the terrible sight blurs at the edges, and a strange numbness comes over me.

Should it really hurt so much to lose him?

I never knew him. For years, I thought he was already dead. Just days ago, I hated his guts. But that could've been overcome with a good enough explanation for his absence.

He could've come back. He could've been part of our lives, in time.

But now…

My head spins with chaotic thoughts, unable to focus on them now that alcohol has been added into the mix. My mind whirls, making me dizzy.

Closing my eyes, I try to block it out, but somehow that makes things worse. I no longer see the mug or the bar. I see only my eyelids, painted the shade of Ness' lonely, little cave.

She was, what, 15? 16?

Kirk died when she was 12. Or maybe she was 13… Was she really alone all that time?

In that dingy, little cave?

The cruelty of the world makes my stomach churn.

No wonder she got quiet when I asked if she'd look for the Pack if she was in my place. She's been in my place, and she certainly went looking. Getting answers, in her case, just meant summoning a Demoness rather than confronting a werewolf.

The guilt that pervaded that memory, seeing it all through her eyes… feeling it the way she felt it…

The snap of ribs, the melting skin… the ripping of fingernails from flesh…

I shudder as it all washes through me, once more.

She didn't even try to ease her own pain, even though I'm sure she could. Instead, she healed the werewolves and eliminated the Hartan Knights.

She pulled the silver pellets from my father's dying body…

The barmaid sets another mug in front of me.

Chapter 18
Nolan

Swallowing the last bite of my meal, I fumble with my father's old sundial absently. My thumb slides the knob back and forth, lifting and lowering the style. Not for the first time, I wonder if Ness still wears the one I made for her.

Sipping my tea, I let my fingers trail over the dents and scratches which adorn the sundial's surface. The timeworn disc fits easily in my palm, and I run my thumb over its edge.

My mind drifts back to the invasion of Rettland and the first Hartan Knights I ever saw. Again, I watch them kill my father, then take my mother, sister, and I as slaves. My father's dark eyes stared blankly at the sky, a spear sticking out of his chest. My mother clasped my sister, seven years old at the time, to her chest and clutched my hand tight.

She didn't want me to do something rash. She wanted me to live.

And live, I did.

Mother is gone, now, but my sister and I carried on with a bit of help from the Nether. I hid the sundial throughout our time as slaves, keeping it safe. I watched as the Knights lugged my family around, forcing us to leave Rettland.

And I carried this little piece of metal with me. My only reminder of my father, my only reminder of home and peace.

Then…

I take another sip of tea as that night washes over me.

I see the Evaylan Knights, so poorly prepared for an invasion, riding and running toward us. But the slaves of the Hartan army fared far worse. Barely armed and given even less in the way of armor, I was pushed to the front line.

24 seems like a lifetime ago.

I suppose it was. In jus' a few months, I'll turn 124, celebratin' a hundred years as a werewolf…

A lifetime ago, or not, it repeats in my mind, now, fresh as ever. And again, I fall into the memory.

The spongy moss wraps around my feet as I run to battle, *knowing* I'm on the wrong side of the fight. But for my mother, for my sister, I have to survive. I have to find a way to get them out of this mess.

So I run, sword held aloft.

The sun doesn't glint off its rusty surface. The leather armor I wear doesn't clank like the metal armor of the Hartan Knights riding on horseback behind the ranks of slaves. The men in front of me meet the enemy, the people who will likely be forced to fight alongside us in coming days, and the sound of metal on metal erupts into the air.

Everywhere is chaos.

Screams and shouts fill the air. Blood splatters the ground.

A few Evaylan Knights break through the ranks, taking down anyone in their path. One squares up with me, and I narrowly avoid having an arm taken off. His miss throws off his balance, and he nearly falls.

But he's better equipped than I.

The sunlight bounces off his steel armor and nearly blinds me. Throwing an arm up to block the glare, I struggle to get my bearings.

Not that it matters, all that much.

An arrow soars down from the Ether and sinks into the Knight's neck. Guided by a miracle, divine blessing, or magic, it slips through the crack between his helmet and chest plate.

I move through the ranks, fighting just to survive. But I've fought so many times before.

My luck had to run out eventually.

A nasty cut on my arm and a heavily armored hit to the face… And I go down. I don't remember the hit. I don't remember falling.

Or being dragged back to camp.

Now, bits and pieces float up through the blackness of that afternoon.

My mother begging someone to help me, though I had no idea who it was at the time. My sister, Kate, crying over me. Her soft brown hair caked with my blood.

I remember one of her tears falling onto my cheek and the unbelievable effort I put into touching her face.

No' that it worked. I couldna lift a finger.

The next thing I remember is the pain. My shoulder felt like it had been ripped free of my body. Sound tore its way through my throat, and I struggled so hard to get up, to get away from the agony.

But a solid weight held me down.

Orwen is good. Even in wolf form, he deftly managed my thrashin' bulk.

But I was so far gone…

I close my eyes against the tavern, and my mind paints a crowd around me. A few men and women from the battle, several sailors, and a few people from Tarn, Tivoli's homeland.

A high feminine voice echoes out of the blinding light enveloping us, saying, "Of all who've died today, your souls are unplaceable. In your lives, some of you were logical and practical because of strong emotions. Some of you were highly emotional for logical reasons."

What? But… Mom and Kate…

I canna be dead. Who'll protect them?

My heart shambles along, barely able to carry the weight that's just dropped upon it. My palms sweat, and I choke back a sob.

This… canna be…

I glance at the man next to me, a slave that fought alongside me in the battle. His face is no longer smudged with blood and dirt. His clothes are miraculously repaired. But panic shines in his caramel eyes, echoing my own.

"What? We're… dead? I'm dead?" he asks. "What about my family?"

I have no answer for him.

The voice speaks again but doesn't address his questions. "Your actions in your lives were balanced in such a way that no clear path into the Afterrealm revealed itself for you. So, you must choose."

The space around us shifts, shimmering as it does. Suddenly, solid ground appears far below us, no longer the insubstantial white that rested beneath our feet mere seconds before.

Shrieks rise from the throats of several amongst the crowd as the momentary panic of being so high shatters their fragile control. A woman near the front of the group begins to sob. Vertigo pushes my brain out on an angry sea, bobbing and floating to and fro.

My limbs flail, but I don't fall. My stomach flips, threatening to be sick. But nothing comes up. I close my eyes and breathe, trying to quell the uneasiness writhing within me.

It doesn't work.

"The land before you is the Netherrealm," the voice says, though it sounds distant, now.

I open my eyes, unable to miss this visage.

Below me, the landscape ranges widely. People mill about, laughing and touching and dancing. Far away, in an arid land, fire burns everything, and screams reach toward us. Demons roam freely throughout the lands, indulging in whatever their emotions beg them to do. And humans mingle with them.

Everywhere I look, intensity, emotion, and excess rule. Tables laden with more food than a country could ever consume, beds filled with people and Demons alike, writhing together. Streams list lazily through forests, with all manner of people draped languidly along the shores, soaking up the light.

In that far off place, the fires burn hotter, crackle louder than any in the mortal realm. And the screams freeze the blood in my veins.

Then, in an instant, it all disappears, replaced by a cold, monotonous landscape. Nearly drained of color and completely flat as far as the eye can see, pale grey stone stretches out before us. People drift about its surface, purposeless beneath an empty blue sky.

No one screams.

But no one sings, either. Laughter is a forgotten concept here, replaced by logic and restraint.

"This," the voice says, loud and booming, "is the Etherrealm."

The people below us appear serene, content. Their faces hold no longing, no desire, no need. Barely speaking, they move about from one simple white structure to another, things I can't bring myself to call homes.

When their mouths open, only the most basic, civilized greetings come out. No love is expressed, but neither is hatred.

"You will not miss emotion if the Etherrealm is your choice. If you choose the Netherrealm, you will feel emotion, all the joy and love you could ever want. But you'll also feel more pain, more heartache, than you can yet imagine. You must decide for yourselves which you prefer, now, as you refused to do so with your actions in the mortal realm."

The Etherrealm disappears, and we're surrounded by the blinding light of death, once more. My mouth dries out, and I swallow hard. I try to close my eyes against the light of this strange place, try to forget this moment, my death, but to no avail.

I try to forget just how wrong we've all been about the Afterrealm.

But the light peeks in between my eyelids, prying its way into my brain. A thunderous roar cracks the world open, rumbling in my chest, and I open my eyes, raising my hands up to block my face.

Two doorways rip the blinding light open in front of us, revealing both the Etherrealm and the Netherrealm. Through either door, I see impossibly far in every direction, even where the two realms should overlap. This alone is enough to send my mind into a tailspin.

"Make your choice," the voice says, "and enter."

Jus' like that? We dinna get ta figure out our feelin's on any o' this?

I scoff, thinking that fitting of the Gods and the Etherrealm.

Why should our feelins matter to us when they apparently mean so little to them? The choice should be obvious, as far as they're concerned.

I guess it's obvious ta me, too…

My eyes gravitate toward the Netherrealm, pulled by the laughter and the singing. The agonized screams shake me to my core, but…

I look at the Etherrealm, at the blank faces and the aimless wandering.

Why would anyone ev'r choose that?

But they do. Lines form, and people pass into the Afterrealm. And far more line up for the Etherrealm than for the Netherrealm.

Are they so des'prate to forget the pain o' leavin' their loved ones behind that they'd give up their love fer them? Or can they no' see that the Knights were wrong?

Either way, I know my decision. I shuffle toward the Netherrealm, falling in line behind the caramel-eyed slave.

But as he passes through, the high feminine voice speaks. "Nolan, be still. You have one more decision to make. It may not be your time, after all. The Nether in your mortal body calls for you. Will you answer it?"

Without a second thought, I nod and find myself coughing and spluttering on a wooden table, far from the Afterrealm. A massive wolf stands over me but jumps down, letting my mother and sister embrace me, even as my body shudders with pain. My blood coats them, but it no longer flows from my body.

A burst of laughter in the Golden Tankard pulls me from my reverie. Blinking away the past and the Afterrealm, I stow the sundial back in my pocket.

Letting the tavern filter back into view, I sigh. Voices ebb and flow, and laughter bubbles from lips throughout the room. Nearby, a group of Order Initiates shouts and chuckles and jokes. The sign of the Knights blazes on their brand-new armor, not yet scuffed or dinged.

Or bloodied.

One raises his mug, bright-eyed, and says, "To the righteous people of Evayla! May we never succumb to the wickedness of the Netherrealm, again!"

Alina raises a brow and shakes her head. Her hands never stop, though, cleaning mugs between customers.

I scoff, rather louder than I intend to.

Naturally, the Initiates turn. The one who made the toast, a young blonde with peach fuzz on his chin, asks, "What's the problem?"

His tone isn't confrontational, though a few of his fellows clearly wish it were, if their expressions are anything to judge by. Yet, he merely seems curious.

And I can't help myself. I say, "People are no' more righteous er less wicked, now. They're jus' no' as des'prate."

Several people in the tavern turn to look at me. One, in particular, a man at the bar, stinks to the Netherrealm and back. Burnt sugar falls from him, and his green eyes are clearly bloodshot from crying.

But what I've said seems to be distraction enough for him.

He stares at me for a while, and…

Do I know him? The lad looks familiar.

But that's a topic to explore later.

"What do you mean?" the Initiate asks.

After finishing my drink, I say, "Och, lad. Have yeh fergotten ev'rytin' yeh learned in school? Yeh canna have been out long."

His eyebrows knit themselves together.

"I was a sickly child. I wasn't in school much. I only recovered my health a few years ago," the boy answers. Face brightening, he adds, "It was like a miracle. The Gods finally answered my parents' prayers."

I nod slowly and give the boy a knowing smile.

A miracle. That, er yer parents turned ta the Nether…

"Well," I begin, "a hundred years ago, even fifty years ago, the Hartan Empire was taxin' people right out o' their homes. No'ne could afford food, much less potions fer sick babes."

I raise one eyebrow to drive my point home, then continue, "People prayed ta the gods. They begged, ev'ry day fer salvation. But none came." Pausing, I shake my head and let out a deep sigh. "Tis hard ta get a God ta feel. Even harder ta get them ta act. Their emotions are weak, and their self-control is unrivaled."

Again, I pause. I glance at my plate, then back at the boy, very aware now that the whole tavern awaits my next words. My dark eyes smolder with a bit of momentary mischief.

"Tis a lot easier ta make Netherspawn feel some'tin. And if yeh make Netherspawn *feel* some'tin, they *do* some'tin."

"Sure," I tip my head to the side, "They dinna always do what yeh want, an' sometimes the result is more extreme than yeh wanted. Sometimes it backfires, completely." I lift one hand, palm up, and shrug to allow for the possible negative consequences.

"But *some* response from the Nether is bett'r than *no response* from the Ether. Makes people feel like some'tin bigg'r cares about them, like they're no' alone. The Netherspawn even helped wit' the revolution. Gods know the Hartan Knights were more extreme than the Evaylan ones."

Rising, I approach the bar, carrying my dishes to the counter. "Times are different, now. No'ne's hangin' in town square b'cause they couldna afford the taxes, raised twice in as many weeks. Kids dinna wither in the gutt'rs."

I turn to face the Initiates.

"So, I repeat… People are no' more righteous. They're jus' no' as des'prate."

The boy never had the opportunity to learn the lessons I've paid so dearly to learn and doesn't appear ready to lose his chance, now. "Then, why were the Knights needed before? Harta wasn't always here."

"Och, boy. There was a plague! People get plenty des'prate durin' plagues. Netherspawn were runnin' ramp'nt. They nearly outnumbered the mortals. Know yeh nothin' o' the Order yeh plan to pledge yer life ta?"

A glance at the boy finds him disheartened. The jubilation and confidence which filled him mere moments ago have vanished.

"No, no, dinna get all down. The Knights are no' *all* bad. Least, not the Evaylan ones," I smile wryly, and the boy smiles back. "They do a lot o' good tings fer people, and balance isna the worst ting to fight fer."

The boy visibly brightens. But I have places to be.

"Look, I 'ave ta go, now. Come back tomorrow, same time. I'll teach yeh some more if yeh want, and yeh can make an informed decision. Sound good?"

The Initiate nods, and I make for the door.

Rising onto unsteady feet, the heartbroken man from the bar follows me out the door.

"Nolan?" he asks, voice thick with alcohol.

Turning around, I squint at him and nod. Again, the feeling that I've seen him before hangs over me. "Do I know yeh?"

He shakes his head. "You knew my father."

"Nether take me..." I exclaim, realization dawning on me.

He looks jus' like his father.

"Elias? I'd given up on yeh comin' here a long time ago. Figured yer mum poisoned yeh against us."

Now, it's his turn to squint confusedly. "What?"

"Isna that why yeh stayed away?"

If no' that, then what?

"No. She didn't know dad was dead, only told us he was to spare us. She—" a hiccup cuts off his words, "thought he abandoned us. She still does, actually," he says, looking down. "My letter won't reach her for a few days."

Anger and pity weave together in my stomach.

"No wond'r she never made it ta the funeral. We disowned the poor woman fer nothin'… We sent a lett'r…" My chest rises and falls quickly. "I told them we shouldna 'ave done that. I told them, send one o' our own. But there was the war… and that night…"

I trail off, eyes widening for emphasis.

The night Everett died was a mess. We 'ad our hands full, ta say the least.

My hands clench, and I close my eyes. I take a deep breath to push away the sight of Solvi and the Knights, slaughtering my packmates. Another deep breath to push away the image of a young Ness, so broken, yet trying so hard to heal everyone.

Even wit bloody fingers and a melt'd neck, she tried so hard ta save them…

Her compassion nearly pulls a bittersweet smile to my face, but I hold it back for Elias' sake. He's clearly upset. Me grinning at him isn't going to help that.

"I know what happened," Elias says, words slurring.

Sighing deeply, I say, "So, yeh've been ta see Orwen and Nissa, then?"

"Who?"

"The Pack Alphas. How…?" Incredulous, I trail off.

How could he know if he hasna met them?

"I met Ness. In the woods. She showed me, told me I could find you here."

And suddenly it makes sense. The charred sugar scent of him, the knowledge he shouldn't have, all of it. I nod, and my nostrils flare as I take a deep breath.

"And the two o' yeh…?"

Jealousy rages within me, hot as a wildfire. My hands ball into fists, and I have to stretch them out a few times.

My eyes rake over Elias, and I reconsider. Shaking my head, I say, mostly for myself, "No, she wouldna. But yeh… Yeh would have, had she let yeh."

I grit my teeth. My chest rises and falls rapidly as anger begs me to punch Elias.

She wouldna. He's mortal. She wouldna be wit' him.

"How do you know that I…?" Elias asks.

"Please," I say, tapping my nose. "I can smell it on yeh. My nose never lies. And this," I tap Elias' chest, "reeks."

Pulling the sundial from my pocket, I turn to face north and check the time.

I dinna have long. Orwen and Nissa are expectin' me. Liam should be back, wit news o' the Howlers and whether we need ta worry.

I turn back to Elias, and his eyes linger on the sundial.

Is he curious? Or has he seen the one I made for Ness? Does she still wear it?

Sucking in my lips, I stall. My heart is a frantic, discordant mess of hope and riotous jealousy.

If Ness brought Elias here, which she musta done or he wouldna 'ave made it through the woods, she must be close. If she sent him ta me…

She had ta know I'd smell his broken heart…

That I'd know she wouldna have been wit' him…

My lips try so hard to lift into a smile.

Stop it! Don't let yer hopes carry yeh away.

First tings first. Elias needs ta meet the rest o' the Pack. After he sleeps off the alcohol.

"Come wit' me," I finally decide. Placing my father's sundial back in my pocket, I say, "We need ta talk."

Without another word, I lead Elias down the sloping, winding road out of town, stopping occasionally to allow for his inebriated state.

Chapter 19
Ness

I drift to Liam's cottage, barely noticing my surroundings. I'm not sure why my feet lead me there. Maybe because it's close. Maybe because I know I'll be alone for a while. He'll be busy at the foundry, and school will claim his wife and children for many hours to come.

Nolan will be at the foundry all day, as well, and Elias will claim his time this evening. Otherwise, I'd just wait in his cottage. But I won't be able to see him until tomorrow evening when he comes home.

I meander into Liam's garden and put myself to work. Idle hands will give me time to think, and I'm certainly not ready for that. I don't want, or need, to dwell on whether Nolan will take me back.

Or how pitiful or stupid I'll feel if he doesn't.

Never mind the damage I've done to Elias and his family...

Sighing, I try to keep my mind on the garden.

Trouble is, I quickly run out of ripe fruits and vegetables to gather. Placing the basket on the small porch, I wander into the little yard around the back of the house and lay down in the plush mixture of moss and clover.

My hand finds the small sundial on my necklace. It rests heavily against my chest, a weight I've long since grown to find comforting. Closing my eyes, I let my mind drift back.

In my mind, Nolan stands at my door with a beautifully wrapped parcel half-concealed behind his back. Little drops of sweat glisten on his forehead from the run to my cottage, and I know he must have left the Pack house as soon as the sun chased the full moon away the night before last. The pace he must have kept to make it in time astounds me.

A day and a half for a journey which should have taken well over twice that long…

All to see me…

My heart skips a beat.

He did say he'd be here for my birthday.

I smile, and my face warms, color brightening my cheeks.

"Hello, love," he says, dark eyes shining.

My arms throw themselves around him, no longer under my control. Not that I'd stop them. He pulls me against him, burying his face in my hair. His long, tangled mane tickles my face, but I nestle into it, breathing deeply.

It's been too long…

"Well," he says, pulling back to look into my eyes, "Can I come in, er must I stand outside like a strang'r?"

Taking his hand, I lead him indoors. The relative darkness of my cabin envelopes us, and I open the curtains further with a flick of one hand.

Stepping in close, Nolan releases my hand and lifts my chin with one finger. Eyes like smoldering coals burn just inches from my face. He brushes his lips softly against mine, and waves of heat surge through me. My eyes flutter, and my lips part with a gasp.

"Happy birthday, love," he says.

Finally, his lips land on mine, so soft, so delicate. Sliding his hand to my neck, he pulls me in for a deeper kiss, and suddenly, I forget that it's my birthday. I forget the full moon that kept him away with the Pack. I forget the world, everything but our lips and his hand against my skin, his thumb on my jaw.

Nolan pulls away, and a soft moan breaks through his lips. "I'd bett'r give yeh this, b'fore I end up… preoccupied."

He places the parcel in my hands, and I smile at him.

"You really didn't have to get me anything," I say, still unaccustomed to birthday gifts. Or… any gifts, really.

He doesn't speak, only smiles.

I make quick work of the beautiful wrapping, a luscious red fabric with a black bow tied around it, and find a small wooden box. Popping the lid open, I see a little metal disc, very much like…

"Is this… your father's sundial?" I ask, incredulous. My eyes find his, desperately seeking an answer and unsure what to hope for.

He shakes his head. "I'd give yeh the original, but I'm fairly certain my mum would find her way back to our realm an' kill me. Kate wouldna even have ta do that. She'd jus' kill me. Then, I'd never get ta see yer smile, again. So, I made yeh this one. I hope it'll do."

"It's magnificent. Thank you," I say, lifting it free of its wooden box. Setting the case aside, I hold up the chain and let the beautiful bronze disc spin before my eyes. A little knob on the side waits to be moved, to push the style up.

"May I?" Nolan whispers, huskily.

I nod, and he takes the chain from my hand to unclasp it. I spin around, lifting my hair as he drapes it over my chest. His fingers brush my bare skin as he closes the clasp, and my body burns for his hands to move over me.

I turn to face him with one hand fingering the necklace, and I wrap the other arm around him. A blush spreads over my cheeks, and I smile brightly. His lips brush mine, and my body ignites.

Now, lying on the ground behind Liam's house, I stare at Nolan's cottage. Luscious tapestries hang over the windows in place of ordinary curtains. The scent of him oozes out of the place, I know. I remember it well. But I'm too far away to appreciate it, now.

Another memory rises to claim me.

He swims before me, bathed in the light of the moon in a hot spring in the forest. The water caresses my naked skin, and Nolan dips beneath the surface for a moment, stealing himself from my view.

When he comes up for air, he's closed the distance between us. Dark eyes bore into mine, and his hand slides over my waist. My breath comes in short gasps. My heart skips so many beats…

He looks down at my lips for a second, a mischievous smile lifting one corner of his mouth. Pulling in a deep breath, he peers through long lashes to meet my gaze.

Reaching out, my hand grazes his hard, muscled chest before tangling in his wild mane and pulling him in for a kiss. Skin to skin with warm water lapping against us, we melt together. Hands cupping, eyes burning into each other, tongues tickling skin, we let the moment take us.

His lips burn my skin, and I beg for more.

Pushing me back against the rocky edge of the pool, he lifts me up. My legs wrap around him, and we writhe together in ecstasy.

My horns scrape against the rock behind me as I tip my head back, delighting in Nolan's soft nibbling at my earlobe as my body falls apart. My nails dig into his back, and a guttural moan sends him spiraling down after me.

By the time I come back to myself in the moss, my heart beats unevenly. Breathing feels more like panting, and my stomach coils tightly with lust.

And if that were all I felt for Nolan, it would be so simple. Lust cares not who fulfills it. Moving on is easy.

But I need him for so much more.

I hope it isn't too late to tell him that.

A gentle summer breeze rustles through the leaves, whispering to me, but all I can do is wish for Nolan's voice. Warm sunlight caresses my skin, yet it pales in comparison to the heat that his touch once brought me.

My hands trail through the moss, and patches of clover lay down at my touch.

But I want his skin beneath my hands.

I want him.

But what if he doesn't want me?

Another night from our past comes back, unbidden, to haunt me. This one, far more recent, aims to break me.

My eyes well up, anticipating the memory.

The night Nolan proposed floats in the shining glaze of tears.

My hands are warm in his, and his eyes sparkle with the question he's just asked. It hangs in the air between us, and he waits patiently for me to speak. The moon shines, half full, outside my window, and for a moment, I stare at it.

Can I really make him do this?

I can't tie him down. I can't let him commit to… me.

A shiver rolls through me at the full breadth of what I am.

"Ness?" he asks, uncertainty making his voice waver over the single syllable.

I drop my eyes to my lap, knowing I would wither beneath his gaze. Beside me, the fire crackles, keeping total silence at bay. The soft fur rug suddenly feels too warm beneath me, but I can't move. Paralyzed by my emotions, I close my eyes.

He deserves so much better…

But I can't speak.

"Ness?"

The anguish in his voice, the way it breaks… That does it.

I buckle.

Brows furrowed, my eyes seek his, only to find his lips drawn downward and his eyes strained. His hands tighten on mine.

I have to say something.

I know this, and yet, not a word comes to mind.

"You…"

No good. Start over.

"Nolan, I can't let you… This…"

I shrug. It's the wrong thing to say, and I know it. But I say it. "This can't possibly be what you want."

Moving one hand to the side of my face, he stares into my eyes. The logs in the fireplace shift, tumbling and sending a shower of sparks up into the chimney. Neither one of us spares it a glance.

"I want a future, Ness," he says. "I want a future *wit' you.*"

"There is no future for me, Nolan. I could be killed the next time a Knight sees me. I probably should be killed, honestly. It's just a matter of time."

My words aren't meant to hurt, but they do. We both flinch from them.

He pulls his hand away, and I ache for his touch. Glancing at the ceiling, he sucks in his lips.

"I see a future fer us," he says earnestly. "But… if yeh canna see it…"

Smudging a hand over the bottom half of his face, he steels himself.

A pit of despair, so much like nausea, opens within me. Because I know where this conversation leads.

Unable to meet my gaze, Nolan takes a deep breath. "If yeh canna see a future fer us… Then, what are we doin'?"

Words tumble from my lips, heedless of my preference for silence. "I don't know."

My eyelids flutter, and I slam my lips shut before I get sick. My body revolts against this conversation, against the path I know it leads to. Palms sweating, I clasp my hands together on my lap.

"I…" Nolan's voice breaks, and he runs both hands through his hair. Eyes averted to hide the tears forming within them, teeth gritted against the agony I can smell pouring off him, he takes another deep breath.

"I canna…"

Helpless, I watch him stand up.

"I canna do this," he whispers as he walks to the door. It opens so easily, letting him walk out of my life. It shuts behind him, even easier.

Leaving me should have been more difficult, should have held more obstacles. But the door swung wide to let him pass, without even a creak of protest.

That night fades to black in my mind, then slowly transforms into the red of sunlight seen through eyelids.

What if he doesn't want me, anymore? What if I hurt him too badly?

The weight of those words falls upon me, forcing air from my lungs and tears from my eyes. Inhaling sharply, I give myself over to the pain of knowing that after tomorrow, I may never hold the hope of being with him, again.

My hands release the clovers, and I roll onto my side, curling into myself. Knees drawn up to my chest like an infant, I sob openly, loudly. Were anyone home, I'd be embarrassed for making such a spectacle of myself.

But I wouldn't stop.

The idea of it, the ache of meaning so little to him that he could block me out in the blink of an eye fills my blood with ice. My heart stutters in the sudden cold, and I lay there, aching for him.

Slowly, I wear myself out. Tears dry on my face, and the shuddering sobs come less often. A strange numb feeling overtakes me for a while, and I lay there, watching the tiny bugs in the clovers.

They crawl over the leaves and venture toward my sundial. It rests upon a small mound of moss with little white flowers sprinkled around it.

I reach for it and blow the little bugs from its surface. Holding it tightly against my chest, I try to think of the good that could come of this. Eventually, the agonizing hope that maybe, after tomorrow, I'll have Nolan back in my life seeps in.

I can finally tell him that I... love him...

Maybe we could move in together. We might have to find somewhere new to live, though, if Elias brings the Knights down on me.

My stomach sours once more at the thought of leaving my home, the only place I've ever grown to love.

But no.

Even in my agony, I can't lay that at Elias' door. He wouldn't do that. Impulsive he may be, but coldhearted actions are beyond him.

Another sharp breath pierces my lungs, a remnant of the sobs which wracked my body moments ago, and I close my eyes against the sun. For I know what Elias will do.

He'll go home and move on. Elias will find someone else and forget I ever existed. His life will go on without me.

As it should.

As everyone's probably should. I shouldn't be here, shouldn't exist.

I slide a hand through the clovers and pluck one at random. Through the blur of fresh tears, it appears to have four leaves.

Not that it'll make a difference.

My life, my very existence is a curse, and no amount of luck can undo that.

I glance over at Nolan's cottage, still empty, and sigh.

Cursed or not, I'd be a fool not to make the best of the life I have, the life Kirk and my father died for.

I can't squander the chance I've been given.

I have to start living.

***

Sari comes home first and sends the boys into the house. She finds me laying in the yard, silent and unmoving, but no worry seeps off her. I healed her through her transformation. When I'm near, she feels my heartbeat in her bones. She knows very well that I'm alive.

The acrid smell of burnt sugar pours off me, and as she draws near, it hits her. I watch as her nose scrunches up at the unpleasant stench of an aching heart. I see the way her brows reach for each other, hoping to extend a bit of comfort in the face of pain.

She pulls me from the ground, drawing upon the strength granted her as a werewolf. Her mortal body would have struggled to lift a child, but since she joined the Pack a couple decades ago, her small frame has the potential to shock.

Her dark hair flutters against my arm, as do the strings from where Elias tore off my sleeve. Without a word, she leads me into the house she and Liam share. Her grey eyes survey me as she heats a kettle. She casts a few concerned looks my way as she corrals her children into their room to practice what they learned in school today.

With their door shut, she pulls the whistling kettle from the hearth and speaks. "Liam should be home, soon." Pouring the tea into cups, she adds, "Whatever happened, I'm sure he'll know what to do. He always does."

Her faith in him to fix whatever problems arise would normally spread a smile across my face. Today, it drags my mood lower.

Will I ever have that?

I guess I'd have to count on someone to take care of something for me, first…

My gaze drifts to the window as she begins preparations for dinner. Nolan's house stares at me through the pane, begging me to venture across the yard and pay a visit, regardless of Elias' looming arrival.

My previous nights with Nolan parade through my mind. Nails digging into flesh that regenerated easily. His thick lashes hanging low over dark, smoldering eyes. His accent caressing my ears as he moved over me, pulling me tight against him. My hands clutching his hair before sliding across his muscled back.

His laugh, low and musical. The husky lilt his voice always held when he called me "love."

The endless discussions of what's best for Evayla no longer seem so abhorrent as they once did. His need to help others, even at great cost to himself or the ones he loves…

I can tolerate the uncertainty. I can ride with him into any battle… if it means I get to be with him.

My eyes fall to the table, and my shoulders rise with a deep breath.

Why couldn't I realize all this a few months ago? Why couldn't I realize it through the years that we were together?

Before I can venture much farther down that road, Sari meets Liam at the door. They embrace, and a gentle kiss joins them.

I avert my gaze.

Sitting at the table, I sip my tea as he washes the day's work from his skin. When he returns, free of soot and slag, he sits across from me. His and Sari's sons, Timothy and Jack, play roughly in the living room, bumping into the couches and tables with little consequence.

I open my mouth, and my guts spill out, pouring into their ears. I tell them everything that brought me here, from the day in the meadow to the oak tree confession. I say nothing of my intentions of seeing Nolan, though. I certainly don't mention my continued feelings for him.

Nolan deserves to hear it first.

The idea that Liam would protest sliding back into my past also does a number to still my tongue. He remembers the fighting as well as I do.

Liam places a hand on mine, and warmth soaks into my bones at his touch. It doesn't spread far, stopping at my wrist. He can't change my moods as I could change his. But the effort at comfort is appreciated.

A hush falls over us, and he gazes lovingly at his sons. A smile lifts the corners of his lips as the children make up their own games. They're far more brutal in their games than mortal children. Smacking into the floor or the corner of the table hurts, yes, but they know very well that no lasting harm will come of it.

Living recklessly is just the way of Netherspawn. We know that, with time, our bodies will heal. We know that the pain in our hearts won't actually kill us, even if we sometimes wish it would.

"Liam," I begin, merely curious, "Do you ever wish you were mortal?"

His gaze finds me, and he considers his words carefully. "No," he says, finally. "But then, no one *I* love is mortal."

My jaw drops.

What? He thinks… I love Elias?

"No," I huff.

Though, them thinking that could prove rather convenient… It'll stop them from asking too many questions, at any rate. I'll just explain after I speak with Nolan.

"It seems to be the case," Sari pipes up from the hearth.

I shake my head and run my hands through my hair. I don't like deceiving them, but Nolan needs to be the first person I tell. For nearly a decade, I couldn't say it. I can't tell them, first. So, I say nothing.

For a moment, we all fall silent. The laughter of the children and the chopping of vegetables fill the air. But in my mind, chaos rules. Thoughts spin and twine together, screaming as they run through my head.

The ache builds, and I have to say something.

I can't let them think I love Elias. I just have to… not tell them I love Nolan.

"It's not possible, though," I say, matter of fact. "It's too soon. Love takes longer than this."

Liam smiles at me, eyes gentle. "Love doesn't care about time, dear."

Heaving a great sigh, I challenge him, thankful for the change of pace. "How do you know that, wise old wolf?"

Sari giggles as she pulls dishes from the cabinet, apparently taking more joy in my mockery than Liam does. He quirks his brows higher, feigning offense.

"Because if it did," he says, "I wouldn't have loved my kids before spending even one second with them. Sure, it's a different kind of love, but it *is* love."

I purse my lips skeptically. Grudgingly, I have to admit he has a point. Not that I voice this admission.

For effect, he adds, "If love cared about time, we'd all have to *learn* to love our crying, screaming, *crapping* babies."

The three of us burst out with laughter, and Sari even lets out a small snort. "That would make raising kids a lot harder," she admits.

The mirth deserts us slowly, and silence reasserts itself over me, holding my lips shut. The burnt sugar smell still pours off me in waves, making even *my* nose wrinkle.

Eventually, Liam pats my hand, again. "You love him," he says simply. "That's okay."

A fervent shake of my head gives rise to a near-hysterical laugh.

They're convinced *that it's Elias…*

I tug at another hangnail, ripping it up along the side of my finger before it finally comes away. A droplet of blood sneaks out, beading upon my skin. I watch it grow before lifting my finger to my mouth and sucking the blood away. The metallic taste lingers on my tongue as I try to supply them with another scapegoat for my scent.

"I just… Everett…"

The thought brings tears to my eyes, and I blink away the memory. It really, genuinely is part of my broken heart.

"I can never think of him without… ending up like this."

My heart squeezes painfully in my chest. The air fills with the terrible scent of heartache, reaching out from me all the way to the living room. The boys stop playing and come over to hug me. Cradling them against me, I do all I can to keep waterfalls from opening up in my face, again.

"You need to eat, and you need rest," Sari says, settling a plate of food in front of me. "You can stay here, tonight."

The offer can only come from her. Liam would never extend it, knowing the strain my presence puts on her.

I glance at her, ready to insist that I go to the Inn, but the look in her grey eyes brooks no argument. So, I nod. "Thank you."

The sun fades from Tor quickly, dipping behind Mount Surm. The light from the hearth and the candles around the cottage illuminates our meal. Timothy and Jack keep the conversation light, regaling me with tales of their school time exploits. They even eke a few smiles out of me.

After we finish our food, Sari tucks the boys into bed, and Liam sets up a cot in the living room for me. He and Sari disappear into their bedroom, and I lay awake, staring out the window at Nolan's house.

Taking a deep breath, I fill myself with the scents of Tor. A jumbled mess of people, animals, and immortals makes my head swim, heavy with a million emotions. But the faint scent of sandalwood drifts in through the open window, barely discernable in the mixture.

The ache in my chest eases.

He's home.

So close…

Yet, an ocean lies between us.

My chest collapses as I exhale the town. Another breath finds the scent of cedar and sap, and I know Elias still resides within Nolan's walls.

Another breath pulls him into my lungs, once more, and I find the acrid stench of heartache hanging around.

I've broken him.

But his life and family await him in Everson.

My hands shake, yet the thought of Elias returning to a peaceful life comforts me.

Chapter 20
Elias

Tucked away in Nolan's home and instructed to sleep it off, I settle in for a nap. Nolan promised me answers when he returns from his errand, and something tells me it'll be a long explanation. But at this point, I could use it.

Unable to sleep just yet, I look around at the guest room. The smell of sandalwood incense fills the place, telling me exactly where Ness got hers from. Nolan likely has it brought over directly from Rettland.

It makes me wonder, though.

Does she buy it from him?

Or is there more between them?

My stupid heart jumps into my throat.

Why shouldn't there be more between them? His soul is already headed for the Netherrealm. It was the moment he became a werewolf.

My eyes slam shut, unwilling to picture them together. Yet, I can't help wondering if she'll run back to him. A deep, sick feeling churns in my stomach, the toxic result of alcohol and jealousy mingling freely within me.

Rolling onto my side, I block the world out for a while, willing myself to think of anything else. Alva and my mother come to mind first, but they bring with them another sore spot, my father and the impending heartbreak which has yet to hit them.

Something else.

Taking a deep breath, I think of all the things I'll have to do when I get back to Everson, hoping thoughts of home will soothe me.

Mom will doubtless have a stack of skins for me to tan. She was stocked on leather before I left, but by the time I get back, I'm sure she'll be running low. My job at the mine may or may not be waiting for me, given my sudden absence, but that's fine.

I'll just work with mom and Alva. It's almost their busy season, anyway. Harvest always means plenty of accidents, plenty of wounds to heal. Cooler temperatures bring orders for jackets to replace the ones neighborhood kids outgrew over the summer.

But the tedium of it all, the familiarity that I once loved about Everson, no longer calls to me. It dulls my senses far more than I intended it to. My eyelids grow heavy, but only due to boredom.

The place that calls to me now is Ness' cabin. The soft fabrics frame my thoughts. The pungent aroma of wood smoke which seems to cling to her, following her around even in the absence of a fire… It reaches out for me.

But I know I'll have to go home.

For the sake of my soul, she won't have me, even if my feelings for her may have already settled my place in the Afterrealm. After all, rumor has it that the gods are unforgiving, except for Roata, of course.

Ness'll have Nolan here to comfort her in my place.

Again, jealousy riots within me, burning its way through my veins. Bitterness swells within me.

I'll have no one, and she'll run to him.

Rubbing a hand over my face, I sigh. No sleep will see me through this.

But then, a thought strikes me.

So obvious, so simple.

So perfect.

All I need is Nolan's help. A smile warms my heart. Finally, I drift off to sleep and dream of Ness.

***

My idea finds Nolan slightly less than receptive. One hand finds his hip, and the other ruffles his hair.

"Yeh dinna know what yeh ask. Tis a big ting…" he hedges. "And so suddenly. Aye, it seems foolhardy, if yeh ask me."

But something more lurks behind his eyes. He doesn't just dislike my plan for being fast. His hesitation seems born of something else, altogether.

"Yeh dinna even know her that well," he says, pacing on the other side of his table. "No' ta mention the fact yeh may die. Aye, yer father's blood'll make yeh heartier than most, fer sure. But tis quite a risk, all the same. Fer someone yeh jus' met. Have yeh no prospects back in Everson? Surely, there must be someone."

Then, more to himself than to me, he adds, "Anyone, but her."

Dark eyes falling to the floor, he pinches the bridge of his nose and sighs. The look in his eyes, the way they narrow as they rake over me, confirms my earlier suspicion.

Ness sent me to her ex.

Did she think he'd run me off? Or did she think he'd give the most thorough answers to my questions about my father?

He certainly did that.

He told me more about the Netherrealm than I ever could have thought possible. Apparently, it isn't half so bad as Ness and the Knights would have me believe. It's just more intense than the mortal realm, more emotional. Like Netherspawn are more emotional than mortals.

His description of the Etherrealm, a cold, emotionless place filled with uncaring gods, seems a far cry from the haven of peace I'd been led to believe it was.

Nolan told me all about the man I never knew. He told me that my dad was far older than my mother, that they met when the Pack was helping run the Hartan

Knights out of Everson. He said that, when they met, dad knew instantly that she was the one.

Nether take me, Nolan even told me my mom was distantly descended from a demi-god. As such, she could never be a werewolf. Apparently, they'd planned to tell Alva and I what they each were and allow us to make our own choices. But when mom thought herself abandoned, that plan changed.

Now, I stand here, making my choice and hoping to the gods, or perhaps to the Netherrealm, that Nolan will help me take the woman he clearly still loves. I don't particularly like my odds, but he's the only Pack member I've met, so far.

"Can we jus' sleep on it?" he asks, pain plainly visible in his eyes. "Tis a big ting, after all."

Chapter 21
Nolan

"What am I ta do?" I ask, leading Liam into my home. "Should I go ta Orwen an' Nissa?"

A deep breath fills my lungs, and the scent of cedar nearly chokes me. He's still in the spare bedroom, waiting.

So much fer hopin' he'd wise up an' leave…

"You know my position in the Pack. They trust me with decisions like this, as their beta, and I think you know what I'd do," Liam answers, taking a seat at my table. "You could ask Ness what she thinks of all this. She hasn't left, yet."

My heart leaps into my throat.

She's still in town. I could talk ta her, sort this all out, but…

If she's still here, why dinna she come see me?

"I know her answer. I dinna need ta ask," I say firmly, hoping to convince myself in the process. "If she want'd him changed, she'd o' done it herself, Liam."

"I know," Liam allows. "But if you saw her, you wouldn't be so hesitant."

Silence permeates the walls, soaks into the stones in the floor. I wait on bated breath, unwilling to disturb the stillness until he explains. My heart becomes a chasm, threatening to swallow me up.

"She isn't coming back, Nolan. I know you've held out hope, not that I fully understand why. The two of you certainly had a knack for making each other miserable."

"Yeah, we also had a knack fer makin' each oth'r happy," I say, trying hard to keep my tone from becoming too argumentative.

"I know," he admits, voice soft.

I jerk a chair across the stone floor and sink into it. My fists ache to break something, but I plunge curled fingers through my hair, instead.

"I know we fought," I whisper, voice barely traveling past my lips. "Fer an immort'l, she cares v'ry little fer anytin' past the comin' week. And I always, *always* have ta help ev'ryone. But I'm workin' on that. I dinna insist on goin' ta see ta the Howlers meself, did I? She's the one, Liam. She's it fer me."

"You know why she can't look further than that. She's never thought herself worth hoping for more than next week," Liam says. Then, tone dropping, he adds, "Kirk saw to that…"

My stomach sours. All Ness ever got from that bastard was grief and guilt. He's the reason she hates the Netherrealm so much, him and her mother. They're all she knows of it. She doesn't realize it isn't all bad, certainly not when compared to the cold, heartlessness of the Etherrealm.

Just because her mother surfaced from the deepest, most agonizing pit of the Netherrealm doesn't mean it's all like that.

But thanks to Kirk, her mind is closed to any other view of it.

If the man were alive today, I'd kill him. An' I'd smile the whole damned time.

Yet, here and now, my anger is short-lived. My heart quickly turns to the effect he had on Ness. As usual. Through that filter, Liam's words cut me to the bone.

Because I know exactly how she sees herself. She's shown me a few memories before. The depth of her agony hits me once more, sending a shudder through me.

Bu' she never sees the cruelty in him, the way he twist'd 'er. She only sees the faults he told 'er she had.

"But," Liam continues gently, "she's considered Elias' life beyond next week. I think she wants him around, Nolan. She just didn't want to be the one to turn him. I know you don't want to hear this, but… I think she loves him."

My jaw drops, and my eyes go wide. My entire world shatters, and I fall into the hole within my chest.

"What?" I gasp, deep voice cracking as the air rushes from me. "But she always… I mean, when I told her, she couldna say it… But fer him… *Fer him*, she can?"

"It's not that she said it, but… she's hurting, Nolan. Badly," Liam waits, clearly hoping I'll meet his gaze.

But I can't.

"I… There's something more that I didn't tell the Pack about," Liam says. "I hate having to tell you this… I was hoping I wouldn't have to…"

"What? Jus' say it."

My face scrunches, and my hands ball into fists, wrapping tightly in my hair.

This… This is goin' ta hurt.

A moment passes without a word, without a sound. As it stretches out, I fear insanity may grip me before Liam speaks.

But finally, words fall from his lips. "When I went to find the Howlers… Ness is the one who took them out…"

"Yeh told us that…" Gritted teeth cut my words into a growl.

"Yes, I did. The Howlers got a few bites in. They tore her up. Elias… She let him carry her to a little stream, let him clean the blood away. She let him help her."

"There was… tension between them." Liam's words come out slow, halting.

And each one cuts me, dragging blades over my skin at an agonizing pace.

Then, the killing blow.

"I really think she loves him, Nolan."

It pierces my chest, and for a moment, I fear I may double over. Again, the sensation of falling washes over me in frigid waves, and I forget to breathe, forget what it *means* to breathe.

"Take some time to think it over. But if your feelings for her are the only things stopping you…"

Liam lets his words hang in the air like a noose, waiting for my neck. All I have to do is step into them and jump.

My lungs grapple with all I've learned, struggling to remember how to pull air past the lump in my throat. The sunlight streaming through the window warms my back, but the heat of it does nothing to free my heart from the icy clutches of rejection.

She loves him.

A deep breath lifts my chest, and a tear falls down my cheek.

"Can yeh get her ta stay anoth'r night?" I ask, and my words come out flat and defeated. I wrap Liam's words around my neck, ready to step forward into nothing.

"I'm sure I can think of something," Liam answers.

I hear his chair scoot across the stone as he rises, but I don't look up. I count the grains of my wooden table, focusing on a knot in one of the boards. His hand pats me on the shoulder, and a good, solid sound reverberates through the air.

"You know where to find me if you need anything," Liam says. I listen to his footsteps, pounding across the floor beneath his weight.

The front door opens and closes.

A single sob rips its way up my throat, punctuating the silence.

Footsteps from the bedroom make their way carefully into the main room. Everything in me wants to reach out and break this man, this thief. I want to rid myself of the obstacle between Ness and me. My hands desert my hair and curl into fists on the table. Teeth gritted, jaw clenched, I fight the urge to kill him and be done with all this.

But I know that wouldn't solve the problem.

No' if she loves him.

I choke back another sob.

Elias' hand finds my back, patting far more gently than Liam did in a weak attempt at comfort.

"I'm sorry," he whispers, but the words aren't enough.

I look at him, and my insides churn wildly with equal parts rage and sorrow. Tears shimmer, hovering on thick lashes, partially obscuring my view. Rubbing a hand over the bottom half of my face, I drop my gaze, once more, to the rough wooden table.

A deep breath lifts my shoulders, and two tears fall to darken the wood.

***

Venturing from my cottage, I leave Elias to his thoughts. The sound of him, busying himself in my home, follows me to the back of Liam's house. The scent of him tramples through my senses, wreaking havoc.

So, I take a deep breath and seek Ness out, instead.

I need ta talk ta her, need ta see her.

I need ta know…

The all-consuming need for answers drives me forward, pushing me into the woods after a faint trail of wood smoke. I slip through the trees, silent and searching. My nostrils flare as I breathe her in, trying to savor the scent like I used to.

But my insides quake before the thought that… maybe she's moved on.

A heady mixture of burnt sugar and spoiled food falls from me, and the birds nearby stop singing. Rabbits and squirrels stop in their tracks.

I pull my emotions inward, unwilling to let my personal agonies destroy their peace, as well, but that does nothing to settle my heart. It struggles beneath thoughts of Ness choosing Elias. My lungs falter, and I grit my teeth.

Maybe Liam was wrong...

I grasp that frail hope so firmly that it shatters, digging sharp edges into my heart and mind.

The sun dips toward the horizon, and gray light filters through the leaves around me. Shadows play in the brush, painting the undergrowth the color of my despair. They consume my feet as I step through, clinging to me and wrapping inky black tendrils around my legs.

No path presents itself, but it doesn't matter. The trail of wood smoke doesn't twist or turn. It cuts straight through, meandering only when a tree forces a curve.

She knew exactly where she was going.

I take a deep breath, filling my lungs with the scent of Ness, and my heart beats unsteadily.

But not for the usual reason.

The weakness in my knees finds no home in desire or love. Today, fear and uncertainty shake me to my core.

My stomach churns, and I put a hand on the nearest tree trunk to steady myself. The rough bark presses into my skin with the full force of my weight as I lean weakly against the tree. Desperately, I ache for Ness to tell me Liam was wrong.

To finally tell me she loves me.

A faint wind lifts her scent and throws it in my face, taunting me.

I have ta know. I canna wait aroun' 'ere all day.

Pushing away from my crutch, I carry on through the woods. Twigs crack beneath my feet, and small vines rip as I force my way through them. Animals scurry away, fleeing before my frantic advance. But it doesn't matter.

I need to find her.

As the trail of wood smoke grows stronger, my frayed nerves tie themselves around my heart, and my pace slows. My hands linger on tree trunks, begging them to spare me the pain of losing Ness.

But my feet carry me onward.

The wind blows her scent to me, filling my lungs with wood smoke, but nothing else. No emotions float toward me on the breeze.

A small clearing appears, and her scent grows stronger. It wraps around me, begging me to come closer. I take a few tentative steps forward, and there she is. Her brilliant red hair shines in the waning daylight.

Blue eyes struggle with some emotion, but the air is empty of it, offering no clues.

My feet turn to stone, and I linger on the edge of the clearing, letting the shadows and wind conceal my presence while I gather the courage to ask her…

Him?

Or me?

My heart stops in my chest, frozen solid as I watch her reach out to touch the trunk of a large oak tree. She sobs, shoulders rising and falling in sharp, staccato bursts. Tears cascade over her cheeks, dripping from her chin, and I ache to go to her.

But my feet don't move.

A whisper drifts from her lips, barely reaching my ears, "I'm sorry, Elias." Her voice breaks over the words.

In an instant, the scent of burnt sugar floods the clearing, pouring off her. She sinks to her knees, cradling her head in her hands as she cries.

For him.

The ground opens beneath me, and suddenly, I'm falling, again.

My lungs pull in one sharp breath, collapsing my throat, then they fail me altogether.

Darkness descends upon my soul, and I back away from the clearing without a word. Ness sobs at the base of the tree, but I know, now.

Going to her, holding her… It won't help her.

But I know what will.

***

As night falls, tension builds within me. Dread thickens my blood, slowing its progress through my veins. Elias stands by my table, waiting. I pace before him, growing more and more restless as the full moon rises.

I've told him the risks, several times over. He may die. His father's blood makes it less likely, of course, but the danger is still there.

No' ta mention the fact I may lose control…

Instinct an' emotion are hard'r ta resist under the full moon, especially in wolf form.

I'm no' entirely sure o' meself… No' sure I'll be able ta resist killin' the one who's takin' Ness from me…

Once I taste blood, his blood…

Deep breath. Just… focus.

Fer Ness.

I nearly buckle, knees growing weak beneath the weight of my grief.

This… is what she wants…

Elias watches me as I move from one side of my home to the other, unable and unwilling to stop myself from moving about, and he grows nervous. I smell it on him.

Have his choices ev'r forced him ta stare so closely at his own mortality before?

Finally, I force myself to stop stalling. I turn to face him.

"Are yeh ready?" I ask, voice low and empty. My dark eyes hide in shadow, but his shine like emeralds in the firelight.

He nods.

I venture into my bedroom, leaving the door slightly ajar. "Stay here," I say. "I'll be back. I'd prefer no' ta ruin my clothes if I dinna have ta."

The darkness swallows me. I slowly undress, laying my clothes on my bed and trying my damnedest not to think of her… Lying in my bed, smiling at me. Pulling my shirt up over my head or ripping it off. Her hands on my chest, her lips on my skin…

My hands shake. I close my eyes, wishing it were that simple to close out every thought. I wish, with every fiber of my being, that it were that simple to just forget.

But she wants him…

An' I can nev'r forget that.

Standing in my room, stark naked and staring at the moon through my window, I feel it pulling at my soul. My eyebrows knit together, and I take a deep breath.

Jus' get it ov'r wit'.

It's the only ting yeh can off'r her, now.

My spine goes cold, sending shivers through me.

With tears rolling freely over my cheeks, I peer at the shadows of the moon and begin the transformation. My bones break at my signal, shifting, shrinking, and growing to become a wolf. My skin stretches and tears, only to piece itself back together.

The pain of it barrels through me like a rockslide, but I grit my teeth against it to keep from screaming. Falling to all fours, I feel the Nether surging through me, burning and soothing, all at once.

As the transformation draws to a close, anger courses through my veins, and my blood cries out for Elias' death.

Chapter 22
Elias

Waiting in tense silence, I ball my hands into fists to keep them from trembling. Moonlight streams in through gaps between curtains, eager to watch the birth of her newest servant. The light emanating from the hearth flickers over me, every bit as restless as I am.

A groan squeezes past gritted teeth, barely making it out of the bedroom. My ears strain to hear it. Though I know what's happening, though I know it's real, my brain struggles to accept the change as the sound morphs into a canine whine.

I've never seen a transformation before, never even met a werewolf in person until this week. Now, my blood, my father's blood, cries out for it, pulling me toward the bedroom. I even take a step forward, despite Nolan's insistence that I stay put.

The moonlight hits me as I take that step, and my veins cry out, begging me to open the curtains. No full moon has ever affected me so. My heart beats strong and hard against my eardrums, and my skin tingles.

The door to the bedroom creaks open, and a massive black wolf steps through. Head dipped by calculation, he stares at me. Eyes like the night bore holes in my flesh.

I gulp down a mixture of fear and excitement, suddenly unsure of my instincts for the first time in my life.

But… This is what I'm meant to be.

Just like my father before me. This is my birthright.

The black wolf moves in closer, and my heartbeat drowns out the world. Nolan stands on two feet, putting his front paws on my shoulders easily. Teeth bared, he sniffs my neck.

I find myself panting as his nose brushes my skin. Fear slithers down my spine when a low growl rumbles near my ear.

Then, his jaws land on my neck, and it's too late for second-guessing.

Chapter 23
Ness

Sipping at a steaming mug of tea, I gaze at the stars through a little window. Sari and Liam sit at their table, casually discussing the boys.

They urge me to come away from the window, to join them. At long last, I do, but I ache to look out once more. Perhaps it's the pull of the full moon. Perhaps it's the bad feeling that's been brewing in the pit of my stomach for the better part of the day.

Or maybe it's the hint of worry beneath Liam and Sari's words.

They've buried it carefully. I can barely smell it on them, but it's there, like the stench of sweat and something spoiling. They plaster cheap smiles across their faces.

For a moment, it angers me.

Do they really think they can sneak this past me? Another werewolf, maybe. If they're young. A vampire, almost certainly.

But a demi-demon? No way.

The anger passes quickly though, overrun by the anxiousness growing in my belly.

Talk of Timothy's progress in school becomes a murmur, clouded over by the thoughts in my head as I try to figure out what they could be hiding. But I come up empty-handed.

My eyes drift to the window, yet again, having only briefly left it. My gaze skips past the dark green curtains, forsaking them for the trees and the stars outside. Suddenly, staying cooped up here seems the worst possible thing in the world. I have to move. I need to stretch.

"I think I'm going to take a walk," I say.

"Okay," Liam says. "Just don't wander too far." He laughs, trying to play it off as a joke.

But I don't see the humor in it, and the scent of something rotting slips free of his control.

Why is he so anxious?

It nags at me as I leave their cottage, coiling the knots in my stomach ever tighter. The fresh air and the light of the moon do little to calm me.

Glancing back at Liam's cottage, I make sure they aren't staring through the window before I turn for Nolan's house. With my heart in my throat, I walk the path to his door. The velvety scent of sandalwood floats out of the place, wrapping around me. Cozy and luxurious, I breathe it in, letting it comfort the ache in my soul. It teases the knots out of my back.

My nerves calm, and something, perhaps my own deluded hope, tells me that I'll have him back, tonight. I lift a hand, ready to knock on the door. Eyes closed, I breathe deeply.

And there, underneath that most beloved aroma, lies the scent of cedar and sap.

My eyes snap open, and frustration coils tight in my belly. My hands ball into fists. Heart skipping along far too quickly, my muscles tense.

Elias is still here? Why didn't he leave?

All I want is to see Nolan. Is that so much to ask?

Eyes rolling up to stare at the moon, I turn and lean against Nolan's door. The terrible feeling in my stomach seems to have found its cause and steadily intensifies. I close my eyes to stave off the dizziness and the tingling sensation crawling up my neck.

Then, an agonized scream rips through the air inside Nolan's cottage. I jump, and my heart freezes. Another quieter shout follows closely on its heels, and I turn to face the door. Terrified of what I'll find on the other side, paying no mind to the pounding footfalls of Liam and Sari running to meet me, I stumble back a few steps.

My stomach flips over on itself, sickened with worry. Elias' hoarse whimpers leak through the door.

I just… I never thought Nolan would hurt him. I wouldn't have sent Elias to find him if I thought that…

If Elias dies, it'll be my fault. I sent him here.

My hands tremble, one wrapped around the other in front of my face in a horrid mockery of prayer. The blood drains from me as I stare at the door.

If he dies… I'll never forgive myself.

My heart burns with the resolution to save him. I grasp the doorknob, knowing I'm not prepared for what I'm about to see. Rage boils my blood, and the metal doorknob crumples in my hand. I push, and the door swings open, slamming into the wall with a loud bang.

And my heart drops so far that it trips me, sending me stumbling forward.

Elias lies in the middle of the kitchen floor, bleeding from a massive bite on his neck. I shuffle forward, mouth agape, and fall to my knees at his side. With a gasp, I take his hand in mine.

The Nether in the air shifts, gravitating toward Elias. Cold sweat beads on my skin and drips down my spine as the scene dawns on me. My mouth falls open.

Nolan transformed him? But… Why?

Elias' heart beats faintly in my ears, and his eyes slip in and out of focus. With some difficulty, his gaze lands on me. Blood is smeared over his face. It mats his hair into clumps, even as it spreads across the floor. Pulling forth all the Nether I can drum up, I channel it into him.

He can't die like this.

Footsteps barely register as Nolan meanders out of his bedroom, wearing only pants and Elias' blood. He isn't even surprised to see me, but a deep sadness tugs at his lips. It furrows his dark brows and taints his eyes.

He reeks of burnt sugar, and it makes my hands shake.

Clinging to Elias' hand, I raise my other arm, intending to pin Nolan to the wall by his neck. But even now, even with Elias bleeding on the floor before me, I can't hurt him.

"What did you do?" I whisper, wishing I could shout to force the worry and the guilt out of my body. My hand falls uselessly to my lap.

Croaking the words out, voice hoarse and broken, he says in that irresistible accent, "Only what he asked me ta do."

Tearing my eyes from Nolan, I force myself to the task at hand. Tears roll down my face as I gather more and more Nether, pouring it into Elias. My skin warms and tingles with it, akin to the early stages of a panic attack.

Yet, I savor it. It's my only way to help him.

Elias' eyelids flutter and fall shut.

For the last time?

NO! It can't be.

My bones riot at the thought of bringing another person to their death.

The bleeding slows. A bit of savaged flesh closes, but the damage…

Oh, the damage…

The pool of blood spreads to soak into my dress as if this garment were simply meant to be stained with Elias' life.

His grip on my hand weakens, despite the small progress his neck makes, and I press a hand to his forehead. Skin slick with sweat and blood, he's cooler than he should be.

Sobbing, I beg the Etherrealm and Netherrealm alike to spare him. Dousing him with Nether, I will it to rinse the blood from his flesh, all the while fearing it's too little, too late. My brittle heart aches with the loss I know is imminent, and the world appears black before me.

Breath hitching in my throat, I cough and sputter until my ribs hurt.

I've led him to his death. He'll never see his family, again. He'll never move on. He's dying...

Because of me.

A gentle hand on my back nearly gets broken as I shove it away. Undeterred, Liam crouches beside me.

"What happens, now?" I ask, hoping he knows something I don't.

Rubbing my back softly, Liam says, "Now, we just have to wait."

Fear wraps ice-cold hands around my heart and gives it a squeeze. Placing a tender hand on Elias' unusually pale cheek, I lean over him to peer at his wound. My tears fall onto his bloody skin, but he doesn't so much as flinch.

Nolan's voice drifts down to me from somewhere far away. "I jus'… I jus' want yeh ta be happy, Ness."

And then, I see this for what it is.

Rejection.

My body recoils as waves of agony wash over me.

He doesn't want me…

Blinded by sorrow and rage, I spin to face him, prepared to launch into a rampage. But he's gone, pulling the door shut behind him even as I rise onto my knees.

A fresh wave of tears cascades over my cheeks, and I settle myself into the pool of Elias' blood. Lying down beside him, the only person I have left, I drape one hand over his chest and press myself to his side. My head fits nicely on his shoulder, but it leaves me staring at the wreckage of his neck, barely touched by the Nether.

My eyes slam shut, unable to bear the weight of it. His heart struggles to beat beneath my hand and makes little to no impression on my ears.

This can't be it. He's supposed to go back to Everson. He's supposed to have a future.

And I'm supposed to have a future with Nolan…

Another sob rattles my ribcage, and my entire life unravels within me. Lukewarm blood soaks into my dress and hair. My tears do little to wash it from my face.

Desperation alone compels me to dig deep. I pull the Nether from the dirt below this place, from the air around us. I rip it from the blades of grass beyond the walls and the branches which hang over the roof. All of it enters me, and my skin grows hot with it.

Beyond me, voice so quiet as to be insubstantial, Liam whispers, "Ness, I think we've got company."

The door opens, and Nolan rushes in. Words tripping over themselves in their urgency, he says, "Someone's comin,' an' they've brought the Knights. She canna be here." Then, "Nether take me. What's she doin'?"

But their revelations and questions are inconsequential.

Nolan's voice only serves to push me further into darkness, chilling my soul with the knowledge that he *wants* me to move on.

The pool of blood I lie in begins to sizzle where it meets my flesh, but I don't care. I pull Nether from the clothes upon us, from the cottage we lie in. Rid of the Nether, it all glows, lending my nightmare the light of the Etherrealm.

When it becomes too much for me to hold, when the skin of my hands grows dark, my form reveals itself of its own accord. The air around us rumbles with my change, rattling my unsteady chest along with everyone else's.

And still, I gather the Nether, only barely managing to keep myself from pulling it from Nolan's bones...

Now that I can't have him...

Only when my muscles ache and my bones threaten to explode do I touch Elias' broken, battered neck. The flesh gives beneath my touch in a way it never should. With all the shimmering buzz of a lightning bolt, my hand burns his skin. A thin veil of smoke rises from his wound.

Forcing the Nether out of me, I push it forward. The skin on his neck darkens as the Nether enters him, but his body responds.

His heart strengthens, hammering in my head. His lungs pump with renewed vigor, and his lips part to pull in a deep breath.

My body quakes with the effort of dispensing so much Nether, but I don't stop. I can't.

I can't have Elias' death on my conscience.

Even as the door slams inward and chaos erupts behind me, I keep going. The bleeding stops completely, and Elias' skin, muscles, and veins reassemble themselves.

The world behind me is comprised of shouting and the sounds of battle.

But I'm here.

With Elias.

The only person I have left...

A tiny hiccup of anguish bubbles up through me, and I sob deeply. Chest clenching, I shudder.

Nolan doesn't want me.

My heart shrivels into a tiny ball, squeezed tight by the prospect of a life without him.

Elias' skin tries to close over my hand, so I pull back, sliding my hand to his collarbone.

Suddenly, a blade slices into my side, burning as it pierces skin and muscle, and I'm dragged away from Elias by the ankle. Two Knights pour a ring of salt around me, and instantly I feel myself grow weak.

Self-control wanes, and fury takes over. Eyes wild with rage, I snatch one of them up by the neck. Tightening my grasp, I smile at him, watching his eyes go wide as he struggles for breath, then I throw him across the cottage.

I try to grab the other, but the salt and silver have done their job. I'm too slow. He skips out of my reach, tumbling to the floor as he does.

Desperate, I grab the hilt of the dagger with the aim of pulling it from my stomach. But it burns my hands. I can't hold it, can't pull it free of my flesh, and the world around me slips out of focus.

Red rims my blurry vision, and black spots drift lazily across my eyes, concealing the forms of Nolan and Liam fighting off the Knights. My stupid, silly little heart wants so badly to protect Nolan, even though he doesn't want me.

But my ears ring, and suddenly silence screams louder than any mortal or immortal ever could.

Falling to my knees, I watch my blood drip to the floor.

One of the Knights begins the incantation, and I nod, accepting death if I can't have a life with Nolan.

Chapter 24
Elias

Lightning bursts across my skin. The world flashes in and out of focus alternating between bright white and the darkest black I've ever seen. The darkness calls to me with Ness' voice, and I'm helpless, giving myself over to it without a shred of hesitation.

Pain arcs through my body, twisting me into unnatural positions. My bones snap, and my skin stretches. My lips part in an agonized scream which worsens as the sound grates through my damaged neck.

That little scrap of memory brings the world careening back into focus. My neck. Nolan and the moonlight that pushed his teeth just a bit deeper. My scream, and him saying Ness will be along soon.

Then, her. Crying over me, forcing my body to heal itself when it desperately wanted to give up. Until…

My eyes snap open to find Nolan's cottage awash with blood. The scent of it, strong and potent, flows through me, and my mouth waters. Nolan and Liam each fight off several Knights. A few stand off to the side, muttering strange words that make my skin tingle.

My feet, no… My paws…

Nether take me, it worked!

Shock pulls my eyes down for an assessment, and I find myself transformed. Dark brown fur coats all four legs.

Four legs!

But my paws are slick with blood.

And it isn't all mine.

The smell of wood smoke rises from the puddles and smears, leading to Ness. She lays in a ring of salt. A gleaming silver dagger protrudes from her stomach.

Every muscle in my body tenses, and a growl rises from my throat. Rage like I've never felt before burns my veins, and my lips curl into a snarl. The scent of molten iron drips off me. Dipping my head low, I ache to tear into the one who did this.

Nolan shuffles backward and swipes at the ring of salt surrounding Ness with his foot. She gasps as the circle breaks.

Launching myself forward, I follow suit and slide across the salt nearest me. It makes my paws tingle uncomfortably, but Ness moves. She rolls onto her back, and that simple movement delights me.

Nolan shoves his attackers away, face contorted in anguish. He falls to his knees at her side and reaches for the dagger in her stomach. He pulls it free, skin sizzling where it meets the hilt. His face relaxes when the blade slips free of her flesh, despite the pain his hand must be in. I watch as he gulps down a lump in his throat, gazing at Ness with tears in his eyes.

The smell of something acrid and burnt oozes from him. He reaches out, but a Knight grabs him from behind before his hand touches Ness' cheek.

The blade flies free of Nolan's grasp as the Knight spins him around. It clatters to a stop at my feet, and the hideous odor of the one who stabbed her rises to my nose. Vinegar and dill flood my senses, sending a shiver of hatred down my spine. One of the men speaking the language of the Gods reeks of it, and Ness' blood still coats his hands.

Three Knights stand in full armor with pouches of salt hanging from their belts and silver shining in two out of three sheaths. They eye me warily. One even takes a step back. The one whose dagger lies at my feet, the man of vinegar and dill, draws a shining silver sword from a sheath on his back and takes a step forward to meet me.

Yet, he worries. He sweats beneath his armor, and it smells rotten.

A shiver of anticipation sweeps through me as I curl my lips back, ready for my teeth to meet his flesh.

Near the door, Liam shouts at Nolan. "Get them out of here!"

But I don't want them to leave. My insides burn. My heart cries out for their blood to spill across the floor.

Nolan knocks a few Knights unconscious, then drags them from the cabin.

Liam screams at the remaining Knights, easily heard over their broken, whispered chanting. "Get out of here! It's his first time! It's not going to be good."

I take a step forward, sizing up my prey.

They hurt Ness. They want her dead.

But I will be their end.

"Elias, stop!" Liam yells.

But I feel the Netherrealm coursing through my veins, screaming for vengeance. Another step forward and the chanting ceases completely. Silence rules the cottage.

The Knight who stepped back first makes a break for the door, but I can't allow that. I spring forward, blocking his path, and a sharp bark bursts from me. He skids to a stop, clanking in his heavy armor.

Footsteps pull my attention away, but only partly. Wood smoke drifts closer and closer, soothing my temper, just a bit.

Ness steps between me and the Knights. Her hands are up, palms facing me. She speaks, but not to me. "Liam, Nolan, get them out."

Then, beautiful amber eyes meet mine, and she says, "Elias, it's okay. I'm okay, see?" She moves the torn flaps of her dress to reveal her torso. The wound no longer bleeds, and the skin is closing.

"I'm healing. Don't hurt them," she pleads, eyes full of past sorrows. "You'll regret it. They'll haunt you, just like Kirk and your father haunt me." She holds my gaze and lifts a hand to the side of my face.

She doesn't see the nearest Knight, the dumbest Knight, raise his sword behind her.

But I do.

Rushing around her, I leap on him, knocking the sword from his hand. Before I can bite down, she pulls me up into the air. My stomach flips uneasily.

Damnable floating.

Nolan yells, rushing forward. He jerks the Knight to his feet, spitting, "She's tryna help yeh, slaggin' fools!" He slams the man into the wall. Bottles and trinkets on a nearby shelf rattle with the impact, tipping and rolling into the floor.

Teeth bared, Nolan hisses, "What did I tell yeh abou' informed decisions, jus' days ago? Thought that might appeal ta yeh 'logical' types." He slams the Knight into the wall, again, earning a satisfying whimper of pain. Practically growling, Nolan says, "Guess not…"

He shoves the man past me, and the other two follow, willingly. They stare up at me as they pass, eyes wide behind the slits of their helmets.

When they've all gone and the door shuts behind them, Ness sets me down. She stares into my eyes again, but her face is unreadable.

"Elias, you can't hurt them. I know, *I know*, you want to. But you *have* to resist."

Closing my eyes, I take a deep breath, chest expanding until it aches. Ness' hand finds the side of my face. Warmth spreads from her palm, seeping into me. A shiver runs through me, and her warmth reaches out, loosening the muscles and untying their knots. The anger melts from me, and I open my eyes.

A gentle nod, and then, I transform.

Again, pain surges through me. Bones shatter and rearrange. Skin tears and reattaches. I fall to the floor, a writhing mess of agony, praying that it gets easier to handle. After what feels like an eternity, I lay naked in Nolan's floor, human.

Ness kneels beside me. Tears slip from her golden eyes, falling into smudges of blood. "You shouldn't have done this," she whispers. "This isn't the life you're supposed to have…"

"Yes, it is," I say.

Placing one hand on the side of her neck, I lean in close. Breathing deeply of the luscious scent of wood smoke, I press my lips gently to hers.

She sniffles. Once, twice.

Hunger consumes me, and my hand wraps itself in her hair, pulling her in for a deeper kiss. After a moment of hesitation, she wraps her arms around my shoulders. But even then, she holds back, and a wisp of burnt sugar floats up to my nose. Then, nothing more than wood smoke.

Ness pulls back, golden eyes heavy with emotion. She dredges up a scrap of my clothing from the pool of blood beside her, and I drape it over my lap.

I open my mouth to speak, meaning to ask Ness what's wrong. After all, we can be together, now. But a knock at the door silences me. Liam peeks in through the partially opened door. He walks in with Nolan following moodily behind.

The big man won't meet my eyes, keeping his gaze on the floor. He doesn't even glance at Ness, though her eyes never leave him.

She sits there, in a pool of *my* blood, in *his* floor, weeping quietly.

Anger rolls through me.

She should be happy. We can be together, now.

Why isn't she happy?

Because of my stupid soul?

Sighing, I try to stifle the anger. I rub the back of my neck and focus on my breathing.

Movement at the window catches my attention. Eyes like a spring sky stare in at us. Simen, Alaric's pledge, glowers at Ness and Nolan. Cold fury simmers in his eyes.

I take a deep breath, still trying to cool my temper, and the scent of vodka wafts through the open window to greet me.

Simen spits on the ground, but his eyes never leave Ness and Nolan.

His meaning is clear enough.

This isn't over.

***

After a lengthy discussion with Liam, cleaned up and clad in clothes borrowed from Nolan, I head toward Liam's house with Ness at my side. I don't make it far before Nolan stops me with a hand on my arm. Ness looks back, concern edging her eyes.

"I'll only keep him a moment," Nolan assures her.

Her eyes bore into Nolan for a long moment, looking so much like… betrayal? But he doesn't meet her gaze.

I nod, and she releases my hand. In the absence of her touch, my fingers seek the black scar on my neck, burned in like lightning bolts. The skin stings, but whatever she did, it's pieced back together.

Silhouetted against the glow of his cabin, Nolan struggles for words. All the scents of the Knights linger, mixing with his and making him hard to read. His eyes hold mine for only a second before falling to his hands. They worry at each other, moving ceaselessly.

When next he meets my gaze, his dark eyes glisten in the soft light of the full moon. Voice thick with tears, he says, "Be good ta her." His eyebrows raise in an open threat.

"I will," I say, fighting off the lump forming in my throat. Though I know the words aren't enough given all that he's put himself through today, I say, "Thank you."

248

"I dinna do it fer yeh," he says. His gaze falls to the soft moss at his feet. Without another word, he turns and ventures back into his bloodied cottage.

Lifting my eyes to the sky, I inhale deeply. The moon sings in my veins, begging me to change. My bones yearn to break and rearrange themselves. But I refuse them. Something stronger pulls at the Nether surging through me.

Tearing my eyes from the moon with far more effort than I ever expected it to take, I wander toward the smell of wood smoke with one more glance at Nolan's cottage. Through the window, opened to air out the scent of so much blood and so many people, I see him standing motionless near my bloodstain.

A sob racks his massive frame, and his hand rubs the bottom half of his face, dragging itself over the stubble of the day. Guilt wars with happiness in my stomach, unsettling me.

Yet, my feet carry me toward Ness, tugged along by the gravity between us.

Chapter 25
Ness

The lush moss behind Liam's cottage calls to me, begging me to lay upon it. Cleaned and freshly changed into my nightgown, my legs drink in the cool night air.

Silence rules the nearby woods, either because all the animals are asleep or because they fled when my true colors came out to play. I haven't gone back, not yet, at least. My eyes still sparkle liquid gold, and my horns yet pierce the night sky.

I know I'll have to hide tomorrow, but for now, I can be free.

My eyes fall shut, and I inhale deeply. The wind can't whip away the chaos of scents next door fast enough. Though, something about them seems off. The bourbon, I expect. For Alaric to have brought the Knights to us, after his stupidity with the Coven, rings true.

But the scent of vodka lingers amongst the others, hiding where it shouldn't be.

It means a second vampire was here. But I can think of none stupid enough to follow the Knights into the home of a werewolf on a full moon, to attack his demi-demon ex-lover, during the transformation of a new wolf.

The stakes are too high, and the motive… doesn't exist. Vampires aren't exactly altruistic, so helping Alaric wouldn't move one to such extremes.

The Knights' presence make sense. They tolerate the Pack alright, mainly because they hold jobs and don't go around killing people.

Vampires… kill people. Routinely. Tivoli keeps their murderous intentions limited to wanderers and ne'er-do-wells, but the Knights still don't trust them. Killing a vampire isn't their top priority, but they don't hesitate.

Demi-demons, however, they kill on sight, regardless of the risk to themselves. Leaving someone like me alive typically proves far worse than any danger they could face in the pursuit.

So of course, the Knights would come.

But for another vampire to have been here?

It just doesn't make sense.

I take another deep breath, seeking clarity, but all I find is Elias. Cedar and sap overrun my senses, and I turn to face him. He stands there, staring at me, and I wonder how long he's been there. The Nether scar on his neck, peeking out from the collar of his shirt, makes my skin tingle sympathetically.

Even in low light, his green eyes shine for me, roaming freely over my bare legs before working their way up to my face. A delicate shiver plays over my spine as my body reacts, but my heart wants no part of it.

With the moon smiling down at him, he closes the distance between us. My heart quivers painfully, and my mind forgets the oddity of vodka on the wind.

Nolan doesn't want me…

The words whisper through my mind, repeating, again and again, taunting me. I hold my emotions inside, carefully concealing them even as they threaten to rip me apart.

I close my eyes, taking a deep breath.

Nolan doesn't want me…

But Elias does.

So, I reach for him. My fingers graze the fabric of his clothes, and I push away the knowledge that they belong to Nolan. I push away the thought that my hands, my lips, my *everything* belongs to a man who wants nothing from me.

For a moment, I hold the pain at bay. My heart races, and my breathing becomes shallow as the world narrows to exclude everything beyond Elias and me.

Sliding my hand to his waist, I pull him to me.

After all, his soul is as damned as it can get.

My skin tingles with anticipation as he reaches for me. Fire burns across my skin when his hands reach my neck, tilting my head back with his thumb.

Sliding one hand up his chest, I graze the erratic Nether scar with one golden talon. He shivers, and a tiny droplet of blood makes an appearance, pricked free by my nail. His heart beats an overwhelming rhythm in my head, pounding my thoughts into submission, if only for a moment.

And for now, all I need is a single moment of peace.

Inching closer, eyes heavy with desire, he presses his lips against mine. We come together, and one of his hands finds my waist, pulling me to him. My body screams out for more, but I tumble back into reality.

He isn't Nolan...

The thought cripples me.

Elias laces a hand in my hair and breathes deeply. His gaze darts between my lips and my eyes, and he tips his head to the side to brush his lips across my skin. Barely touching, he grazes my neck, and his grip on my waist tightens, crushing me against him.

A soft moan escapes my lips as my body betrays me, growing impatient. With wild eyes, I pull back to look him over, letting my hand slip free of his hair. My thumb caresses his strong jaw.

He isn't Nolan, and he never will be.

But he's all I've got...

His chest rises and falls in staccato breaths. My own lungs work furiously, halfway between a sob and a pant, pushing my breasts against him. My heart threatens to drown out the sound of his.

Apparently, the ache becomes too much for he crushes his lips to mine. Skin burning, hearts racing, we melt together. His grip on me tightens, and I throw my arms around his neck, giving myself over to the moment, if only to forget.

Desperate kisses become ravenous. I pull his shirt up over his head and kiss the newly exposed skin. My body buzzes, promising release from the agony that wants so badly to swallow me up.

His hand slides down to my hip, then reaches back to grasp my buttock. Gripping tightly, he pulls me against him.

At long last, our lips come together again, and the sun explodes across my skin. Then, Elias' hand moves lower, gripping my thigh, hiking it up to his hip. His hand on my bare skin sends my heart skipping along and makes me thankful that the front of my gown is so short.

I always used to love that with Nolan… His hand on my skin, touching me so easily…

NO! Focus! He made his choice.

Now, please…

Just forget.

I beg my mind for a break, for relief, but he circles through my mind, haunting me. Even as Elias and I lower ourselves to the ground, Nolan fills my thoughts.

Clovers and moss press against me, cool and shocking against bare flesh, as Elias moves over me, pushing up my nightgown. He presses against me, gasping as he does, his breath hot against my neck.

Aching and hungry with the moon howling in his veins, he pushes my nightgown up further still and pulls it off me in one swift motion.

Desperate to move further, to push past the ache in my chest, I undo his pants and push them down. He kicks them away with no care for where they land. With one hand on my breast, he grinds against me, hard, but slow.

And suddenly I can't take it anymore.

I roll him onto his back and straddle him. The moonlight plays beautifully over his muscled torso, and sparks of excitement glow in his eyes.

But I look away, glancing at Nolan's cottage.

Just pretend.

Just this once, pretend he's Nolan.

I close my eyes, and settle myself down over him, taking him in. His hands grasp my buttocks, squeezing tightly, and we move together as one.

But whenever my eyes open, they merely glance at him. Pulled like a moth to the flame, my gaze seeks Nolan's cottage. He doesn't appear in any of the windows, so I close my eyes, imagining him beneath me.

Pretend he's Nolan.

I imagine his hands on me and recall the sound of his moans. I imagine him sitting up beneath me, raining kisses over my chest. I think of his long, unruly hair tickling my skin as he nibbles gently at my ear lobe. I see the smolder in his dark eyes as he smiles up at me, glancing through thick lashes.

I need to forget him. I need to move on.

But all I can do is think of him.

And only when I let my mind roam over Nolan can I enjoy any of this.

Chapter 26
Nolan

Houses pass by in a blur, insubstantial. Businesses, shops, places I frequent daily, are reduced to shapes, meaningless stacks of wood. My feet drag me to the Golden Tankard so my mind can resemble the slurred edges of the world around me.

The full moon shines bright overhead, but I keep my eyes on the ground, watching my feet as they place themselves, one in front of the other, on the cobblestone road. People laugh in the houses around me, unaware that life can become so meaningless, so quickly.

My heart shambles along in my chest, every bit as aimless as my life.

Ness is it… She's it fer me…

But she's…

My throat closes, and I swallow the words down, unable to finish the thought. But I feel it, slithering through me, chilling my veins. I shiver with the loss. My bones, my muscles, they all freeze solid. Each step fractures me, splintering the ice that's slowly replacing my body.

She's in love wit' Elias.

Ness is… wit' him, now.

The feeling claws its way into my mind and bursts like an acidic bubble. It splatters over the inside of my skull, and I shudder with its impact. Everywhere the thought touches burns, and it melts me down to a puddle of grief.

Throat constricting, chest collapsing on itself, I wander through the moonlit town. A few people amble on late night jaunts, arm-in-arm with loved ones and lovers, but I pointedly pay them no mind. Bearing witness to such happiness could be lethal.

The scents of them, all sugar and lilac and the thick luscious scent of lust, swirls in the air around them, and I close myself off to it. Much like closing my eyes, I reign in my senses and walk faster to get away from them.

Eventually, the Golden Tankard looms ahead, raucous and noisy with the late-night crowd. Perhaps that will help me blend in. Conversation isn't exactly a pleasant prospect, right now.

Once inside, I push through the crowd. The smell of bodies, the crushing weight of their emotions hits me anew, and I dull myself to it.

My own emotions weigh quite enough at the moment, thanks…

Sighing, I settle in at the bar, staring once again at wood grain. Alina saunters over, cheery on such a busy night. The tavern will do well tonight, surely, and she'll share in that.

"Missed you at dinner," she says. "Finally, hungry?"

"No. I jus' need a drink. Sometin' strong." I barely look up, glancing at her through my eyelashes.

"On a full moon? You're already going to be Lun-y." Her head tips to the side, and her nostrils flare as she tries to separate my emotions from the crowd. "You sure that's a good idea?"

"I know it's not. I jus' dinna care."

Pulling a coin from my pocket, I lay it on the bar. I slide it to her and try to focus on the way its edges grate over the pocked, scratched wood. Better to focus on that than the pit in my stomach or the hole where my heart used to be.

Pulling a second coin from my pocket, I say, "On secon' thought, bring me two."

My mind swirls with images of Ness, lying beside Elias in my cottage.

Crying over him.

Healing him.

A million times, I watch her touch his face, his neck. A million times, the hole in my chest expands, swallowing more and more of me.

Each time I blink, I picture them together. In her cottage, in the stream. I see them laughing.

I see them… touching each other.

I nearly gag as my mind conjures images of kisses and gasping breaths. A sob shudders out of me, and I drop my head into my hands.

Alina settles two small glasses in front of me. Clear liquid fills them to the brim, the strongest alcohol available. It smells like the poison it is.

I toss them back quickly. It burns all the way down, but I don't care. I could use a little warmth in my chest.

Two more coins on the bar, and Alina brings me two more drinks. I down them, aching to forget. But nothing happens.

Still, I see Ness walking away from me toward Liam's house. I see the blood on my floor, a mixture of hers and his.

I see the hurt look on her face when she found him, bleeding in my floor. I smell the heartache, leaking off her.

Another coin for another drink.

"Nolan, you really should slow down…"

I shake my head and push the coin across the counter. "Please, Alina. I canna think, right now. I jus'… canna do it. I *need* anoth'r drink."

Whether my pleading wears her down or the brittle tone of my voice, I don't know. But she doesn't question my decisions, anymore.

I lose count of the drinks I buy, and barely notice when she takes a shot or two, as well.

Slowly, the world inside blurs every bit as much as the world outside. Visions of Ness with Elias no longer fill my head. They barely form before the alcohol burns them away. An amorphous blob of sorrow expands within me, grey and featureless, oozing to fill every part of me. But the sharp edges have worn away, dulling the ache.

Hours pass, and Alina leans in close. Alcohol taints her breath.

Er maybe tha's my breath?

"It's time to go, Nolan," she says. "We've got—" a hiccup interrupts her, "—to close the tavern."

Her words come out slow, labored. The sweet smell of love wafts off her, layered with lust. Heavy eyes flicker over my face, only to settle on my lips.

"Time ta go…" I mumble, eyes barely open.

Rising unsteadily to my feet, I knock something to the floor with a clatter. I spin around to apologize to whoever I've just bumped into but find no one.

Jus' a stool…

I giggle, then clutch at my spinning head. Taking one step, I put my arms out to steady myself as the world dips to the side, dodging my foot. I start to go down, but Alina is there, catching me.

"I'll walk you home," she offers.

I open my mouth to protest, to insist that I'll be fine. But the floor dodges my foot again, trying to crash into me.

So, I nod and let her help me.

Why do I live so far from the tavern? Has it always been this far?

"I need a differen' house," I say.

"Why's that?"

"It's too far… fro' the Tankard," I pause to steady my stomach. "An' it's shiny, now."

"What are you talking about?" Alina giggles.

"No more Neth'r…" I mumble.

Near the door to my house, I take a wrong step, and Alina catches me, though just barely. Her arms wrap around me. One hand grasps my shirt, and it pulls upward as I slump down. Her other hand lands low on my waist, touching skin that hasn't been touched by anyone but Ness in nearly a decade. My heart shrinks from it, desperate for this not to be my life.

But she stops my fall.

Her eyes stare into mine, so close, and her breath warms my skin.

I swallow back a nervous laugh.

Ness swims in the back of my mind, and I start to pull away from Alina. But Elias swims there, too, and suddenly, I can't look away. His hands reach for Ness, and she kisses him tenderly.

I can almost hear her say it…

My eyes search Alina's. Dark brown looks so little like Ness' beautiful golden eyes. Her dark hair doesn't hold a candle to red.

Then, I hear Ness' voice utter the words she never spoke to me. "I love you," she whispers to Elias in my mind, eyes burning with intensity.

And I kiss Alina.

She throws herself into it. Our drunken stupor pulls us through the door and past the now-dried blood splattered across my home.

She wrinkles her nose at it but doesn't question it for long. Her lips quickly give up on speaking, finding mine with renewed vigor as we stumble to my bedroom, knocking things from counters and tables as we go.

Our clothes fall to the floor quickly, and she pushes me down onto the bed. Staring up at her, bare skin glowing in the moonlight, I feel guilt welling up within me. Her dark eyes rake over me, and I fight the urge to shy away from them.

She isn't Ness…

But I can't be wit' Ness.

So, I stuff my feelings down and prepare to settle.

Chapter 27
Ness

Lying on the soft ground with my head cradled on Elias' shoulder, horns tucked away for easy sleeping arrangements, I drown out all that happened yesterday. The sun shines brightly overhead, painting the backs of my eyelids bright red.

Elias tightens his arm around my shoulder. His other hand slides from my knee to rest on my thigh. His breath comes easily, still evened out by sleep.

I inhale, expecting cedar and sap to flood my senses. While it isn't the scent I hoped to wake to this morning, I'm prepared for it.

But the stench of death fills my nose, instead. The sudden shock of it chokes me. My eyes burst open as I cough, and Elias startles awake. He sits, bolt upright, and I roll onto my back. My nightgown tangles around my legs as I push up onto my knees.

"Nether take me," he says, oblivious to the irony of his words. "What is that?"

"Death," I say simply, heart as cold as ice and as heavy as stone.

My eyes follow the trail straight to Nolan's cottage. My blood runs cold, and something greasy slithers through me. The fear that something could have happened to Nolan takes hold of me, and I'm on my feet in an instant, sprinting for his door.

My heart pounds against my eardrums, and my world narrows to a pinpoint.

He has to be okay.

Please… Let him be okay.

The thought spins in my head, expanding to take up every scrap of space. I know precisely how durable Nolan is, but… the Knights have weapons tailored just for Netherspawn. It would be easy enough for them to kill him.

And he certainly played a role in keeping my existence a secret from them.

My heart stops, but I keep moving.

Elias runs side by side with me, a feat he never could've managed only yesterday. We round the corner, and there it is. Cold and lifeless, a body rests upon Nolan's doorstep.

I fall to my knees as the air rushes from me. Dark eyes stare up at the sky, but in a face framed by short blonde hair. No wild curls reach down to the ground. A wiry frame drapes lifelessly over the stairs rather than the strong, sinewy muscle I feared I'd find.

Relief washes through me, chasing away the thought that somehow… it might have been Nolan.

Yet, it isn't just *any* body.

It's Alaric.

Every scrap of color has abandoned his skin, drained out through an ugly gash in his neck, far darker than the scars I left upon his face.

Nolan's door opens, and my heart skips a beat, hoping to see him. I lift my gaze, but it isn't him. Alina, a woman Nolan transformed years ago, stands there, clearly startled by our presence. Big brown eyes, usually sultry, go wide with shock and confusion.

Suddenly, I understand that Nolan wanted me to move on… Because he already has. Ice water runs through my veins, and the color drains from my face.

But… We weren't apart that long…

How could he replace me so quickly?

My heart plummets, falling so fast that it buries itself in the ground. I only wish I could join it.

Why must death be so difficult to come by?

Not that it is… I just need to find a Knight, turn myself in…

Then, Alina sees the body at her feet and shouts for Nolan. Her tousled hair falls chaotically about her shoulders as she turns her back on the body. Instead, she stares back at Nolan's approaching form, covering her nose and mouth with her hands.

Rushing through his cottage shirtless, he grumbles something about it being too early for screaming. Yet, he stops in his tracks when he sees the dead man at his door.

My heart twists painfully in my chest at the sight of him, knowing he spent his night with her. Pulling myself to my feet, I reign in my feelings, determined not to let him know how much this hurts me.

I have *some* pride, after all.

Alina rushes to him, burying her face in his chest, and he wraps his arms around her, smoothing her hair protectively. His eyes fixate on Alaric's lifeless body, bloodless and shining with a thin layer of dew.

Yet, I can't tear my eyes away from the man who's torn me to shreds twice in less than a day. The little bit of light which filters through the windows of his home finds him restless but beautiful. Hair a mess of curls hanging down beyond his shoulders, eyes intense and brooding, he's still the only one I want.

I long to kiss the crease between his eyebrows until it smooths itself out. I need to touch the side of his face, to lift it until he looks at me.

But Alina stands where I should be.

And his eyes are drawn to the dead man at his feet, instead of drinking me in like they used to.

When Nolan finally lifts his gaze to meet mine, a shadow of pain flickers within him, even as he kisses the top of Alina's head. A spear of pain pierces my heart, and I fight to keep my face placid.

Alina isn't soft, she's seen her share of trouble, but she's never had a stomach for death. Her arms wrap around his naked waist, and she turns her face to the side to gulp in a breath, despite the stench. The early morning shadows which fill the cottage conceal the parts of her face not covered by her hair.

Every move, every bit of her that touches him, every time he pats her back, every time she leans further against him breaks me. The pieces of my heart fracture further until they're nothing more than dust.

Finally, I can't bear to look. My eyes fall to Alaric, staring at the careless way his arms fall across the stairs and the curling of his fingers, clawing the air. Elias places a hand on the small of my back, clearly meaning to offer comfort.

But it reminds me just how far I am from where I want to be.

A small part of me begs to look up, to see how Nolan reacts to Elias touching me so casually.

But I don't dare.

What if he's smiling? What if he thinks… this is for the best?

The thought alone hits me like a landslide. Seeing that thought shape his face would be too much. So, I study the dead man intently, hoping for some clue as to what happened.

Several moments pass before any of us notice the note stuck to the frame of Nolan's door. A small knife, buried in the wood up to its hilt, holds it in place.

Elias steps over Alaric's body and pulls the blade free with ease thanks to his newly acquired strength. I watch him, wishing desperately that yesterday never happened. Rooted to the ground by dread, I know that nothing good can come of this.

He unfolds the note and reads it aloud. "It says, 'I got what I wanted, after all, Uncle.' It's from Simen," he says, turning to look at me. His brows scrunch in confusion.

But my eyes find Nolan.

Even in the shadows, I see the panic fill him. It tenses his arms around Alina's shoulders, stilling his hands and their comforting circles on her back. His mouth falls open. Dark eyes fluttering, he shakes his head in disbelief.

I curse myself for having missed it. I haven't seen Nolan's nephew in years, though, maybe even a couple of decades. The Pack refused his appeals for transformation, several times over, because of his temperament. Never mind the so-called accident that befell Nolan's brother-in-law, Simen's own father, after they fought over that very topic for what must have been the millionth time.

Simen was the one I should have worried about, all along, not Alaric.

"Gods 'ave mercy on us all," Nolan says.

Overhead, birds chirp, oblivious.

Chapter 28
Simen
The Previous Night

Only Alaric's muffled cries and the crackling of the campfire break the stillness of the night. The light of the full moon fails to filter through my Nether wall, leaving us in a world of shadow.

I'm so close. Finally.

It's certainly taken long enough, thanks to Uncle Nolan and those filthy mongrels he calls family. But soon enough, the bastards will wish they hadn't turned me away. And the Knights will surely take out Uncle Nolan, now that they know he's been hiding that bitch, that demi-demon.

I watch my potion bubble angrily as the ingredients combine in a pot kept carefully away from the fire. Slowly, the acidic liquid grows darker than a moonless night. It boils of its own accord, and a few drops slop over the side. The patch of moss they land upon sizzles and glows a dazzling yellow as it burns.

It's more than I'll need, just a few mouthfuls will do the trick. But I'll have to force it down Alaric's throat, and I can't risk him swallowing too little.

My eyes leave it for only a second, glancing up at the predator who only recently learned he was the prey. Sweat beads on his forehead and he strains at the bonds which pin him to the tree. But even his vampiric strength is no match for the Nether I invoked.

A smile spreads my lips wide, and Alaric shivers. Reinvigorated by fear, he curses me through his gag, and jerks at his bonds.

Just a smile. That's all it took.

Power sweeps through me, warming my blood. I've always had power over him. He's dumb as a rock, after all, but seeing the smug look drip from his face in little trickles of sweat as he begs for his life…

My breath quickens, and I laugh. He knows just how outmatched he really is, and I can't get enough of the feeling.

His blond hair mats itself to his scalp. His eyes practically glow with fear. It rolls off him in waves, filling the camp so strongly that I can't even smell the putrid potion. The air around us is acrid, the scent of a cornered animal.

My eyes fall shut as I breathe it in, savoring it. It tells me the potion I made for myself earlier is working, preparing my body for the coming change. A little shiver of pleasure traverses my spine.

Beside me, my latest potion slowly stops bubbling, and I tease, "Thirsty?"

A smirk decorates my features as I rise. It's a question meant for both of us, really. I'll have to drink a great deal of his blood once he's consumed the potion.

Invoking the blessing of the Netherrealm again, I mutter a couple of words and sprinkle a few herbs into the palm of my hand before blowing them toward Alaric.

His head jerks back, held firmly against the trunk of the tree.

Ripping the gag free of his mouth, I let it dangle around his neck. He screams and shouts, but the Nether wall blocks his cries, holding them in so only I can enjoy them.

I pull my dagger from a sheath at my waist and cut away the gag, exposing his neck. After putting on some gloves, blessed by the Nether, I stoop and lift the potion.

Alaric tries to turn his head, struggles to move at all, but fails. My skin tingles in anticipation.

Finally, I'll have what I've always wanted… I'll have the power of the immortals. I'll be stronger than any of them. And I'll be able to make the Pack pay for making me wait so damn long.

Pushing the potion against Simen's lips with one hand, I pinch his nose shut. He tries so hard to hold his breath.

But he can't keep it up forever.

Tears track down his face, getting caught in his scars.

When he gasps, I pour the potion into his mouth, smiling gleefully. It sizzles, burning his lips and tongue. Smoke wafts into the air.

"Drink up."

Chapter 29
Nolan

"Alina, go on home," I whisper, unwilling to trust my voice not to waver at a higher volume. The aching in my head pulls my lids low over my eyes.

She takes the combination as compassion and reaches up on tiptoes to kiss me.

My heart tries to pull me away from her, but the events from last night hold me still.

What have I done?

But… Ness is wit' Elias, now. I may as well give Alina a chance.

Yet, I don't kiss her back.

I can't.

Sobered up, I know I can't lead her on. She feels me tense, sees the way my eyes can't help but dart to Ness… And she pulls away.

My head pounds with the agony of having imbibed a bit too freely last night, and the tensions of the morning certainly don't help matters. Not that I expected a cheerful, easy morning. I fully expected to be driven back to the Tankard, tonight.

Now, I have no doubt. Were it not for the necessity of dealing with this corpse, I'd head there, now, if only to ease the ache in my skull.

As it were, that isn't an option.

Ness stares at the fallen vampire with her gorgeous red locks falling to block her face. I wait, hoping she'll look up, hoping she'll meet my gaze, but she doesn't. I take a deep breath, trying to read her, but when I push past the scent of death, past the scents of Alina and Elias, all I find is wood smoke. She guards herself, reigning everything in.

Elias' hand rests gingerly on her back. He reeks of honey and chamomile. Sympathy. His bright green eyes are pulled tight with it.

Does he tink her unused to death? Does he tink her soft?

He doesna know her well. She doesna shy away from tings like this. She doesna like death, but she can stomach it.

But what's she be hidin' from?

She's got ev'rything she wanted...

Bitterness chokes me, and I drop my gaze.

Beside me, Alina nods solemnly, more to herself than anyone else. She reaches up to touch my face, apparently unable to help herself, and says, "I'll see you, later."

Covering her nose and mouth, she leaves, stepping carefully over the dead body. She waves goodbye to Ness, but those beautiful blue eyes never look up to see it.

Unable to stop myself, I say, "Elias, could yeh fetch Liam and Sari? I need ta speak wit' them." I clench my hands behind my back to keep them from trembling. Well, to keep them from trembling where Ness or Elias can see them.

I need a moment wit' Ness... I need ta know what's botherin' her.

I hate my own weakness, but I know I've never been able to fight it. Not with her.

She's the one. If she's hurtin,' I have to help her.

Whether she wants me, er not.

Her eyes meet mine for a second, and somehow the brilliant blue seems brittle. Maybe it's the tension which narrows them. Maybe it's the furrowing of her brows or the conspicuous absence of any emotions in the air around her.

Beside her, Elias nods his assent to my request, and for a moment, I think I'll get my chance.

"I'll come with you," she says, pulling in a deep breath. She turns from me, so quickly, and leads him away.

Taking a step forward, foot almost hitting the dead man, I lean out the door to watch them go. A tiny bit of emotion leaks off her, barely discernible, but I'd know that scent anywhere.

A broken heart is hard to hide.

My knees buckle, and I grasp the door frame to keep myself upright. I take another deep breath, desperate to make sure I didn't just sense what I wanted to find.

I want her ta hurt fer me, petty as it may be. I want it so badly... Maybe I imagined it in the wind.

But it's gone.

And she doesn't look back.

Her feet lead her steadily across the grass, around the little garden, and up to Liam's door. She doesn't even look at me before going in.

But Elias does. His brows draw together when he sees me, leaning over a dead man to stare after them. They're quickly out of sight, tucked away within Liam's cottage, and I'm left to wonder.

Was I jus' lookin' fer it? Was I jus' hopin' she'd be hurtin' ov'r me?

Or is she?

Ducking into the relative darkness of my home, I sidestep the dried blood in my floor, *her* blood, and venture to my bedroom. Rummaging through the wardrobe, I find a shirt and pull it on.

Does she jus' no' like me wit' Alina?

Anger flares within me, singeing my flesh.

She canna have it both ways. That wouldna be fair.

But... She knows that.

Tha's why she never came after me.

Right?

Pacing, I knot my fingers together, hands atop my head. A deep breath fills me with the stench of blood and death and honeysuckle, rather than the peace and clarity I seek. Reaching out, I shove the door of my bedroom shut and sit on my bed. Elbows find knees, and my head drops into my hands.

Exhausted, head aching from far too much alcohol, it takes me too long to drive this last knife into my chest.

Was Liam wrong?

A bit of hope flutters through me, but it's quiet and small, stifled by a bigger agony. Its wings reach out at the edges of the massive stone which crushes it.

If Liam was wrong...

Then, I drove her to Elias.

The possibility, however small, threatens to drive me mad. It taunts me with equal parts hope and fear. The former makes my skin itch, makes my muscles burn to go to her. The latter... holds me still in the darkness of my bedroom.

Then, guilt settles firmly on my shoulders, and I spring from my bed. Turning around, I stare down at the mess of blankets, tangled from things I shouldn't have done.

In a frenzy, I tear them from the bed. I throw them to the floor, wishing I could burn them and my whole, shining house along with them just to be rid of the constant reminder of last night.

Snatching my pillows up one at a time, I launch them across the room. They smash into the wall with such force that they burst, spewing feathers all over the place, but I don't give a damn.

In one swift motion, I wrench the mattress from the bed frame and fling it against the wall. It doesn't pop like the pillows, and that makes my hands curl into fists.

Blood boiling, I flip my bed frame, and it splinters when it hits the floor.

But it isn't enough.

Suddenly devoid of things to break, my anger smacks me square in the face, finally landing where it should have been the whole time. Nothing in this room made me do what I did last night.

That's my fault.

Buckling beneath the weight of guilt, of pain, of not knowing what to believe, I fall to my knees. Reduced to a heap on the floor, I sob with my hands gripping my scalp.

One way er anoth'r, she's lost to me.

Whether I drove her to him yest'rday er three months ago…

This is my fault.

Chapter 30
Ness

The day passes in a blur of introductions as I lug Elias around. Orwen and Nissa, to their credit, disguise their slight discomfort at the unplanned addition to the Pack. Apparently, Liam took it upon himself to inform them yesterday shortly before Nolan…

I swallow back another wave of nausea, making sure to keep it contained within myself. It wouldn't do to show them how I feel about the situation. It certainly wouldn't help matters.

What's done is done.

Sure, they'll notice the absence in the air where my emotions should be. But I'll let them think what they want to.

Finally alone, I wander through the Pack house. I look over the old weapons and armor, made for human and wolf forms, which they've preserved since the revolution. Though the Knights have glazed over our role in the war, the Pack has taken special care to keep the proof.

The Netherrealm symbol burns upon the chest of every suit of armor. Three vertical lines, with the tallest in the center, united by an x, all in dark green soapstone, carved and laid into the metal. Even all these years later, it sparkles with remnants of Nether magic. The same symbol burns in the hilt and handle of every sword, axe, and dagger which line the walls.

Plush red carpet cradles my feet as I meander through the Hall of the Forgotten, staring up at one tapestry or another, all depicting scenes from the Evaylan revolt against Harta. Stupidly, though I've stared at these tapestries many a time, I still find my eyes searching for the one fighter that means everything to me.

Everywhere, armored men and women run to battle, their weapons gleaming and the bloodlust clear in their posture. But somehow, I still expect to see him, for him to stand out as much in the history of Evayla as he does in my own history.

On the sidelines of the battle depicted in one tapestry, I see wolves lurking in the shadows, waiting for the Evaylan Knights to drive the Hartan soldiers to them.

In another tapestry, the wolves, shrouded in armor which swirls with dark green Nether, descend upon a camp of Hartan soldiers. Before the alliance between the Netherspawn and the Evaylan Knights, it was no holds barred. Any time, any place.

Hartan Knights could expect no mercy.

The alliance restricted things to more *civilized* means, facing each other on a battlefield in the light of day.

Only, the Hartan Knights didn't agree to the terms of civilized war.

Which brings me to the next tapestry. A fire, set in the middle of the night, right here in Tor. It nearly claimed the whole town. Some of the local buildings still hold the scars, smoke-stained wood and all.

I don't need the tapestry to remember that night, though. I was there. I'd come to see Ren, the wolf who taught me to make a few healing potions.

And... of course... to see Nolan...

Even then, even with as little as I'd seen of him, I knew he was special. I just had a feeling he'd be important to me.

I was only 17 at the time. I'd been living alone for so long, so living in the little cottage they found for me out in the woods was no problem. It was a far sight better than running from one cave to another.

It was such an odd visit, too. I hadn't been summoned, nor had I any real reason to go. I didn't need to buy or sell anything at the markets. I just thought I should go see Ren.

My eyes glaze over, and that night descends on me, again. I sit at Ren's old table, laughing gaily about Nether knows what. That part has blurred with time.

Transformed later in life, Ren's smile crinkles the skin around her eyes. Streaks of grey decorate her black hair, shining in the light of the fire. The nearby hearth crackles with it. Having long since taken on the role of Pack grandmother, Ren's table is full of younger Pack members.

And, of course, Nolan is there.

He sits across from me, and I can't help but smile every time he looks at me. My stomach erupts with flocks of butterflies when he smiles, dark brown eyes smoldering in the flickering candlelight. His hair touches his jaw, recently cut.

Then, we hear it.

A few shouts break through the din of our laughter. All eyes dart to the window, and I lean over to pull back the curtains. Far too much light pours in, and fire shifts to encompass more and more of the market. Hartan Knights flood the place, spreading the flames from one building to another with torches.

Never one to hesitate, Nolan jumps to his feet instantly. He has no armor with him but knows he'll be stronger in wolf form.

It takes me far too long to avert my eyes when he starts pulling his clothes off. The hard muscles of his chest hold my attention, but Ren clears her throat, giving me a significant look. I blush and drop my gaze to the table.

As the Pack members strip and transform, groaning as their bones rearrange themselves, I fiddle with my fork, too young to face a battle. In my head, I hear the arguments between Pack members over whether they should use me against the Hartan Knights, despite my age.

But the heat of the moment is hardly the time for discussion.

They leave me behind, falling into familiar patterns as they run out the door. Shouts and screams tug at my ears, pulling my gaze to the open door. My heart aches to help.

These people accepted me. They took me in, despite what I am...

And they're out there hurting, fighting...

Staring out the window, I see Nolan, a massive black wolf, lunge at a Hartan Knight with teeth bared. He lands a solid bite on the Knight's neck, but another Knight kicks him in the chest. He flies through the air and slams into a market stall.

Wood splinters and rains down over the market, little slivers silhouetted by the fire burning behind them.

I jump to my feet, heart in my chest. The Nether calls to me, begging for blood. I feel it, coursing through my veins, burning me alive.

And a Knight rushes in through the door.

Hands balled into fists, I slam them down upon the table, forcing the Knight to his knees.

"Ness! Don't!" Ren cries out from the head of the table. She doesn't want the Hartan Knights, or the Evaylan Knights for that matter, to know the Pack has been harboring a demi-demon.

But they'll have to survive to tell anyone.

I bring my hands up, feeling the itch just beneath my skin, the need to hurt the people hurting my friends.

Well, the people who tolerate me, at any rate.

A simple motion, like opening a jar, twists his head around backward. The Knight falls to Ren's floor, head still turned the wrong way.

It should take more effort to kill. This isn't enough. It doesn't satisfy the ache in my bones.

But it'll have to do.

Walking around the table, past the counter where herbs and bones wait their turn to be made into potions and salves, I step out into the night. The moon shines, half full, but its light pales next to the fires consuming Tor. My eyes find the Knight who kicked Nolan, and I lift my hands.

"Ness?"

Nolan's voice startles me, and I turn from the tapestry, glad to look at anything other than that night. Yet, I'd look away from anything for him.

And he's so close.

My heart gallops unsteadily in my chest, and my stomach flips.

Nether take me… Get ahold of yourself!

Lifting my chin, I stare up at him. He opens his mouth but says nothing. Full lips parted, he struggles for words.

Kiss him…

My body begs me to step forward, to touch his chest, slide my hand to his neck.

To show him why I'm better for him than Alina...

My lungs work furiously, trying to decide whether to shiver with the heavy breathing of pleasure or to shudder with sobs. My heart splinters, opting to struggle in both directions. But I lock it all inside.

Dark eyes a mess of emotions, Nolan whispers, "Ness, I... need to talk to yeh."

But a flash of this morning washes over me. I see his arms around Alina, and anger and despair rattle my bones.

Taking a step back, I look at his tan arms. They hang, empty, at his sides. So innocent, as if they didn't push me away, as if they didn't reach for someone else, instead.

Wiping his hands on his black trousers, he struggles, yet again, to speak.

But what could he feel so awkward about? This is what he wanted, isn't it?

He wants her.

Not me...

My knees nearly buckle. I grit my teeth against the pain of my broken heart, limping along to get me through the day.

I've got to get away from him.

I can't... I just can't...

"It's fine," I lie, keeping my tone level. "There's nothing to talk about."

I meet his gaze, weak and wanting to see something in his eyes that might suggest he still loves me.

But all I find is shock.

He closes his mouth abruptly and drops his eyes to the floor.

"Ness..."

Clenching his hands into fists, he squeezes his eyes shut.

Run. Just run.

Nothing he says next can help me. It'll only hurt worse.

Now, run!

Before he says why he wants her...

Whether he senses my impending retreat or whether by luck, he takes a deep breath and opens his eyes, again. The second his gaze finds mine, I freeze. Retreat is no longer an option.

Eyes fluttering, he looks to my neck, and despite my better judgment, I ache for him to reach out.

And against all odds, he does.

My heart stops, waiting for his touch. He pulls in a deep breath, letting it out in a rush, but my lungs are still. Every bit of me, every fiber, is paralyzed.

Run, you fool!

But I can't.

His hand finds my neck, and his finger traces the chain at its base. Lifting it from my skin, sending white-hot tendrils throughout my body, he tugs the sundial from its resting place within my gown.

I gulp down the regret of having worn it here, for there's no use regretting something I couldn't change. I know I couldn't have taken it off. The backs of his fingers rest against my collarbone, and my lungs decide to work now that their efforts will press my skin harder against his.

He peers at the sundial, turning it over in his hand, and my heart breaks into a gallop. I try so desperately to breathe in his emotions. But he's locked them away. Instead, I'm filled with the luxurious velvet of sandalwood, coating my lungs, filling my chest.

When, at long last, he meets my eyes, a deep line etches itself between his brows. He searches my face for something, but only he and the Gods know what.

Sorrow pulls my brows together into a mirror of his expression, but for entirely different reasons. I need to know why he chose her, and yet I'm terrified to learn why.

He merely wants to know why I still dare to wear his necklace.

Does he want it back?

Oh, gods, no. Please, Nolan... Don't ask me to give it back...

Panic pulls my eyelids shut, closing me off to whatever expression might grace his features.

Would he give it to her?

Just rip the necklace from his hands and run.

He's fast but not as fast as me. Just go.

Surely, he won't chase me.

Nether take me... He wouldn't chase me...

And suddenly, I wish, more fervently than ever before, that the Nether would *actually* take me. Because I can't face this.

But I'm spared.

A door at the end of the Hall of the Forgotten opens, and my head jerks toward the sound. Elias and Orwen, olive skin glowing with pride, enter the Hall, deep in conversation about the history of the Pack.

Elias sees us first, sees Nolan's hand still resting against my chest, clutching my necklace. With green eyes narrowed, he almost speaks. His lips purse as he takes in the scene, and this forces Orwen's grey eyes in our direction.

Of course, our scents let him know we were here long before he entered the room. But now, his head tips to the side. This isn't the scene he'd expected to walk into, not now. A few months ago, he doubtless would have expected a lewd vision entering a room with only the two of us.

But now?

With my new *lover* standing right beside him?

With Nolan's new lover somewhere else in the Pack house?

My stomach lurches, and I recoil from the thought.

Finally, I step away from Nolan. The sundial falls from his grip and thuds against my hollow chest.

It slides down over my skin, still warm from his hand, and comes to rest between my breasts as I walk to Elias' side.

Just act normal.

He's with Alina, now.

I'm with Elias.

My heart twists painfully, as I realize what I have to do.

I have to give the necklace back.

My spine shivers with the thought.

At least, then, I won't have to hear him ask for it...

Chapter 31
Elias

Standing in the garden of the Pack house, I study Ness. She sits alone at the base of a large tree, picking at her nails. She keeps her horns tucked away, and her blue eyes shine beautifully in the sunlight.

"Elias?"

My attention refocuses on Nissa, one of the alphas of the Pack. Her warm brown eyes favor me with less and less patience each time I get distracted.

Her full lips purse with mild irritation, and she says, "Must we go somewhere else?"

"No, that's not necessary," I answer, bowing my head instinctively.

Strange, that the Nether pulls my eyes to the ground in deference to this woman I never knew before today. It knows she's my alpha.

She's my master, in a way.

Suddenly, I wonder if I've willingly entered into a form of slavery, bound to serve my alphas and the moon. And these rowdy emotions…

My mind recalls the scene in the Hall of the Forgotten.

Nolan touching Ness' necklace, his hand resting against her chest… Again, anger courses through me, stiffening my spine and curling my hands into fists.

Nissa's chest rises with a deep breath.

"Is there a rebellious streak in you? I've asked only for manners and for you to pay attention as I teach you, yet you're *furious*?" She laughs derisively. "Do *not* test me, boy."

And suddenly, I can smell it. Her anger seeps into the air, hot and metallic. It tenses my muscles and bows my head deeper, forcing me to stare at the grass beneath our feet. Her bare feet set up a dark contrast to the vivid green, and my body nearly collapses before her.

"I wasn't angry at you," I hurry to explain. "My mind wandered… again." The admission is sheepish.

But it cools her temper.

I breathe a sigh of relief as the tension eases out of me. Her whims have far more power over me than I expected.

This may well be more than I bargained for…

My eyes drift to Ness, one last time. Her head leans against the tree trunk, and her eyes are closed. If not for the scene in the Hall, I'd convince myself easily that she was thinking of me.

I let the jealousy pass through me for only a moment and ignore the distinct lack of emotion in Ness' part of the garden. Then, I lift my head.

Meeting Nissa's gaze with my chin down, I say, "I'm ready to try again."

Her lessons on reigning in my emotions and my transformations last throughout the afternoon and leave me drained. Ness and I dine in the Pack house with a few of the other members, though I hardly register their names. The long day of practicing with Nissa left little room in my brain for anything else.

Though it clearly causes a bit of distress for a couple of wolves, Ness and I are put up in the Pack house for the night. Of course, I'll be leaving soon to see my family, so we won't be staying long. With so much to tell them, with the introductions I have to make, I need to see them soon. Nissa and Orwen didn't feel right sending me off without a lick of training, though.

I'll just come back for the rest of my training afterward. They understand the pull of family, know the bone-deep ache which pulls me home, so they don't question it.

In our room, Ness ducks behind a screen to change into her nightgown, which baffles me.

I've seen her naked. She's seen me. Why be shy? Why hide?

But she does.

Tucked away in a comfortable bed, Ness pulls away from me. I roll onto my back, staring at the ceiling until long after sleep claims her.

***

Exhausted once more, I shovel food into my mouth at dinner. Orwen took me under his wing today, and his methods are far more vigorous. The big man pushed me to my limits with transformations many times over, sending my bones breaking, over and again.

Now, I gulp down more food than I've ever eaten in a single meal before. Plate after plate, I keep going, voracious in my hunger. I spare no glances for the people around me or the finery of the place, though there is certainly a surplus of expensive goods.

It's a shame that I don't care to look them over. I've seen roast goat and vegetables many a time, but it fascinates me more than the high ceilings or the works of art which line the interior walls.

Halfway through the meal, well, halfway through *my* meal… most everyone else sits before empty plates with napkins draped over them…

The atmosphere changes.

A strange scent wafts in through the windows. Somewhere between sweat and rotting onions, mingled with the stench of rotting meat and molten iron, it wrinkles my nose.

Glancing up from my plate for the first time in several minutes, I peer down to each end of the table only to find Nissa and Orwen looking decidedly strained. Their eyes narrow, and their shoulders tense. Beside me, Ness closes her eyes and grips the arms of her chair.

A tall woman with her head shaved bursts through the door, naked from her recent transformation back to human form. Her chest heaves with rasping breaths, quite a feat. The wolves here seem to have endless endurance.

What could she have done to wear herself out?

"Selby?" Nissa cries, springing to her feet. She rushes over to the naked woman and places one hand on either side of her face. "What's happened?"

Still panting, the woman named Selby struggles to form words. "Tivoli..." She gulps down a breath. "He's... dead. Simen... killed him... took over the coven."

Bending forward, she braces her hands on her knees. Small breasts hanging forward in points, she huffs, "Tried to kill me."

Huff.

"Barely made it out."

Another shuddering breath, though less severe than the previous ones. Already, her unnatural endurance is soothing her body.

"They're coming for us," she says. "Simen wants us dead."

My heart freezes.

"Sniveling little weasel," Nissa hisses. "And he wonders why we didn't want him in the Pack in the first place..."

Chapter 32
Ness

After another trying day of hiding, I sit near the fireplace in our room, a silent statue perched on the edge of a richly upholstered chair. For nearly half an hour, I brood over the news of Tivoli's death, pained by his loss and the implications it has for the whole of Evayla.

Strong and honorable, he ventured into vampirism with ideals and purpose. His willpower was all that kept the vampires under control. Without him, they would have descended into murderous frenzies far more often throughout the years.

Now, a man viler than most vampires, even in his mortal days, has wrested the reins from Tivoli. A black cloud hangs on the horizon, threatening a storm which could break Evayla.

And this time, I can't run from the fight.

Staring into the fire, I pray, stupidly enough, that no harm will come to Nolan in the coming days. But I know the gods won't intervene on his behalf. They certainly won't interfere for my sake.

This falls on me.

My chest rises with a soul-shaking breath, and I lean back into the chair, silent as ever. Elias foolishly tries to wait me out, apparently certain that I'll speak eventually, but my patience is far better than his.

Newly transformed, his strengthened emotions get the better of him. Pacing at the foot of the bed, he asks, "What is it?"

My eyes span the dark wood walls, glazing over the paintings that adorn them. That is, until they land on one specific landscape hanging in the corner. Rising, I seek it out, crossing the room in a few quick strides. My fingers trace the intricate frame as my eyes linger lovingly over the scene it depicts.

Harsh waves beat against a cliff, and the forest atop it shimmers with countless flecks of wondrous blue light. The glowfly migration in Rettland.

My time in that very clearing with Nolan floods my memory, warm and inviting. The words he whispered to me reverberate in my mind, a bittersweet melody.

I see him, lying beneath my hand as I stroked his chest, staring up at me with wonder in his eyes. I hear him say it, over and over, as I have in so many dreams since that night.

But I never said it back. I was too caught up in my own problems, my own insecurities.

I hurt him.

A bit of burnt sugar slips past my control, wandering into the air around me as my chest implodes. My fingers tremble against the golden frame, and my eyes slam shut against the sight of the glowflies.

It's the first bit of emotion I've let out all day, and it prompts a spike of jealousy from Elias. The hot, acrid scent of it burns my nose, and I swallow hard, regretting my lapse in control.

Determined not to let my voice waver, I clear my throat before finally answering his earlier question. "I can't go to Everson with you, Elias."

"What?" he mumbles, surprised by the topic. "Why not?"

"You heard what's happening," I say, turning to face him.

The firelight flickers over him, lending him a bit of ruggedness. He wears only his trousers, and somehow, that makes him… fit. This place, this way of life seems to have claimed him, already.

Maybe he was *meant for this.*

But… Does that mean he was meant for me? Wouldn't it be so much simpler if that were the case?

Yet, my body, my heart, my mind, my very soul… They all reject the thought.

He cannot be for me.

I am meant for Nolan, and since he's clearly meant for Alina… I'm meant for no one.

A fitting turn of events.

Sighing, I force my mind back to the world, back to Elias.

"The *Coven* is coming," I tell him, trying to convey the proper weight of such a thing. A battle between the Coven and the Pack will shake the core of Evayla. Unless I step in and end it.

"I'm sure the Pack can handle a few vampires," he says, petulant. Yet, even as the words cross his lips, he recoils from the thought of deserting the Pack in a moment of need. Every muscle in his body tenses, and his eyes scrunch as the Nether burns him for his treachery.

"There are a lot more vampires than werewolves. They're less… selective." My eyes drop to the floor. "The Pack is outnumbered, by a long shot. Besides, this is partly my fault."

Guilt oozes off me, sour and acidic. It pulls Elias closer, despite the jealousy simmering within him every time his eyes drift over my shoulder to the painting of the glowflies.

"I could have killed Simen the day you and I met, but I didn't. Had I looked a bit deeper, had I tried to figure out more of him… Had I recognized him…"

My hands move furiously as I pick at a bit of skin beside one nail, ripping it free of my body. The sting centers my mind, and I go on. "If I hadn't been blinded by my own stupid anger, I would've seen him for what he is. I could have prevented all of this."

Finally meeting Elias' eyes, I say, "I have to stay. I have to help fix this."

I have to protect Nolan…

Elias reaches for me, right as my hand goes to my necklace, fiddling with the sundial. And there it is, a fresh wave of jealousy, overlaid by fury. It singes my nose, but I don't flinch.

For a long moment, he stares over my shoulder at the painting. He may not know the exact memory, but he's clearly pieced together that I went to Rettland with Nolan. Gritting his teeth, he squeezes his eyes shut.

Does he regret his choice to transform? Does he regret his choice to be with me?

Would anything have been different with Nolan if Elias had never come around?

Taking a deep breath, I shove that last question away.

I can't blame Elias for this.

Nolan wants Alina.

My knees shake beneath me, but I steady myself with a hand on the wall. My necklace thuds against my chest, making a terrible, hollow sound.

At long last, Elias opens his eyes. Making a conscious effort to control his breathing, he reaches for the sundial. But his hands should never hold it.

Acid drips over his words as they creep out through his clenched jaw. "Yeah, I'm sure helping *the Pack* is the only reason you want to stay."

He curls his hand into a fist around the sundial, and I'm gripped with the fear that he'll break it. I almost snatch it from him but manage to hold myself steady.

At long last, he forces himself to go on, saying, "Are you going to tell me what happened in the Hall? You've been acting weird. What's going on?"

"Acting weird?" I hiss.

He barely knows me, but he thinks he knows when I'm acting weird?

He has the nerve to hold my necklace, to grab it up and squeeze it so hard he might break it? The necklace Nolan gave me? And now he's the one asking questions?

Fury roils within me, souring my stomach and turning me distinctly stubborn.

"Do I *owe* you answers? Do I *owe* you anything?" I ask.

Gritting his teeth, Elias begrudges me, "No."

"Then, drop it. Believe me, you don't want to fight with me. My anger runs deeper and burns far brighter than yours ever could."

The true gold of my eyes begins to reveal itself, brought out by the rage boiling in my veins and all the other things I've been repressing today. I can't hold it all back indefinitely.

The firelight bounces off my eyes, shimmering as it reflects onto Elias. He drops the sundial against my chest, and it comes away tainted by the warmth of his hand. He purses his lips and locks his jaw, holding in the challenge he clearly wants to issue.

But I've healed him.

Now that he's a werewolf, that gives me a measure of control over him. Even if he tried, even if he wanted to speak against me, he couldn't. The Nether that courses through his veins is there because I put it there. It will not run against me.

The strength of his emotions is all that let him get this far into the argument.

So, he turns and stomps to the bed. Tossing the covers back, he collapses into the mattress with a huff and turns away from me.

Unwilling to share the bed with him, I rip blankets from a wardrobe near the window and haul them over to the glowfly painting. Spreading them out beneath it, I curl up in the corner and drift off to sleep staring at the specks of light on top of the cliff.

Chapter 33
Nolan

The sigil of the Evaylan Knights glows in brilliant blue soapstone on the wall at the head of the table. A circle encapsulates an X, and a horizontal line strikes all the way through. Captain Weln sits beneath it, wearing full regalia. His helmet rests on the massive table beside his clenched fist.

"This cannot stand," he spits. "Not only have you brought the Coven down upon us, but you've been harboring a demi-demon?! And yet, you expect us to just *trust you*?"

His face reddens beneath his short brown hair, and the air swirls with his anger.

But after the countless ways he's debased Ness throughout his previous statements, my own temper flares, as well. My hands grip the arms of my chair, turning them to splintery dust. They stab my poor palms, but I don't care. My stomach churns, and my jaw locks firmly into place.

"That beast could've killed us all, any time, and you all kept us in the dark," the Captain shouts.

"And yet, she didn't, which tells me we've been right to trust her," Orwen gentles, but his hands ball into fists in his lap.

Too bad the good Captain canna see them.

"That *bitch* does not deserve trust. She deserves extermination!"

On my feet in an instant, I send my chair flying backward to the floor. My fists pound the table, shaking the whole damn thing. "Dinna ev'r call her that, again," I growl.

"Or what, mongrel?" Captain Weln spits, slowly rising to his feet.

My skin bristles with the ache to transform, to tear this filthy bastard to bits. Orwen stands, as well, blocking my periphery. His mouth moves, but no words makes it past the sound of my blood rushing through my veins.

Baring my teeth, I hiss, "If anythin' happens to her, yeh'll—"

"Nolan!" Orwen shouts.

And this time, I feel it in my bones, rattling my teeth. It jerks my head in his direction.

"Outside. Now." Grey eyes strained with fury, the big man glowers at me.

He's one of the few men in the Pack who would rival me in a fight, not that it could ever come to that. My head bows obediently as the Nether in my veins flows with his will, and I stomp out of the meeting room. As soon as the door shuts and the sparsely furnished hall envelopes us, I spin on my heel to face Orwen.

I canna let him speak first. He'll jus' send me away.

Of course, he tries to speak, but I barrel over him before he can demand my silence.

"We've got to stand up fer her. We owe her that," I say, voice firm. "*You* owe her that."

I've never come so close to challenging him or Nissa before. The Nether in my veins burns me. His outrage singes every muscle.

Yet, he flinches, and I know my words have found their mark. Only for a second do I regret dredging up such a painful memory, and then the overwhelming need to protect Ness from the Knights reasserts itself.

Any cost.

He holds his jaw tight, but his lips tremble. "I have not, even for one second, forgotten what I owe Ness."

And then, I see it in his eyes, see the way that night haunts him. I remember taking turns carrying his daughter as we ran, hell for high water, through the forest for Ness' cottage. I can still see her tiny body, a mess of blood and sizzling gore, splayed out on Ness' table. She'd gotten into the storeroom and toppled a rack of silver weapons over onto herself.

She was so weak when we finally got her to Ness. She'd been battling her wounds for a full day. Ness barely managed to save the girl.

But she did it.

She never hesitated, never asked for anything in return.

No' that she ever does.

My heart twists painfully at the thought. The very notion of Ness falling into the clutches of the Knights, only to be snuffed out despite all the good she's done.

They canna take her...

Voice low, Orwen says, "I've been thankful for Ness *every minute* for the past 17 years. I know *exactly* what I owe her."

He steps closer. Eyes like monstrous storm clouds peer through mine, staring straight into my soul. My body aches to bend before his will, but I force myself to hold steady. My lungs struggle for air, and my heart beats erratically.

"But," Orwen says, eyes brimming with tears he won't let fall, "losing our heads with the Knights will *not* help our case."

Reason finds me, and I see that, of course, he's right. Much as I hate to admit it. So, I let my eyes fall before him, silently thanking him for reigning me in.

"They know the Coven's numbers. They know the practical advantages of having her on our side. They're just mad that we didn't tell them about her, and now they're making a show of it. They'll come around," Orwen says.

My shoulders fall slack, and I unfurl my hands.

He's right. He has to be.

Nether take me, he has to be right.

"Now," he adds, voice considerably softer, "do her a favor and *go home*."

I nod, accepting his words for the order they are.

As I walk away, footsteps echoing through the barren hallway, I say, "If yeh canna stop them…" My entire body trembles with the thought of the Knights hurting Ness.

"I *will* kill as many o' them as I have to, er I'll die protectin' her."

I open the door, and as I cross the threshold into the sunlight, Orwen whispers, "I know."

Chapter 34
Ness

I march to the local chapter of Knights with my heart in my throat. Everything about this feels stupid, *is* stupid.

But Orwen insists there's no other way.

Nolan walks close at my side, and Elias takes it as an invitation for competition. He tries to take my hand in his, but I wrap my arms around myself, instead, withdrawing from him. It isn't *his* touch that I crave, nor his comfort that I need.

We trudge through a nearly empty street in Tor. A few people talk outside the Ether temple, but they pay us little mind, barely sparing a glance for what must surely be my last moments.

My gaze falls as we round the temple, and an innocuous little wooden building peeks into view. When the front stairs appear, they draw my eyes upward, and I shudder. This plain cottage seems harmless from the outside. And to anyone else, it is.

But in its halls, my predators lurk.

I fight myself, willing my arms not to reach out for Nolan. I even keep myself from fiddling with the necklace that hangs heavy with dread and rejection around my neck.

I close my eyes and allow myself one last moment of peace, for I'll surely never see another.

Ignoring the door in front of me, waiting to open and swallow me up for good, I take a deep breath and listen.

The birds throughout Tor chirp happily, freer than I've ever been or ever will be. A nearby sparrow sings a hauntingly beautiful melody, perched in the branches of a solitary pine. The mid-morning sun warms my skin, and a gentle breeze teases my hair. Inhaling deeply, I focus on the scent of sandalwood.

Somehow, despite everything, he's here.

My icy heart melts, just a bit. One tiny corner thaws, and the blood running through it warms, just a touch.

Maybe he still cares.

Maybe just a little.

Pain spears my soul, but why deny myself that feeble fantasy, now?

It's not like I'll survive the day…

A hand on my elbow, Nolan's hand, pulls me from my reverie. Warmth like I haven't felt in months oozes into me, seeping into my bones and sending delicate shivers over my skin. I meet his gaze.

Dark eyes fierce, he whispers, "I won't let *anythin'* happen to yeh."

Before I can wonder at his words or his soft tone, the door before us opens, and the Captain stares down at me. A man I've feared for decades looms over me with the sigil of the Knights emblazoned proudly upon his chest.

Yet, in his sharp, brown eyes, a healthy dose of fear mixes with the hatred and mistrust that I expected. Only then does it occur to me that this meeting might be every bit as worrisome for him as it is for me.

Nolan releases my elbow and places his hand on the center of my back, far higher than he used to touch me. "Captain Weln," he says, tone carefully controlled, "this is Ness." He takes a deep breath and softens his voice. "Ness, this is Captain Weln."

I shiver for half a second before I get a hold of myself, and Nolan's hand dips lower, sliding to the small of my back. A far more pleasant shiver moves through me, but agony follows quickly on its heels, slicing my heart to bits in my chest.

Even with my death almost guaranteed, I can't fool myself into thinking it means anything to him, anymore. Much as I want to, much as I need a final delusion to ferry me safely to the Netherrealm, the truth wrests the dream from my hands.

All I see are flashes of Nolan's arms wrapped around Alina, his lips touching the top of her head as he presses her to his bare chest.

Even with the end staring at me through Captain Weln's eyes, I can't pretend Nolan wants me to spare myself a bit of pain in my final moments.

Because I know better.

My stomach falls into my shoes, and my frozen heart goes with it, shattering into a million jagged pieces. And suddenly, the end doesn't seem so bad.

Aching to get it over with, desperate to end the anguish of being without him, I step forward to meet my death. The brittle, broken shards of my heart crunch beneath my feet.

Holding out my hand, I offer to shake.

The Captain stares down in horror, and I withdraw the invitation. I'm only glad that my true appearance is still concealed. Had I come here, claws and horns shining in the sunlight, and offered to shake hands…

He likely would've cut my hand off.

Though, I suppose I should've expected as much. I chide myself for thinking he'd treat me like anything more than what I am…

The spawn of a demon.

A heathen.

Worthless.

***

With a plan set in motion and my heart somehow still beating, we all sit together in the meeting room. Our gazes roam over each other uneasily. Bonds of trust which have been in place nearly as long as I've been alive have been tested today.

Because of me.

My eyes run another quick lap around the room. The massive table easily accommodates the lot of us, but it can't possibly put enough space between me and the high-ranking Knights at the other end. All seven of them stare daggers at me.

Beside me, at the head the table, Orwen leans back in his chair and pinches the bridge of his nose. Across from me, Nissa lays her hand atop his, curling her fingers under his palm. The contrast of their skin tones strikes me as beautiful, and I try to carve it into my memory. Still convinced that the Knights could begin their chant at any moment, I hope that one last pleasant image will help me tolerate the Netherrealm.

To my right, Elias shifts in his chair and puts a hand on my knee. The comfort he intends it to fill me with doesn't come across. For I know, deep down, that once I've outlived my usefulness, the people at the other end of the table will kill me. I can only hope they won't kill anyone else on my account.

After all, they did bring me here.

Shouldn't that earn them leniency, or perhaps, some sort of pardon?

My eyes find Nolan, finally, and a weak smile lifts my lips.

Maybe they'll let him live. Maybe he'll go on without me…

My heart convulses in my chest, shriveling as the ice closes around it once more.

Maybe he can be happy.

"Well," Captain Weln says, breaking the tense silence. "Let's get this started. We don't have forever. None of us do if the Coven is coming for us."

I look over at him, surprised. Whether that was his way of motivating us, or whether he really is concerned for the survival of the Pack, I can't tell. With so many emotions filling the air in this tiny, closed-off room, it's impossible to sort out what comes from whom.

Clearly dismissed, we all rise to do our part. Four of the seven Knights venture off to issue orders and move the entire population of Tor into a single sector. Two others are sent in search of their Ether witches with orders to help with the partial evacuation, then meet at the entrance of the Ether temple when that's done.

Those witches will have to work with me, something that's never been done, but we don't have a choice. Too many civilian lives are at stake not to try.

Each Knight stares at me as they pass. Their hands reach, unconsciously, for the silver weapons at their sides, resting on hilts, and hatred burns in their eyes. But their fear shines brighter.

Captain Weln bids us a temporary farewell and disappears into the depths of the chapter house. "Get your people ready," he tosses over his shoulder.

And by some miracle, I live to walk out of the chapter house.

Outside, the sun is just as bright as it was before I entered this place. Birds still sing. People mill about at the entrance of the Ether temple, just as oblivious to the danger which threatens them as they were an hour ago.

The little sparrow, or perhaps a different one, perches in the branches of the lone pine. It cocks its head to the side, appraising me.

But it no longer sings.

Orwen and Nissa set our pace, leading us to the Pack house, and Liam and Sari fall in behind them. Nolan and Elias stare at each other for a moment, and I start walking without them, letting them fall in line behind me. I've no time to watch Elias piece together my past with Nolan.

And I haven't the strength to watch Nolan offer me up to him.

With my arms crossed over my chest, wrapping up to grip my shoulders, I rest my chin on my wrists and press my necklace against my skin. I'm weak. I have to touch it, have to *feel* it, and this is all I can do to keep myself from gripping it tightly in my fist and hurting Elias further.

The only thing I can do to keep from showing Nolan just how much I wish he would wrap his arms around me.

One last time.

Because deep down, I know I won't survive this day. I can feel the Netherrealm calling me. My body aches to show itself for what it is, to let the Nether slither freely through me.

Concealed by my hair, I let my finger trace the chain of my necklace, my little bit of comfort. But soon, I'll give it up, so Nolan can give it to Alina.

He can be happy…

Without me.

Chapter 35
Elias

Jars clank together as Alina piles them into my arms. She takes one after another down from the shelves of the Pack's preparation room. Their contents range from simple, easily identified flowers and herbs to scales and bits of bone from creatures I've never seen.

Her eyes roam over them restlessly as she carefully considers each one, weighing their contents and usefulness for… whatever she and Ness will be up to later. The sweet scent of honeysuckle floats through the air, wafting on an undercurrent of something burnt.

Somehow, she smells… like rotten food, too, and it makes no sense to me. I'm not entirely sure I've smelled this emotion before, so I can't pin it down.

"How are you feeling?" My head tips to the side, and my brows scrunch together, sizing her up.

Her dark braid slaps her shoulder as she jerks her head around to stare at me, hand still reaching for something on the back of a high shelf. Her brows furrow, and she narrows her eyes.

"Gods, you *are* new, aren't you?"

I blush, fully aware of how rude I've been thanks to my newly weakened self-control. Swallowing, I drop my gaze.

"Sorry," I whisper.

"It's fine," she says with a laugh, turning back to the shelf.

With a hop, she finally reaches the jar her hand sought for nearly a full minute.

Thank the Gods. Watching her struggle with that was eating at me. Not that I could help with my arms full...

My eyes fall to the jars populating the space between my arms and my chest. She places this newly acquired specimen, a red and black claw with one side flattened as if grated down, on top of them in a careful balancing act.

Her hand brushes my arm, and my body reacts to the touch, craving more. A little shiver rockets through me, rattling the jars in my arms. Something devilish flashes in her eyes, but quickly vanishes.

Ness has been ignoring me, and my desires are certainly elevated. Taking a deep breath to settle the bone-deep ache inside me, my nose fills with honeysuckle and musk, though the second part disappears with the mischief in Alina's eyes. The bitterness of burnt sugar returns, strengthened by its own temporary absence.

"Since you *are* new, and you clearly need to learn…" Alina trails off, reaching for yet another jar on the top shelf. "These things should be somewhat intuitive, but it can't hurt to tell you. It'll speed up the learning process. And I must say, I have a lot of experience with this. I've smelled pretty much everything at the tankard."

I glance up and down the length of the room, tracing the walls of shelving, and hope we won't need many more jars from the top shelf. Though, considering how many find their homes at that height, the odds aren't great.

"First lesson, it isn't polite to just *ask* people outright what they're feeling. Smelling it is already pretty invasive," she says. "Generally, people let you know if they want you to know."

She jumps again, trying to reach the same jar.

I shift my feet on the stone floor, impatient. But there, in a dark corner, I find our salvation. A table. Shuffling across the floor, I gently settle my cargo upon it and make my way back to Alina.

Placing a hand on her back, I say, "Please. Let me." But the contact sends another rush of electricity bursting through me.

She turns to look up at me, chest rising and falling quickly with the effort of jumping for jars. Her eyes fall to my chest, and she nods. Again, something rich and earthy floats up to my nose, this time tinged with the bitterness from before.

"The one with the blue flowers."

Turning, I grab the jar easily, and we proceed like that. She indicates the many jars she needs from the top shelf, and I fetch them for her.

"I'm… hurting," she says. "That's what the burnt sugar smell is. A broken heart."

She swallows loudly in the otherwise silent room. The sigh which follows is louder.

"Broken heart?" I ask, recalling the same scent drifting off Ness. A pit of despair opens within me, pulling me inside out.

Alina nods. "Nolan… Well, I'm sure you know how he feels for Ness."

Numb, I nod along, wondering for the first time if…

Does Ness still have feelings for Nolan?

Then, I realize just how instinctive these scents are. The anger that swept through me last night screams back into focus, explaining itself to me.

I was jealous.

Somehow, I knew. When I saw her staring at that damn painting, fiddling with that necklace…

I knew. And I hated it.

I told myself I was just mad that she hadn't bothered to speak to me, but… This makes so much more sense.

She still loves him.

And… I'm right in the way.

I gulp down a lump in my throat.

But can I do what he did? Can I give her up to make her happy?

Logically, I *should* step aside. There isn't much point being with someone who doesn't want me, but… My body aches to be with her, again. The Nether in my bones begs me to forget Nolan and go to Ness. To put my happiness first, to do what I have to do to be with her.

For a second, the vision of Nolan's desecrated corpse floats before my eyes.

Before me, Alina's nostrils flare rapidly, analyzing everything I fail to hide. Voice soft, she asks, "Does Ness…?"

I can't answer, can't speak the words. I can't tell her how deeply I've screwed up, or how badly I'm hurting Ness. I can't tell her that I can't give Ness up, or what that must mean of how I actually feel for her.

I can't tell her that I'm willing to put my own selfish happiness ahead of Ness' broken heart. Or Nolan's.

So, I grit my teeth and stand there with my hands curled into tight fists.

But that same mischief lurks within her gaze, accompanied by a luscious, earthy scent. She reaches out and lays her hand on my arm, and my body reacts. Another jolt of electricity, another shiver quakes through me. My blood quickens, and the air fills with a thick, earthy scent.

"Breathe. It gets easier to reign this stuff in," she says. She doesn't pull her hand away, but she goes on. "The rotting smell is fear. The musky, dirt smell… That's lust."

I stare at her, shocked at her openness.

But she says, "And you…"

Alina slides her hand up my arm, over my shoulder, all the way to the side of my neck. Her thumb caresses my jaw, and my heart stutters.

"You smell about like a freshly tilled garden…" She steps closer to me, lifting her other hand to my waist. "Of course, there are other things in there…"

Her eyes drop to my lips.

My body tenses, muscles coiling tightly. My hand falls away from the shelf, abandoning the jar I'd intended to grab. Instead, it lands on Alina's hip.

"Jealousy, worry. Guilt…" She steps closer, pressing herself against me. "They're all there, too. But now…"

Tipping her head to the side, Alina pulls her bottom lip between her teeth. I suck in a breath as she slides her hands along my torso to the top button of my shirt. "Now, those other things are fading."

Ness… Ness… Think of Ness.

I close my eyes as Alina pulls the second button loose, then the third, and the fourth. The Netherrealm cries out for me to do this, to live in the moment. To forsake the jealousy, and the anger, and the guilt.

To do what *feels* good.

After all, Ness doesn't want me. I'm just an inconvenience to her.

And this…

Fire burns my skin as Alina undoes another button, the final button, and slides her hands over my bare chest.

This feels good.

My hands grasp Alina's hips, pulling her hard against me.

The Nether in my blood surges through me, and the rushing of it drowns out the world beyond this room, beyond the feel of Alina's hands on my chest and her soft, warm body pressed against mine.

Leaning my head to the side, breathing heavily and filling my lungs with the pure scent of want, I crush my lips to hers. Hungry mouths burn together, aching for something deeper, something to make us feel okay.

Slipping my hands around to her backside, I squeeze, and she lets out a breathy moan. That's all the invitation I need. I lift her up, and her legs wrap around me instantly. Every muscle in my body aches so sweetly, begging for more, and I pin her against the shelves.

Moving against her, using the shelves for leverage, I slide one hand up to cup her large breasts. Her head tips back, and I kiss her neck. Honeysuckle fills my head, pushing my thoughts away.

Alina's hands slide around to my back, moving beneath my shirt and leaving trails of fire along my skin. She nibbles at my ear, and a guttural moan crawls through my lips. I rock against her, moving and grinding.

Then, an eerie wail shivers through my bones. My blood runs cold, and I shake, suddenly hollow.

Not again...

Letting Alina slide back onto her feet, I meet her gaze. The wildness of the past moments lingers in the corners, but her eyes are strained.

Another howl rattles my spine. Then, another.

Thrown from the burning heat of desire, I land in a pit of ice water. My heart shrinks from it, trying to find some way out, but I find none.

I know that sound. I just didn't know I'd feel it happen, feel their creation. Dread settles heavily on my shoulders, and I sag beneath its weight. As my body quakes with the lingering deaths of two more Howlers, I turn my gaze from Alina to the jar I was neglecting on the top shelf.

She nods, fully aware of what we need to do, and I think our little dalliance forgotten.

But she speaks, once more.

"If you were wondering..." she whispers, "If you really loved Ness, *really* loved her... if you knew she loved you..." A sob chokes her, cutting off her words momentarily. "If things were right between the two of you, this," she gestures at the both of us, "never would've happened."

I stare at her, openmouthed. Shock rumbles through me as I realize the test she's just put me through, the test I just failed.

Turning on her heel, she moves to the table and gathers up some of the jars. "I can't make him happy," she says, and one jar clanks against another in her arms. Their contents slide against the glass and clink into the sides. "You can, though. You can make them both happy."

Alina turns to face me with tears glistening in her eyes. Burnt sugar fills the room. The candles throughout the room flicker, shining in her gaze. She swallows hard and reigns herself in. Slowly, the tears dry, and the room smells of nothing but cedar, sap, and honeysuckle.

"You know what you need to do," she says. "Are you strong enough?"

Chapter 36
Ness

My hands tremble as I seek him out. The scent of sandalwood guides me through the Pack house to the Hall of the Forgotten, but I pause outside the door. Reaching behind me, I unclasp the chain and take off his necklace.

After closing the clasp, I stare down at it. The sundial looks out of place, like it aches to rest against my chest rather than my palm.

But night is falling, and the Howlers were made nearby.

Without the weight of mortality, the Coven cleared the distance between Remin and Tor in no time. They'll be upon us within the hour. Maybe two. I still have work to do as the witches are ready.

I might not get another chance.

The chain dangles from my hand, and I grip the sundial tightly. With my heart in my throat, I pull the door open. Sandalwood fills the space, no longer just a thin wispy trail lingering in the halls, and the bitter reek of burnt sugar hits me like a hammer. I suck in a breath, shocked, and it nearly chokes me.

Nolan stands, staring at a tapestry that I usually avoid. One of the final nights of the revolution. The only battle I took part in. My role has been actively concealed from the Knights, but it's been immortalized in a tapestry they'll never see.

His eyes linger on the image of me, horns out and eyes blazing yellow, though I was concealed that night. Soft waves of anguish roll through the air, but they make no sense.

Is he hurting over me? Or has something happened with Alina?

Which would I prefer?

I have no answers for my questions.

Somewhere in the Pack house, a window opens, and the air within the place shifts, blowing my scent into the Hall. Nolan looks up, dark eyes strained. He sets his jaw, and retracts his feelings, no longer comfortable airing them out.

His withdrawal stings me, recalling the days when nothing was hidden between us.

Lugging leaden feet through step after step, I cross the room. My heart falls out somewhere along the way, trampled underfoot. Every step is a chore, a new agony dragging frigid claws over my skin. My chest collapses, unable to sustain my weight, and I clutch the sundial tighter.

I have to do this.

It doesn't belong with me…

Tears prick at the corners of my eyes, but I blink them away. Stopping in front of him, I stare into the same eyes I've stared into for years, now. But today, they're closed off. They don't sparkle with the love I used to see there.

So, I hold my hand out. The chain swings freely, and though it pains me to do so, I unfurl my fist. The tiny piece of bronze lies there, a stone weighing me down. It begs me to drop my hand, to take it and run.

I can't.

The image of him with Alina flickers in my mind, a flame burning me alive. Her hair tickles his chest, shielding her face from my view. I watch his hand smooth her huge mane, and my heart twitches, somewhere on the floor behind me.

Nolan's façade cracks, and his jaw falls. He shakes his head.

"No. I gave this to yeh. I *made* this fer yeh."

Taking a deep breath, I say, "Maybe Alina will like it."

I try to steel myself, expecting to hold back torrents of sadness. But that's not all that hits me. My stomach roils with jealousy, and… That slips through. Hot and bitter, it scorches the air.

A flash of something lights his eyes, but only for an instant. It disappears long before I can place it.

"Are yeh mad about Alina?" he asks, voice tight and eyes narrowed.

"No, of course not." My words drip acid all over the floor, and I hate that I'm not better at hiding from him. My emotions keep bleeding out, leaking all over me.

He pulls in a deep breath and grits his teeth, small fissures in the mask. His hands curl into fists at his side.

"How can yeh stand there, an' be mad at me o'er Alina when yer wit' Elias?"

And there it is. A tiny slip, just a hint of molten iron tinged with something bitter. His breathing accelerates, and his heartbeat hammers at my ears.

"I wasn't. Not until *you* changed him." Curling my fingers around the sundial, I step closer. Bits and pieces of my armor fall away, and I watch his brows furrow as the full force of my agony hits him.

I've already messed up. I've already said too much and damned myself in his eyes. So, I don't try to stop the words that rush out.

"I sent him to you for a reason," I spit, jaw tight, but eyes welling with tears. "I thought you'd know I hadn't been with him. I meant for it to show you I didn't *want* someone else."

Nolan's heartbeat falters, stumbling as it runs through my mind, drowning out even the sound of my own heart's useless flailing.

"I thought you'd know…" My voice breaks, and I clear my throat. But the words keep coming. "I didn't expect him to want to be changed to be with me, especially since he's only known me a couple weeks. And I definitely didn't think *you'd* change him…"

The color drains from my face, and a chill settles deep in my bones as I say, "Not... so *he* could be with me."

Voice small and feeble, I stare into Nolan's beautiful, dark eyes as I say, "You got your point across, though. Don't worry."

Grabbing his hand, I force the necklace into his palm and do everything in my power to ignore the desire to press his hand to my cheek. Dropping his hand before the temptation becomes too much, I whisper, "I'll leave you alone, now."

My cheeks flush, and a few tears abandon my eyes, jumping free to meet their end. Unable to hold his gaze anymore, I turn and force myself to walk away.

A weight in my chest, some stone that fell in when my heart fell out, tries to keep me in place. It begs me to be still. But I can't stay here, withering beneath the eyes I used to love staring into.

Behind me, voice shriveled and small, Nolan finally speaks. "But... Liam said yeh'd want him changed... He said..."

He falters, voice breaking, and I stop in my tracks.

After a moment, he begins fresh, but his voice is no more than a hoarse whisper. "Liam said yeh were in love wit' him."

I turn around, stunned by the hurt in his voice, only to find his face awash with it.

"He saw yeh in the stream, said yeh let Elias help clean yeh up… and after the stream… yeh held him…"

Face twisted, Nolan clears his throat again and rubs a hand over the bottom half of his face. The hand holding the sundial hangs at his side, and the chain sways freely.

"You mean when I was sad and lonely and broken? I couldn't carry myself to the water if I'd tried, and he insisted. But nothing happened that night. All that *ever* happened was a stupid kiss when we woke up the next day… I just… I just didn't want to be alone… I didn't want to hurt anymore…"

Guilt chokes me before I can say anything more, pulling my eyes to the floor. I can't bear the betrayal that must surely darken Nolan's eyes.

"Nothing else happened until you changed him. That stupid kiss made me realize I didn't want him, or anyone else." Fresh tears drip from my eyes to splatter on the stone floor.

"And anyway," I say, wiping at my eyes, "I never said I loved him. Liam assumed. I tried to correct him… He just… I was hurting. Because Elias wanted to *see* his dad's death, so I had to relive it. I was hurting because I *destroyed* Elias by showing him."

My voice lowers further, almost inaudible, and I pick at my nails. Our heartbeats ramble on in unsteady rhythms, filling my mind. "I was hurting because I was nervous about how you'd react. I didn't think Liam would *tell* you. It's not like I could tell him how I actually feel about you. Liam, of all people, knows how terrible we were together. He heard, or heard *about*, every fight."

Footsteps, far closer than they should be, finally break through the wall of heartbeats surrounding my eardrums, and I look up. Suddenly within arms' reach, Nolan searches my face. Another step brings him even closer, and hope shines within his eyes, filling the air with the scent of lilac.

In a husky voice, he says, "Liam also knows, bett'r than anyone, how good we were togeth'r."

He reaches up and touches my neck. I gasp, stomach full of glowflies.

Surely, I must be dreaming...

But his touch feels real enough. My eyes flutter, searching his gaze for anything that might reveal this to be a joke or a fantasy. The sincerity I find is disarming, and I drop my eyes to his chest.

"He knows how happy we made each oth'r. Yeh know, when we weren't tryin' to rip each oth'r's throats out, that is." He laughs, nervously. "Why... dinna yeh come see me when yeh came to Tor?"

His tone is nonchalant, but I can see that this hurt him, that it played against me in his decision to change Elias.

"I was going to, the second night. I knew you'd be with Elias the first night." Sighing, I say, "I was at the door, just about to knock when you..."

I can't finish the sentence.

To think that I was so close, just a few seconds off from sparing us both this terrible mess…

It shatters my last vestige of self-control. Overwhelmed as I am, I feel the Nether within me rising up. It bubbles through me, forcing my true form toward the surface. And I don't stop it, knowing Nolan won't shy away. Our chests rumble with the thunder which shakes the air as the Nether rearranges itself, and we breathe faster.

Tipping my head back with his thumb, he stares into my golden eyes. A single tear rolls over my cheek. Nolan's other hand, still balled around the sundial, finds my waist.

My breath quickens as he moves closer. Nolan presses against me, leaning his head down to kiss me, and I rise to tiptoes to meet him. Our noses touch, and my hands slide into his long hair.

Our lips brush together, softly. He draws that little moment out, moving his lips side to side, ever so slowly, over mine. My lips part with a tiny gasp, and tears pour freely from my eyes. He kisses the tracks left in their wake, and I shiver beneath his lips.

But a voice at the doorway cuts our reunion short.

"You never wanted to be with me, then…" Elias croaks.

Nolan and I turn our gazes to the door, only to find Elias and Alina standing there, open-mouthed. They stare at us, and the air around them swirls with horror and heartbreak and… guilt.

"So, this," Elias gestures to himself, "this change, risking my life, all of it really was for nothing?"

I shake my head, hating my role in the damnation of his soul. And my only defense slips out of my mouth. "I didn't ask you to do this. I never would have expected it of you, either. Nether take me, Elias, we only knew each other a couple weeks…"

My gaze drops to the floor. "Your soul is just another stone around my neck."

The words hit like a fist, and the air rushes out of him. He turns to leave, but Nissa appears behind him. Her umber skin shines in the light of the torches spread throughout the Hall, but her eyes are serious.

"That's enough, for now. Whoever survives can sort out this drama later. Ness, Alina, we need you, now. They're almost here, and we have to get that barrier up." Her eyes soften, as she takes us in. "This has to wait," she adds before turning on her heel.

None of us dare keep her waiting with so much at stake.

But Nolan takes my hand, lacing our fingers together as we walk.

Chapter 37
Nolan

We follow Nissa into the courtyard with the shrieks of the Howlers far too near and far too numerous. She immediately sends Elias to the armory. We may not have anything that fits him exactly, but something will be far better than nothing.

Nissa turns to me, and I expect her to send me away, as well. I open my mouth, ready to argue if her tone even suggests it, but she cuts me off.

"Get your armor, and then get back here. Bring Ness' armor with you," she says. "After that, you're not to let her out of your sight. I don't care *who* comes for her. Keep her safe."

Well, at least I have her blessin' to take out a few Knights, if need be. No' havin' it wouldna have stopped me, but it's nice to have.

I nod, curly hair tickling my neck.

Nissa's eyes shine almost maternally as she sweeps them over Ness. Surprisingly enough, she pulls Ness into an embrace and whispers, "If they get too close, fall back. Don't waste too much of your energy on us, okay?"

Nissa flinches at her own words as the Nether in her veins burns her for the sacrifice they hold.

Shocked, Ness puts her arms around the woman she never believed cared about her, despite my insistence. Her golden eyes fill with tears, and she looks to me.

"I told yeh," I mouth. I smile, and my heart warms despite the eerie howls in the distance.

Maybe now she'll see she has a place within the Pack... Maybe she'll stop thinkin' she's a burden to those she's healed.

Pulling back, Nissa puts her hands on either side of Ness' face. A small sniffle escapes her, and she says, "Without you, this'll be a bloodbath."

Smart... Makin' her save herself fer the sake o' others.

"Keep. Yourself. Safe."

Ness nods, shaking a few more tears loose.

Nissa embraces me quickly, then sends me on my way, rich brown eyes staring on through a veil of tears. Orwen approaches them and leads Ness away.

***

Cloaked in my armor, I lug Ness' armor across Tor to the Knights' chapter house. My stomach clenches tighter, knotted up, knowing she's there without me. Sure, Orwen is there, and yes, he'll protect her, but...

I just need to be by her. I need to see that she's okay.

The thought of losing her, now, after just getting her back...

I'd stop in my tracks if it wouldn't keep me from reaching her. Instead, I pick up my pace, jogging with armor clanking noisily.

The unassuming wooden building looms at the end of the street, concealing the one I love in halls filled with people who, mere hours ago, would have killed her on sight. My feet beat a too-quick pace across the cobblestones, passing abandoned carriages and people chatting outside the Ether temple.

Why are there always people standin' outside that place?

Especially now…

"On to the market wit' yeh. Go on," I bark, shouting to be heard over the cacophony of pained howls rampaging through the forest.

Three young kids, no older than 16, any of them, stand there. They look back and forth amongst themselves nervously until a girl with the bushiest hair I've ever seen in my life steps forward.

"I… Well, *we*…" she fiddles with the belt that hangs off her hips, pulled down by a small dagger. Her dress is loose about her bony frame, and her soft face can't have seen more than 14 years.

"We want to help," she says. Behind her, two brown haired boys nod ferociously. But their enthusiasm is misplaced.

Ness' armor feels far heavier than it should, weighed down by my need to be next to her, and I glance at the chapter house. I close my eyes, willing Orwen to watch over her because I can't let these kids fight.

"This is no' the time fer first battles. If yeh want to help, we can talk about joining the Knights or the Pack after this. But… fer now…" I shake my head, imagining the devastation on Ness' face if these kids were caught by the Coven.

"Please, jus' get to the market. A very brave woman is riskin' everything, her life…" A lump forms in my throat, and I finally know how Ness must have felt, all those times when I rushed off to risk my hide. A black abyss waits before me, hoping that I'll fall in or take just one too many steps forward.

The girl looks back at her companions, clearly second-guessing herself and her role as spokesperson.

"Please, don't cheapen what she's doin'. Go. Be safe."

Then, because I know they won't be satisfied otherwise, I add, "If yeh want to help, pray to ev'ry God er Demon yeh know, ask fer their blessin'. We're goin' to need them on our side."

Finally, they nod, rather sheepishly, and I breathe a sigh of relief. Anxious as I am to move, to get this armor to Ness, I watch them walk away. Only when I'm confident that they're heading to the market and have no intention of turning back do I move.

Sprinting around the Ether temple, I vault up the stairs of the chapter house and burst through the door. I ask the first person I come across where I can find Ness, and the woman directs me to the basement.

"They're in the reliquary," she says.

My heart plummets.

Nether take me. Why'd they go there? I hope they dinna actually have the horns of a demon down there.

Gods help them if this is some sort o' intimidation thing…

***

Light steel armor gleams in the sunlight bouncing through storefront windows as Ness walks ahead of me to the door. Even here, beyond the chapter house, her nerves pull her hands together in front of her, awkwardly hugging the helmet tucked beneath her arm.

Stepping up beside her, I place a hand on her back to comfort her as we prepare to leave the safety of the store. I'd much rather hold her hand, but my gloves would pinch her fingers. Not to mention the risk that, given how nervous she is, she could squeeze too hard and drive her nails through the steel.

I'd heal. The gloves… Not so much.

So, I settle for this minimal contact.

She glances at me, and I smile reassuringly, despite the sour feeling in my stomach. Nether knows I haven't seen a *real* battle in decades. I don't think I've gone soft. I've practiced.

But…

Have I practiced enough to be confident in my skills with not only all the Pack's lives on the line, but Ness' life, as well?

I shake my head and hide how terrified I am that maybe I won't be enough, that something may happen to Ness.

That I may lose her.

Chapter 38
Ness

I feel their eyes on me already, and I have yet to set foot outside. My hand rests on the doorknob, desperate not to move. A chorus of agonized wails, far too close to Tor, begs me to go, but I hesitate. I quake with the bone-deep certainty that the people of Tor will kill me and take their chances with the Coven, thinking their odds of survival greater that way.

Nolan puts a gentle hand on my back, and I turn to look at him. He stares into my eyes with such love, such kindness, that I almost can't hold his gaze. Such looks shouldn't be directed at the likes of me.

But I'm glad he disagrees.

The warmth in his dark eyes slowly spreads through me, and I take a deep breath.

Time to go…

Wasting around won't accomplish anything.

Another deep breath and I open the door, steeling myself for the looks of hatred and fear I know will find me. The rusty old hinges creak, screaming for everyone's attention.

Not that they weren't already staring this way, waiting for me to show myself.

One final glance at Nolan, one last attempt to memorize the way his eyes light up as they take me in or the way a few strands of hair fall free even though the rest is carefully tied back…

Then, I step into the light of the outside world. My golden eyes glitter far too brightly, reflecting the fading sunlight out before me, and I glue them to the ground. I cross the small porch and descend three stairs to the ground, counting the tall blades of grass sticking up between the boards.

A few people amongst the crowd in town square gasp. Waves of fear, acrid and spoiled, roll through the air toward me, and my nose scrunches. The hatred I expected is present but diluted by desperation.

The sound of several thousand heartbeats, stampeding at break-neck speeds, assaults my ears and fills my mind. The Nether in my bones wars with itself, torn between two needs. Take advantage of the herd assembled before me, or sate my aching sympathy, the overwhelming desire to solve the problem and end the torment.

I choose the latter and lift my head.

I am better than the Nether in my veins. I will not *hurt them.*

Exhaling long and slow, I rake my eyes over the crowd. Every resident of Tor, men and women, young and old, huddle before me. Some try desperately to hide their fear but to no avail. Their raised chins, their unflinching eyes do nothing to stop their bodies from giving it away.

Dilated pupils, accelerated heartbeats, and the smell…

Nether take me, the smell…

Mortals have no chance of hiding from me.

I breathe deeper, searching for a familiar scent as I cast my gaze about the square. It takes a minute or two, but I find it.

Honeysuckle.

Just yesterday, I would have avoided her like a plague, but so much has changed since then.

I glance at Nolan, once more. A smile lifts my lips. My teeth even peek out, showing my never-used fangs to the world. Happiness fills me. The sky, the grass, the blush beneath his skin… They all seem brighter than they did a day ago.

Reaching out, I touch his face and watch the blush grow deeper. His eyes darken, and he leans into my touch.

A moment of blissful confidence tries to persuade me that maybe we can do this.

Maybe it'll be okay.

I nod, caress his cheekbone with my thumb one last time, and withdraw my hand. Measuring my breathing, I walk through town square, horns out and eyes shining gold.

Alina stands next to a small group of Knights several buildings down, past flowering bushes and a smattering of pine trees. The crowd to my right collectively takes a few steps back as I pass them.

Their fear and worry fill the square with the stench of rotten onions and sweat, forcing me to wrinkle my nose. I need to focus, so I close myself off to it. It's so simple, just like closing my eyes, and my head clears quickly.

Alina stands near a stone statue of Itand with the other thirty-two Ether witches of the Pack and the Knights of Tor gathered behind her. The Goddess of fortitude stands proud, the picture of health. Her hands hold a wolf cub, and a pendant of a horse hangs around her neck. Countless bundles of flowers grace the pedestal she stands upon, sprinkled generously with jewelry, all boasting the symbol of the Etherrealm. Four bowls rest on the edge of the pedestal.

Clad in an enchanted robe, Alina stares at me. She arches one eyebrow, and her eyes dart back and forth between Nolan and me. Much to my surprise, her lips lift in a bittersweet smile, and her ample bosom lifts with a deep breath. She nods once.

Turning, she picks up a stone bowl from the pedestal and sips from it. She hands it around to the other witches, and they all sip from the cool blue potion. When they've finished and settled the bowl back at Itand's feet, Alina lifts another bowl.

Coming together in concentric circles around her, they chant in the language of the Gods. My skin tingles with their words, pricking and stinging. A spike of fear quickens my pulse, but these are not the words that will send my soul to the Netherrealm.

Not yet, at least.

They might get to that later.

Alina lifts the bowl high above her head, and their chanting grows louder. The contents begin to glow, and the crowd to our right falls completely silent, as if afraid that even a breath taken at the wrong time could jeopardize the spell.

And it could.

Magic is such a fickle thing, Ether magic especially so. And the Gods are so hard to appease.

As the chanting goes on, the witches grow louder and louder. Their voices melt together, becoming one rope made of many fibers. All the while, my skin itches with it, and I envy the casual ability of the Pack members to use Ether magic. Sure, they practice Nether magic, too, picking and choosing the one which better suits the task at hand.

But they have a choice.

The Nether has always been a part of me, shaping me from the very beginning. It's laced into the very marrow of my bones, rather than just wrapped around them. It doesn't just whisper through my veins. It *is* my blood.

My choice was made for me, 42 years ago.

At long last, when their chanting is almost deafening, the mixture of herbs and fats and ground-up bones within Alina's bowl ignites, burning itself in tribute to the Etherrealm. The witches near the statue break their circles to allow Alina passage, and she settles the bowl in the flowers at Itand's feet.

In seconds, the bouquets are aflame, shining with the blinding clarity of pure Ether. I close my eyes against it, shrinking away, and turn to face the crowd instead. The smoke of burning leaves and herbs surrounds us, and for a few seconds, they seem to forget my existence. All eyes focus on the brilliant Ether, waiting to be shaped.

Slowly though, one by one, they remember me. Their eyes settle on me, a dark spot set against the magnificent glow of the Etherrealm.

But they don't realize the lengths I'll go to in order to save them, the things I'll give up. Yet, this glowing light is all the Etherrealm will do for them, today.

Stamping out the bitterness lest it spoil me against them, I wait for the witches to finish their spells, of which there are three more. I keep my ears pricked in their direction, listening closely for any sign of the banishing spell, but it doesn't come.

With the Ether refined into a swirling shape, and their chanting changed to a low hum, they send it upward. Shifting and undulating, it moves over town square, shaping itself into a latticework dome to the tune of thirty-three voices.

And here's where I come in.

Chapter 39
Nolan

Ness settles her helmet on the ground at our feet and begins her work. I've never thought to ask her how it works, how she tears the Nether from her surroundings, but she does it now.

I watch in awe as the sky grows brighter and the buildings nearby begin to glow. The bushes, trees, and even the dirt beneath our feet radiates a beautiful light as the balance within them shifts.

Meanwhile, the skin around Ness' eyes grows darker. Black webs branch out beyond the fading borders the Nether normally maintains at her cheekbones. My breath deserts me, and my skin tingles at the sight of her.

The true incarnation of power, and finally, she's using it. Not for terrible things, like she always feared. She's using it for good.

Like I always knew she would.

A lump forms in my throat, and the corners of my eyes prick uncomfortably, even as the corners of my lips curl into a smile. My heart soars.

Maybe we can meet in the middle, aft'r all. Far fewer busy body political trips, but… Maybe wit' her at my side when I go?

I cast my gaze about, amazed at the expressions upon the townspeople's faces. Swirls of bright white Ether move in the air, partially concealing them from view, but as it ripples, I see one face, then another.

All their expressions are the same. They stare down at their clothes and the few possessions they brought into the safety of the dome with them, watching as the Ether shines outward. The imbalance, the *purification* that Ness offers them, gleams brilliantly, reflecting in all their eyes.

A small part of me has to wonder if they'll attribute that to the witches and the Etherrealm, or if they'll see the witches stand still, now. Bitterness sours my stomach, for I know the answer.

Ness must know they won't credit her with this. Yet, she presses on, pulling more and more Nether into her body.

My gaze locks on her, again, only to find the webs of Nether reaching past her jaw, down to her neck, and disappearing under her armor. Little branches of it reach up her neck in the opposite direction, having made it all the way from her wrists. Wisps of faint green smoke emanate from her, drifting lazily into the air.

Her brows reach for each other, and she clenches her jaw. Suddenly, I remember the pain that comes with such intense Nether exposure and regret my earlier thoughts of her helping maintain the peace.

Could I ask her to do this, again?

A tear streaks down her cheek, and her hands ball into fists at her sides. Eyes closed tightly, she focuses through the pain.

I rip my gloves off and drop them at my feet, desperate to hold her, to help her through this. But her armor begins to glow red with the heat of the Nether, and I know I can't touch her.

I listen closely, straining past the wails of the approaching Howlers, tuning into the Nether. I hear her heartbeat galloping along, far too quickly. Her breathing intensifies, and my heart twists in my chest, knowing the pain she must be in.

Glancing around at the radiant town square, I can't imagine there would be much more Nether for her to take in. My eyes dart uneasily between her pained face and the expressions of relief on the faces of the townspeople.

Do they know the sacrifice she's makin' fer them, right now?

Again, bitterness fills me. So many people are completely ignorant of the true workings of our world and the aching trade-off required to use the Nether. There's no excuse.

Beside me, Ness raises her arms, and I breathe a sigh of relief. The pain will end for her, soon. She reaches for the Ether barrier, palms facing out and fingers spread. The Nether flows outward in great black swirling masses, followed by a crack of thunder that shakes my bones. The townspeople jump and cower, stupidly, before her.

Behind us, the Howler army continues its march, but the thunder stops their screeching, striking fear into their hearts. In the absence of their accursed wails, my shoulders feel lighter. I breathe a little easier.

Ness opens her eyes, but the beautiful gold is still strained. I watch as the darkness seeps out of her and weaves into the Ether barrier. Where the two energies meet, they swirl around each other, dancing playfully. The faces of the people in the center of the square, all huddled together, slowly transform into pure expressions of awe.

Then, the barrier solidifies, and the dance ends. Ether and Nether meld together to form a solid dome over the square. The uneven spread and the veins of one color running through the other make it look like marble.

If marble learned to glow.

Faint white light radiates from the hardened Ether in short rays, visible like beams of sunlight piercing clouds. Striking rays of green shine from the Nether, swaying and shifting like an aurora.

My breath deserts me, and my jaw falls open. All around me, choruses of gasps ring out as people finally look up from their spells or their weapons or whatever else they turned their attention toward when the light became too bright for their eyes to handle.

Hordes of glowflies flutter maddeningly in my stomach, and a smile lights my face. I turn to Ness, and her eyes mirror my excitement.

She's done it.

No matt'r what happens wit' the Coven, they're safe, now.

My arms wrap around her waist, and I lift her into the air. Our armor clanks together, and she laughs wildly. The sound is music, it is *life*, and I drink it in.

Hands on the sides of my face, she presses her lips to mine. Fire bursts across my skin. Desire churns in the pit of my belly and pulls my mouth open in a small moan.

I settle her feet back on the ground and pull her tight against me. Her tongue dances with mine, and I weave my hands into her hair. Now, that I've tuned into it, her heart races in my ears, reverberating on the Nether and galloping alongside my own.

A deep need burns within me, but this is neither the time nor the place. So, I pull back, breathless with desire. Ness' brilliant golden eyes are heavy with lust, and I breathe it in, savoring the earthy scent pouring off her.

But a symphony of eerie shrieks assaults us from the edges of the forest, just outside Tor, reminding us that this is far from done.

Though the people of Tor are safe, we're not.

No' that a reminder was entirely necessary.

Chapter 40
Ness

The dreadful screams of slowly dying animals wind my nerves into tiny, frenzied knots. Their suffering pierces my heart and pulls a lump to my throat. Hatred for the Coven, for *Simen* boils freely within me. Each howl, each moan, each and every wail of agony drifts toward us on a breeze far too gentle to bear such monstrosities.

The sun dips below the horizon quickly, ducking behind Mount Surm and the forest as if even that mighty thing trembles at the thought of the coming battle. But the moon rises, unafraid. Stars peer down at us, an audience excited by the spectacle we offer them.

Torn between the chills slipping over my spine and the boiling rage in my veins, my poor body shudders.

Torches burn all around town, staked into the ground along the edge of the forest. Far behind us, in the center of Tor, the marbled dome promises safety to the residents.

But here, on the border of the forest, there are no such guarantees.

Atop the roof of a small home, I look down over my allies, waiting.

Beside me, Nolan stands guard, ready to defend me if necessary. To my left, one hundred feet from the tree line, nearly one hundred werewolves stand ready to meet the Howlers. The local chapter of Knights matches their numbers, standing in formation off to my right in hopes of tricking the Coven.

If they think I've killed the alliance, they'll assume the Knights killed me. Or, so we hope.

Eerie wails fill the air, grating over stiff vocal cords. My blood curdles with their pain, and I ache to end it. The absence of heartbeats withing their ranks chills me to my core, and I shudder beneath the weight of their cries.

No one else seems to fare much better. The tragic howls of what was once a wolf pack set everyone on edge, especially the Pack members who've chosen to fight in wolf form. The Knights seem more unsettled by the choked roars of a mountain lion, mingling with those of a bear or two.

"Ness," Nolan whispers, barely discernible in the chaos assailing my ears.

I turn to look at him. The shadows of his helmet hide his eyes. Every so often, a torch below flickers just right, showing me glimpses of dark eyes drawn tight.

"If anythin' happens ta me—" he begins.

"No," I say, shaking my head adamantly. I stare out at the forest, unable to look at him for fear that I may picture his death. My soul riots at the thought, and my stomach turns sour.

I can't hear his goodbye. I can't face the thought of him dying here. I can't let that happen.

I won't *let that happen.*

"Calm down, love. I dinna mean if I die. I've no intention o' doin' that, today," he says, voice gentle.

His tone pulls my gaze back to him, and he's closer, now. I lift a hand to stoke the fire of the torch nearest us, and his eyes burn into focus. Dark and sultry, they pierce the desperation which threatened to overwhelm me, just seconds ago.

"If anythin' happens ta me," he says, then quickly adds, "if I get hurt…"

I open my mouth to protest, but he presses one finger to my lips. The metal of his glove is cool to the touch, as icy as the thought of watching him bleed.

But the Howlers silence him before he can go on.

A leash of foxes bursts from the undergrowth, all with dirty, dried blood caked into their fur. With no time left to talk, we turn, and I set to work. Pained screams erupt from their throats, but I twirl one finger in the air, binding their mouths shut.

I won't make the same mistake as last time…

The poor animals move jerkily, encumbered by the weight of death. Decaying muscles burden tiny frames, but still, they launch themselves at my allies.

All twelve are dispatched quickly, and I breathe a sigh of relief. Their bodies can rest, and their souls can move on.

But bigger animals stalk the tree line, whimpering painfully and looking for weak points the foxes may have revealed. A great cacophony of wails fills the night, threatening to chase the moon and the stars away.

Yet, the darkness of the forest hides the animals from me. I can't bind their mouths, and no one below dares venture beyond the light of the torches to be swallowed up by their rotting maws in the shadows. All we can do is wait, watching as their eyes shine with reflections of firelight.

Then, heartbeats march into earshot, announcing the coming of the Coven. As they get closer, as their hearts grow louder, the Howlers become more and more restless. They pace and stamp their feet, screeching and whimpering, all the while.

My nerves fray, unraveling like old rope. The forest before me, usually such a serene place, moves with nightmares made real. Their suffering fills the air, carried by the stench of lingering death.

And the heartbeats grow ever closer.

What used to be a wolf howls, voice rasping through a torn throat, and the rest of its pack joins in. Bears and mountain lions roar, and the ferocity of the sound is at once diluted by the pain it causes them and enriched by it.

The Coven joins the Howlers in the tree line. I can't see them, yet, but I hear their heartbeats all too clearly to deny their presence. Between the Coven, the Knights, and the Pack, all I hear are cries of agony and the staccato beats of hundreds of hearts, hammering away at my skull.

A few deep breaths do nothing to push away the sound. Nolan blows out a deceptively easy breath beside me, but I smell his anxiety slipping out between the pieces of his armor.

A gentle breeze tickles the leaves of the forest, temporarily lacing a hushed whisper into the chorus of shrieks which whip through the branches. Faint light trickles down from a sliver of the moon, painting the scene before me a far prettier shade of silver than it ought to be.

When the first bear plows through the undergrowth, it takes me by surprise. Charging the Knights, lumbering far less gracefully than it would have mere days ago, it winces with every step. Yet, it clears the distance quickly, heavy paws pounding the earth into submission.

A few Knights break formation, falling back between the homes at their backs to escape the nightmare beast.

Black veins track over grey skin where bits of fur have fallen off. Blood-encrusted holes adorn its neck, torn wide open by Nether knows what on the journey here. The flesh gapes, hungrily swallowing the light from the torches.

With only seconds to spare, I bind its mouth. It slams into a Knight, but she's more prepared than I was. Sword at the ready, she drives it into the bear's neck, raining black blood upon the ground as the two soar through the air.

They land in a heap, dark blood slick on gleaming silver armor, and she struggles to pull herself out from under the beast. I long to help her, to lift just one finger and pull the beast off her. But that would give away my presence.

So, I try not to watch.

For several moments, silence reigns. Only the clanking of her armor and the crackle of the torches pierce it. At long last, she frees herself. The Knight scrambles to her feet and retrieves her sword with a terrible sucking sound.

She doesn't bother wiping away the blood that coats her armor and weapon. More will soon follow.

All at once, a wave of Howlers storms out of the forest. Wolves and bears sprint for anyone in their path. I bind their mouths quickly, but they push through the ranks, regardless. Their bulk takes down anyone they hit, and bear claws make quick work of any exposed flesh.

Werewolves and Knights set upon them, working as quickly as they can. Dark blood spills over the ground, and the Nether in my veins begs me to jump down, to join the fray.

Then, the Coven stalks free of the foliage, and chaos descends. Nearly three hundred and fifty of them surge forward, some wearing simple leather armor while others wear Nether armor. The black steel shines malevolently in the torchlight. Our only advantage is their decided lack of combat training, for they certainly have numbers on their side.

All around, they pounce on Knights or Pack members who face terrible odds. A werewolf already facing two dying wolves and a decaying hawk is met with three vampires. The poor thing has its throat ripped out in seconds, and little silver pellets pour into the wound.

When the vampires turn their backs, moving on to the next unfair fight, I flick my hand. The pellets tumble out to the ground. Briefly, I wish I had been more skilled at this the night I summoned my mother. Everett and Trinny flash before my eyes.

But I stuff my feelings down. I don't have time for them, right now.

Across the battlefield, similar scenes play out. The blood flows freely, and I struggle to keep our people free of silver.

Then, our archers spring free of their hiding spots, dotted along the rooftops facing the forest. The snap of bowstrings punctuates the howls and shrieks and clashing metal. Arrows soar through the air and slam into bodies.

Howlers begin to fall.

The eyes of the Coven turn skyward, and I struggle not to duck before their gaze. I'm just one more shadow among the archers, just one more dark figure on a roof. If I hide, their eyes will seek me out, following my movement.

So, I hold my ground. Beside me, Nolan faces a similar dilemma. But we know what we're here for.

With the Howlers thinned out, he pulls out his throwing knives, the only weapon he's proficient with at such a distance, and picks a target.

Meanwhile, I refocus my attention. The Knights and the Pack are making headway. Bodies litter the ground. Some of the vampires wearing only leather armor lie on the ground, taken down by silver-tipped arrows, and slowly, the scales begin to tip. The fight is almost equal.

Seventeen vampires drip blood but still breathe, leaving little paths of crimson reeking of alcohol. And finally, I join the battle. Pulling Nether from the ground at their feet, I surge it upward into their bodies and watch as the blood slows.

A sick satisfaction fills me, and I issue my command.

"Stop," I breathe.

Though they couldn't possibly hear me, the Nether knows. Their limbs freeze, midair. Whatever attack they were preparing to launch, halts. In less than a heartbeat, they seize up with mouths open in guttural screams of fury and hands wrapped around throats.

Five more take meager wounds, some at the hands of their own enraged Howlers. Bourbon and whiskey mix with blood, leaving perfect trails. I sniff them out and rip the Nether free of their armor, forcing it into them.

Their wounds heal, and they are mine.

"No more," I whisper.

And the Nether knows.

It carries my order to them, and they stop in their tracks. No longer do they slash at my allies in the Pack.

To preserve my secrecy, and to weaken the morale of the remaining vampires, I say, "Play dead."

And they all lie down in blood-soaked grass, surrounded by the dead.

Still more are wounded, and I heal them, as well. I tell them to stop, and they do. But the Knights see no reason to stop fighting. They use this to their advantage and plunge silver blades into docile necks.

Any vampire who falls near the Knights is met with silver pellets, dribbled into their wounds to finish the deed.

And I don't scrape them free.

My conscience begs me to save them, but I have other matters to attend to. The Nether burns for blood, and this is war. So, I oblige, letting them die.

One of Nolan's knives hits a vampire just below the rooftop we stand upon, and I force the Nether from the house into him. Another whispered command takes him out of the fight. He sits down upon a woodpile and watches the battle go on without him.

I smell his fury, hot as molten iron, and it brings a twisted smile to my face.

Chapter 41
Elias

Too many hearts beat against my ear drums, filling my head with chaos. All around me, blades clash against armor. I jump to the side, desperate to avoid the sword of a furious vampire. Behind her helm, vicious eyes glitter with malice. Released from the morals of Tivoli, the Nether rules her. Simen has no such integrity, so he places no restraints upon the Coven.

If anything, he probably commanded violence…

My thoughts sour, and my bitterness gets the best of me. Shining silver flashes just before my face, nearly crashing into my helmet. Luck alone spares my life.

Even Ness couldn't heal something like that.

Decapitated by a silver weapon… I'd be done.

Jealousy riots within me at the thought of her, throwing far more ferocity behind my next swing of the sword than I otherwise would have mustered. The blade sings through the air, coming down on my assailant's shoulder. It cuts right through her leather armor, finding its way into her collarbone, and she screams in agony.

For a moment, I shudder at the sound, hating that I've caused her pain, that I may have killed her. My blood runs cold as she stares into my eyes and drops her sword. Blood gushes from the wound.

She falls, and my sword pulls free of her body with a terrible sucking sound. Horror shivers in my bones, and I stare down at her, watching the pool of blood spread beneath her. It pours out faster than the ground can absorb it. Resting atop the scuffed-up dirt, it shines in the light of the torches.

But the sound of metal on metal just beside me calls my focus away from her, just as a surge of Nether begins to stitch her back together. She seizes her opportunity.

Sitting upright, she slashes at the back of my knee with a dagger, slipping the blade between armor pieces that don't quite fit me. Pain slices through me, and I scream out. The earth rushes up to meet me, just as Ness immobilizes the vampire.

Staring at my leg in horror, I watch my own blood drip onto clovers and moss. My flesh sizzles where the silver cut me, and the scent of cedar and sap fills the air around me, filling me with dread.

I shouldn't be able to smell that so strongly. It should be stuck inside my body.

I try desperately to move my leg, but it flops, uselessly, sending shockwaves through me. Panic trickles in, and beads of sweat drip down my spine. Looking around, I watch the battle go on around me and pray to anyone that might listen. I beg them not to let the others notice me, laying here, defenseless.

Acutely aware of the danger of my situation, I try to drag myself away from the battle. My leg catches on the arm of the vampire I just fought with, pulling at the gaping wound. I shudder with the pain of it, sick to my stomach and hoping to faint, just to escape it for a second.

But Ness ignores Nissa's warnings not to waste her energy on us. I feel the Nether seeping into me, feel the burn of it as it courses through my veins.

Will my ties to her be strengthened, or am I as bound to her as I can get?

Which would be worse?

I feel the tendon pull itself back up, reattaching inside my knee, feel the knick in the bone filling in. Gritting my teeth, I try to bear it with some sort of grace, just in case she's watching. A glance at the rooftop I know she stands upon reveals her shadowed form, but I can't tell if she looks at me.

Could she possibly recognize me, dressed in full armor? Would it make a difference to her if she knew it was me?

I groan as the muscle tissue begins to knit itself together, pulling and stretching, flooding me with pure, unadulterated agony. I remember watching Ness in the stream as her leg and arm did this very thing. I remember the way she gritted her teeth but barely made a sound.

How often did she endure something like this to learn that kind of control?

Clamping my lips shut, I hold back the whimper that tries to crawl free as the skin reattaches itself. Fire runs through my veins, but the bleeding stops.

Just in time for what used to be a raccoon to turn on me. Dried blood encrusts the exposed bone around its eyes and mats the fur around its neck. A hiss becomes a cry for mercy, and it lunges at me.

Jerking my arm up reflexively, I slash at the poor creature. Dark blood rains down over me, but by the time the animal hits me square on the chest, its soul rests. Again, luck spares me. The unfortunate beast's neck gapes open.

Laying it gently on the ground beside me, I clamor to my feet. My heart rattles unsteadily in my chest, and I stare out at the battle before me.

If only running were an option…

I could turn and run all the way to Everson. I could forget any of this happened and live a mostly normal life. Maybe I could meet a girl that didn't love someone else, maybe we could live happily together, and maybe she wouldn't care that I'm a damn coward…

But the Pack is here, and the Nether in my veins burns me for even thinking of deserting them when they need me.

My hand tightens on my sword, turning my knuckles white. Swallowing back the panic that wants so badly to overtake me, I step forward. The mossy layer beneath the clovers is spongy and soaked with blood. It clings to my boot, begging me to stay here on the edge of the fight, where maybe I won't get hurt, again.

A vampire clad in sturdy armor, black metal gleaming red in the torchlight, slices through the neck of a Knight. Without missing a beat, he turns, and his gaze fixes on me.

I no longer need to trudge toward the battle. The vampire charges me, shield up and sword at the ready.

Just get in one hit.

Ness will take it from there.

I duck and pivot, turning what likely would have been a devastating hit into a glancing blow. But even that has enough force behind it to bash my helm back against my face as the front piece bends inward. Blood drips down my cheek, and panic, all too familiar, stirs my nerves into a frenzy.

Carried by momentum, the massive vampire runs past me, skidding to a stop after only a few steps.

Just one hit.

That's all.

Just one.

Before he can turn, I raise my sword high. Knowing it will never cleave through the armor, I bring the pommel down hard on the top of the vampire's helmet. The strength I gained mere days ago caves the helmet in, making me wonder if perhaps I could have cut through the metal, after all.

But it doesn't matter, now. The vampire falls to his knees. Ness takes him, and he sits on his haunches before me, docile despite clenched fists.

I turn to face the ongoing battle, watching as more and more people fall, some dead, some taken over.

Everywhere, heartbeats assail my ears. And again, the moss sucks at my boots, trying to hold me back.

But…

How long can I count on luck and other people to tidy up my messes?

How many times can I jump into something without expecting consequences?

Arrows fly through the night, usually hitting their marks, sometimes sinking into the ground. People cry out, and a house burns. The smoke drifting into the air smells far too much like Ness, and it pulls a lump into my throat, even as it makes my eyes water.

I jumped into the Pack for her, just like I've jumped into everything else in my life. Just like I jumped into this whole trip, storming away from Everson without a thought. Gods, when Ness didn't want me… I went for Alina…

But now, with this… I can't just change my mind and jump into something else. I'm in the Pack. This can't be undone. It can't be cleaned up.

Taking a deep breath, I shove aside my fickle, impulsive nature. The weight of what I've done settles on my shoulders for the first time. Hands trembling, stomach heavy with panic, I walk toward the battle.

This is it.

This is my life, now.

Chapter 42
Ness

Down below, a bear charges, headlong, through the crowd. It tosses bodies aside to the tune of muffled growls. More wolves and two mountain lions spring free of the forest, giving me no time to bind their mouths.

The bear meets its end as an arrow pierces its skull, and momentum carries its body forward. The massive beast slams into the house that Nolan and I stand upon, collapsing one of the walls. The roof caves beneath us, and we drop. My stomach lodges itself firmly in my throat, and a small scream of shock claws its way out.

Landing atop a pile of rubble in the kitchen, my armor does little to absorb the force. The air rushes out of me in a great burst, and my chest implodes.

Beyond these walls, chaos reigns supreme, barely visible over the corpse of the bear and the mangled remains of the kitchen wall. The sound of teeth clamping onto armor rings through the air, and screams pierce the night.

Taking a deep breath, coughing with the effort, Nolan asks, "Are yeh okay?"

I nod, giving my lungs a second longer to recover before I try to speak.

On his feet in a second despite the fall, Nolan offers me a hand and pulls me up. We turn to face the battle just in time to watch a hawk with the flesh carved from around its eyes swoop down to claw at the exposed eyes of a Knight. Talons like razors make quick work of the man's face.

I twist my hands and snap its neck as it flies away. The Knight presses his hands to his bleeding eye sockets, screaming in pain even as the massive bird plummets. The dead bird plows into a torch, knocking it over.

Heartbeats hammer in my ears as I watch the flames spread, first to a lumber pile, then up the side of a house. My own heart speeds up, mesmerized by the fire. A momentary impulse begs me to spread it, to snap my fingers and set the whole town ablaze.

But I know by now, that's just the Nether talking.

Impulse forces me to push Nether into the Knight, but I regret it instantly. His chance at the Etherrealm disappears as I watch his body knit itself back together. Nolan and I attempt to climb out of the rubble and find the vampire and the woodpile crushed beneath a portion of the wall. His own silver sword protrudes from his chest.

Pity wells within me, but I push it away.

He would have killed me in an instant, given the chance. Don't mourn this death.

But I know I will.

My foot slips on bloody planks, but Nolan grabs my waist to steady me. I gaze back at him. The light of the burning house grants me the beauty of his eyes.

Though they're narrowed with concentration, a smile tugs at them.

"Graceful as ev'r," he teases, helping me climb atop the remnants of the wall.

But the crunch of bone pulls my attention away, and I jerk my head toward the chaos. Not fifteen feet from us, a mangled mountain lion stands atop a fallen werewolf. Her gaping maw wraps around the skull of her victim, and she gives one more crunch before looking up at us. I try desperately to figure out who it is, but the mountain lion steps forward, blocking the gory body from my sight.

Seemingly infuriated by the pain coursing through her, she stalks me, growling all the while. Behind her, a vampire pours silver pellets into the gaping skull in a surprising act of mercy.

All around, swords meet flesh. Fire crackles loudly as the neighboring house succumbs to the flame, casting wild shadows all about.

But the mountain lion spares no backward glances.

In a second, she lunges, clearing the remaining distance in a single bound. I duck and drive my nails up into her dirty chest. Her blood, thick and black, gushes as she flies over me. Rising, I thrust her upward, and toss her off into the remnants of this crumbled house. Grasping my hands before me, I twist them, and her neck snaps.

And then, Nolan and I join the fray. We charge ahead, ripping into the broken bodies of the Howlers. With a single motion, I sweep the birds from the sky and slam them into the ground hard enough to shatter their fragile skulls.

My heart cries out, in joy and in sickness. My blood runs hot and cold, simultaneously. The Nether burns, just beneath the skin, begging for more death, whether it be for mercy or for pleasure.

Driving my hands downward, I push the remaining mountain lion to the earth, stopping it in its tracks before it can claim another victim or suffer another step. One swift motion breaks its neck, and its soul finds the peace it needs.

A dying wolf jumps at Nolan, and my heart stops. The world slows around me as the beast soars through the air. Grey eyes shine behind bloody bone, and bits of flesh hang loose around its mouth. Sharp teeth shine in the firelight.

But Nolan's sword finds its neck easily, just before the wolf slams into him. He pivots to let it fly past, pulling his sword free in the process.

One by one, we put the poor creatures out of their misery, cutting a path to the outer edge of the fight. Any time a pool of fermented blood catches my attention, I trace it back to its owner. Nolan stands guard, fending off any who come near as I heal the vampires and take control of them.

But we're exposed.

And the Coven is getting wise to my tricks.

The firelight, burning brighter now than ever, glints off my horns. Eyes turn my way. A few vampires try to retreat, falling back into the forest, realizing that their odds were never as high as they thought.

Not with me here.

I smell the fear on them as they look around and see the tides have turned. Where they once outnumbered us, we now hold the upper hand.

But I cut off their escape, binding their feet with a twirl of my finger. They collapse, midstride, tumbling to the ground. The Nether in my bones riots gleefully. My hands curl into claws, aching to rip them to shreds.

But Nolan and I fall back, seeking cover.

Stepping back into the shadows beside a cabin, I intend to find a way up onto the roof, but I never get the chance.

A voice reaches out from the darkness, chilling my bones.

"Hello, Uncle."

I spin on my heel, hands raising to bind Simen.

But I'm too slow.

My eyes find them just in time to watch Simen's dagger slide between Nolan's helmet and chest piece.

"NOOO!" I scream.

Sandalwood overrules the stench of vodka as Nolan's blood pours out of him. He gasps before me and collapses.

No, no, no, no, no!

This can't be it. He said he wasn't going to die, today. He can't!

Tears stream over my face, and I kneel beside him. With my heart in my throat, I remove Nolan's helmet.

Unruly hair clings to his forehead, matted down by sweat. His eyes are wild, and his brows furrow with pain. The blood gushing from his neck sizzles and pops against the silver blade.

Grabbing the dagger, I ignore the burning in my palms and pull it free. Nolan gasps as it leaves his flesh, and I toss it away.

"Don't… let…" he chokes, voice far too small.

"Don't talk. It's okay, I'm here. I'll fix this," I promise him, already pulling Nether into my body.

I have to fix this.

I can't lose him.

I can't.

My life without him plays out before me, bleak and meaningless. So, I pull Nether from the dirt and from the cabin beside us. I pull it from the grass and the clovers and the moss.

Nolan shakes his head, wincing at the pain. "No. Get him." But his neck isn't healing as it should.

"Please, Ness—" A coughing fit interrupts his words. "He can't get away. This…"

Nolan clears his throat, but it does little good. Sweat glistens on his forehead, and the stars shine in his dark eyes.

"This has to end, now… Stop him."

With tears pouring over my cheeks, I nod.

If he won't let me help him until I finish this, then I'll just have to finish it quickly.

I look around for the vile thing that did this and find Simen standing in the shadows near the corner of the cabin, watching Nolan bleed.

The smug bastard. Stupid little fool…

I rise to my feet, and he realizes his mistake. But he isn't quick enough.

Rushing forward, I grab Simen by his armor before he manages four steps. I lift him into the air, crumpling the steel in my grasp.

The Netherrealm rampages through me. My heart gallops, and my jaw locks. Every muscle in my body begs me for revenge.

With every ounce of strength I possess, I slam Simen into the wall of the cabin. The wood splinters on impact. A menacing grin splits my face, and I throw him against the wall. It crumbles, and he flies into the cabin. Landing with a great thud, he coughs, desperate for air.

Reaching out a hand, I call his dagger to me. It lands in my palm easily, burning my flesh, but I don't care.

Stepping over the few bits of wall that remain, I saunter through the cabin, watching as Simen turns onto his side, struggling to catch a breath.

But my breath comes fast, filling my nose with the smell of something spoiled.

Fear.

It pours off him, and the demon in me delights in it. Simen raises up onto hands and knees, coughing and spluttering.

Golden eyes glittering with a smile, I shove one hand downward, forcing Simen onto his stomach. Standing over him, I turn him over with the flick of my hand. The sight of him with his dagger in Nolan's neck flashes before my eyes, and the world goes red. He smiled as he did it, but he isn't smiling, now.

"This might tickle," I say, grinning.

With one hand pinning him down, I suck the Nether from him. Closing my eyes, I feel it ripping away from him. It pulls free of every muscle, deserts every drop of blood.

Again, I see him leering at Nolan as he bled on the ground.

I pull the Nether from Simen's skin, from his bones.

Pale blues eyes scrunch tight with pain, and I kneel. A simple hand motion and his helmet flies away. It lands with a clank, somewhere in the cabin.

His face sinks, skin stretching tight over bone as I rip the Nether from him. My heart beats faster. He tries to scream, but even his voice has deserted him. It comes out no louder than a whisper.

I place the dagger beside me and grab the chest plate of his armor. Ripping it as easily as paper, I peel it open. My hands tremble as I pick up the dagger and drive it into his chest.

He gasps and coughs. Blood trickles from his lips.

"I told Alaric how dangerous it was to underestimate me. You really should've listened."

Soft moonlight reaches in through the windows, and I watch as the life leaves his eyes.

Then, I rise, leaving him there with his dagger in his chest. My feet propel me out of the cabin, leaping over the low planks which used to be a wall. I sprint to Nolan's side and fall to my knees.

Gathering him up in my arms, I lean over him.

"Hello, love," he whispers.

My heart cries out in relief.

I'm not too late…

Chapter 43
Nolan

Ness casts her helmet aside and leans over me. Tears stream down her cheeks, dripping onto my face. I try not to jerk away from them, but reflex makes me flinch, pulling at my neck. Bursts of agony rock my body.

Sniffling, she says, "I'll fix this… I can't lose you."

"Ness, dinna do it," I say, thankful that the battle seems to be dying out. The clashing of swords and the blood-curdling howls have mostly subsided, offering my voice less competition.

"What?" she asks, confused. "But I can help you. Nolan, I *can't* lose you," she says, her voice growing in intensity.

My throat constricts, touched by the ferocity of her words. She touches my cheek, and I nestle into it, craving the warmth she offers.

"Relax, love. I've no intention o' dyin' today. Yeh got the silver out fast enough. I'll be fine. But please, dinna heal me, okay? I dinna want the Nether bindin' me tongue." I clear my throat, and say, "I want to be able to fight wit' yeh."

Ness chokes out a small laugh, and my heart leaps. Patting the grass beside me, I push words through my still-broken throat. "Come, love, lay wit' me, fer a moment. They can handle the last bit o' the fight wit'out us."

Words I never would have said before. Just a few months ago, I would have ached to rejoin the fight. I would have dragged my bloody body back into battle, no matter how much it hurt.

But now?

For her sake, I'll gladly sit this part out.

Her shadowed form shifts as she glances in the direction of the waning battle. She lays one hand on the ground. I feel the earth beneath me warm as she dispatches the Nether she gathered to heal me before stretching out next to me. Despite the armor barrier between us, a million glowflies burst to life in my stomach as she slides her hand onto my chest.

Groaning through the pain, I roll to face her. Even if the light here is only strong enough for silhouettes, I want to see her. She pleads with me not to over-exert, but I've waited far too long to lay next to her again to let a stab wound stop me.

Nestling closer, I do all I can to ignore the spike of pain that spreads through my body with each movement. I take a deep breath and let the smell of her soothe me. Wood smoke drifts into me, easing the ache in my neck with soft little waves of pleasure.

"Nether take me…" I whisper as Ness nuzzles her nose against mine. "I've missed this, love."

Stop callin' her that, yeh idiot! Yer goin' to scare her away, again.

"I missed you, too," she breathes, and the darkness suddenly feels substantially warmer. Her hand smooths locks of hair back off my forehead, leaving trails of fire along my skin.

We lay there, for a moment, and I stare into her glowing golden eyes. A deep breath reminds me of my neck, now merely a dull ache. The wound is closing. Slowly. But it's healing.

Well, I guess slowly is a relative term, here... Slower than if Ness did it.

"Nolan..." she begins, bringing my silly musings to an abrupt halt. "I'm so sorry, for before. I should've said it. I should've told you, so many times, I just..."

Her voice breaks, and my heart freezes. Time stops. On bated breath, I wait, hoping so desperately that she means what I want her to mean.

"I just couldn't. Not because I didn't feel that way, but..." Her hand traces my jaw, building sweet tension within me. "Because I wasn't ready to admit how much you mean to me. How terrified I am of losing you."

Ness pauses, and it takes every ounce of my self-control not to beg her to say it. I wait, muscles tense, afraid to move.

"I..."

Ness' hand lifts to my cheek, and her thumb caresses my skin. My heart beats, once, twice. My lungs shudder in my chest, and a ragged breath parts my lips.

"I can say it, now. I hope it isn't too late, but... I love you, Nolan."

My heart expands until I fear it may break my ribs. A tear slides free of my eyes, and a smile plasters itself across my face. "It could never be too late," I whisper huskily before pressing my lips to hers.

She melts against me, and the world is right, again. My entire body responds as our mouths dance together. Her hand knots in my hair, and I moan against her lips.

Grasping her hip, I pull her against me, but the damn armor keeps me from really feeling her. A shuddering breath pulls in the scent of her, and I smile.

She loves me...

***

When my neck has healed enough for me to move with only a little pain, we rise from our patch of grass. Blood crusts my shirt beneath my armor, but it doesn't matter. It's merely an echo, a remnant of something long gone. The wound is closed, and now only a pink line stretches over my neck.

Ness' hand grips mine, and warmth radiates through me. I still feel her lips on mine as we walk into the torchlight.

One house yet burns. Ness does some insanely simple hand gesture, and the flames disappear. A smoking, charred husk remains, its jagged edges casting bizarre shadows over the rest of Tor.

Of everyone still standing, the only Coven members are the fifty or so that Ness removed from battle beyond the reach of the Knights. All other survivors are Knights and Pack members. I cast my gaze about the wreckage, lamenting the uselessness, the waste.

So many lives…

I can't even see them all well enough to know who we've lost.

Captain Weln approaches us, limping and cradling one arm to his chest. I tense at his approach, and so does Ness. Blood seeps out of his armor at his elbow, pouring the scent of citrus into the air, but the smoking husk of a home behind him nearly covers it.

He smiles, despite the obvious pain. "Thank you, Ness."

She jolts at his use of her name, her arm jerking mine ever so slightly.

I, however, breathe a sigh of relief.

He damned well bett'r thank her…

I'd been worried he'd shun her, at best.

Ness gestures to his arm, then says, "I can heal you if you'd like."

"No, no. That won't be necessary. There's still plenty more to do, and you'll need your strength." He takes a step forward, and the sweat which plasters his short brown hair to his scalp glistens in the light of the torches.

His face is amiable as he says, "Besides, I'd like to maintain my shot at the Etherrealm."

Weln carefully lowers his damaged left arm, wincing the whole time. Then, he extends his right hand to Ness.

She takes it, clearly uneasy, and my stomach ties itself into knots. Brows scrunching up with suspicion, I watch him, trying to discern his motives.

But he merely shakes her hand and says, "If ever a demi-demon were allowed into the Etherrealm, it would be you."

Ness gasps, and he releases her hand. She stares after him as he hobbles away, torchlight rippling across his armor, toward the remnants of his Knights.

I know he means it as a compliment, a show of respect, but his words burn me.

The Etherrealm doesna deserve her.

Chapter 44
Ness

Orwen and Nissa assemble the seriously injured Pack members before me, and I do what I must. Their healing takes no time and little effort.

As they take stock of who survived, I call out, singing softly and letting the low tones of the Netherrealm mingle with the higher sounds of a normal human voice. I'm not entirely sure she survived, but she's our best shot at restoring order within the Coven.

Light footsteps make their way across the blood-soaked moss, picking their way through the bodies via torchlight. She approaches, long dark hair loose and swishing against her black armor. Shadows play around her eyes, making them look far more menacing than they normally do.

Though, perhaps she looks this way, now. It's been years since I spent any time with the Coven... Maybe she's changed.

All I can do is hope she hasn't.

"Althea," I say.

She nods warily. Worry creases her brow and drips off her in thick drops like something spoiled as she awaits my command.

"The Coven falls to you, now."

Her jaw falls slack, and I wonder what she expected me to say.

"No one within the Coven witnessed more of the sacrifice necessary to maintain it than you. No one else understands, as you do, why those sacrifices are necessary. This," I say, gesturing to the bodies and blood on the ground, "*can't* happen, again. Lead them in such a way as to make your father proud."

I know the Nether I put in her veins tonight will hold her to my words and thus, Tivoli's will. This command takes a great deal of control from her, forcing her hand in so many decisions.

But with so many lives on the line…

It's all I can think to do to keep the Coven under control.

I'm certainly not fit to lead them, after all. I know nothing of what's happened within the Coven over the last decade.

She bows her head, and her eyes rake over me. A deep breath lifts her chest, and her armor glints in the firelight. Finally, she nods and says, "Okay. Thank you."

Another deep breath, perhaps a sigh of relief, lifts her chest.

What did she think I was going to do?

I don't ask.

Instead, I smile, dismissing her and the Coven to pick their fallen comrades from the mass of bodies. They'll all be buried according to Coven tradition, whether the Knights like it or not.

After all, they didn't want the Etherrealm's blessing or its customs. And we have no way to know how many of them were here simply because their new Coven Master told them to come, stoking the fires of their rage with his own.

They file away, lifting bodies from the moss, and I turn my attention to Tor. Nearby, the witches cast three spells to disperse the Ether from the dome.

Then, I do my part. It takes me no more than a gesture, and the Nether portion of the barrier becomes a cloud, dark and heavy. It hangs about town for a moment, and I stare at it, mesmerized by the way it sucks in the torchlight.

Then, I spread my fingers and push my hands down and out. The Nether redistributes itself throughout Tor, clamoring back to the fibers I ripped it from.

A few of the Knights linger, and the people of Tor flock to them. But they shrug the townspeople off with lame lines of, "It's our duty," and, "All in a day's work."

Those mortals who knew the Pack rush in with smiles spread wide, doling out hugs. Their reception is far warmer, and within their ranks, laughter and joy abound.

The contrast is… striking.

Seeing them side by side and so very different… It draws my brows together. A long-forgotten memory of Kirk dredges itself up from the depths, and I watch him push away the drawing I'd done of us together.

My tiny hands try to lift it toward him, once more, and he snatches it from my grasp. Pacing across the floor of our tiny cabin, one we stayed in no more than two years, he crumples my drawing and tosses it into the fireplace.

My five-year-old heart shrivels within my chest, and I fall to the floor, crying over the doodle I dedicated the better part of an afternoon to.

"I'll not have my likeness captured next to the likes of you, even if it is unrecognizable."

He walks away, and I watch the way the flames lick the paper. The edges catch, and it curls in on itself, shrinking away from its own destruction. Not that it has far to go. It's already been smashed into a ball.

I pull myself inward, mimicking the little ball of paper. My horns disappear, as do my talons. The blackened skin becomes pale white, and gold eyes become blue.

I sit that way for a few minutes, sobbing silently, until he stomps back into the room. "No," he says, "Don't you hide what you are. Don't you dare." His voice rises in volume.

Shrinking from him, I force my horns back out.

"I just want to be normal…" I whisper.

"But you aren't," he spits, and the chill in his words resonates in my bones. "You aren't, and you never will be."

Arms wrap around me, pulling me from the memory. I blink away the past, vaguely wondering how long it's been since I drew anything, and find Nissa holding me tight against her. Tears streak down her rich brown skin, and she kisses my cheek.

Voice breaking now that our duty is done, she whispers, "I was so scared when you fell… I couldn't see where you ended up, or if any of them were near you. And there's no way I could've heard if they were doing the spell… I was just so worried. They had silver, and I'm sure they know the words, and…"

She hiccups through the sobs, and I put my arms around her, stunned. All this time, I never thought she'd care if something happened to me. Now, warmth flows out of her, seeping into me despite the armor between us.

The cold image of Kirk tossing my drawing into the fire flashes before my eyes, and I wonder how I ever thought he cared for me. Next to the warmth of Nissa's embrace, his cold stares and comments about what I am seem… cruel.

For a moment, I hear him calling my birthday the anniversary of his imprisonment, something I'd forgotten all about, and I have to wonder if maybe Nolan was right about him. I suppress a shudder and lean my head against Nissa's, cherishing the moment of comfort.

Over her shoulder, Elias approaches. She smells the cedar wafting toward us and pulls back. With both hands on the sides of my face, she says, "Please, don't be such a stranger anymore."

A lump in my throat keeps me from speaking, so I nod. The tiny movement shakes a tear free, and it slides down the scale of black to purple to white, before dripping off my jaw.

Warm brown eyes dart between mine, looking from one golden orb to the other before she releases me. She turns around, and I take in Elias' battered armor and the blood streaking it. The Nether scar on his neck, pulses with the newest addition of energy. He was certainly among the line-up of the wounded.

He tucks his helmet under his arm and looks back and forth between Nissa, Nolan, and I. Leaving no room for awkwardness, Nissa steps forward, taking charge easily. Her position as alpha has honed her ability to diffuse tension.

"Elias," she begins, grasping his hand. Her other hand cups his from underneath. "Orwen and I have discussed it, and we'll accompany you to Everson. We have some… reparations to make. Your mother deserves a proper explanation for what happened to your father, and it's long overdue. She needs to see his grave. She needs to know…"

Nissa's voice breaks, still recovering from the shocking moment with me, and she releases Elias' hand to wipe away a stray tear. "She needs to know he loved her. He never would have abandoned her. He wouldn't have abandoned you or your sister. Everett was a good man."

"Thank you," Elias says, voice thick with emotion. His eyes fall to the ground, and he nods, slowly.

I bow my head, trying desperately not to intrude.

"If your sister wants her wedding held at the Pack house, she's more than welcome. We'll tell her that when we see her, though. We'll need a few days to square things away here, but after that, we can go to Everson."

Elias nods, again, and Nissa bids us farewell, for the moment. She smiles softly at Nolan, whispering, "Thank you." She squeezes my shoulder gently, as she walks away, heading for Captain Weln. He waits for her, just on the edge of the torchlight. Orwen stands next to him, likely discussing burials and ways to move forward.

Elias kicks at the dirt, nervously. "Ness… I don't see you choosing me…"

My heart plummets. It slams into the ground, trying desperately to bury itself.

How could I have used him…

He doesn't meet my eyes. His chest rises with a deep breath, and shadows play around his eyes. But I don't need to see them to know his emotions. My nose is full of them. A little heartbreak, a lot of bitterness.

"I just…" He shakes his head. Finally, he meets my gaze, but only for a moment. His eyes dart to Nolan, and I worry that he may start something.

"It's for the best, though. If I had the choice, I'd have you to myself, but he gave you up… so *you* would be happy. Even though…" he trails off and runs a hand over his face. "Gods, the way it hurt him… I couldn't do it. Not if I had a choice."

Looking back to me, he says, "Goodbye, Ness." He glances at Nolan and whispers hoarsely, "Be good to her."

"Always," Nolan answers, deep voice quiet but firm.

I lift my eyes to Nolan's beautiful face as Elias walks away and say, "I should probably go with them to Everson. It's my fault Everett died… They should hear it from me." Sighing, I lean against him.

He tugs my chin up and stares into my eyes. "*Solvi* killed him," he says, smoothing my hair back. His fingers trace my horn, reminding me that I have yet to hide them. "Yeh tried to save him, love. His death is no' yer fault."

Dark, sultry eyes peer into mine, so genuine, so warm. Pulling me against him, he nuzzles his nose against mine. "Orwen an' Nissa can handle this, I promise. They can take Liam and Sari wit' if they need to. We dinna have to be involved in everything the Pack does."

The idea of living our lives, without constantly rushing off for official Pack business, fills me with hope.

"Besides, I've an idea far bett'r than goin' to Everson."

His lips brush mine, sweet and agonizingly slow. My lips part, and I breathe him in. Wrapping my hands in his hair, I try to hold myself in place, waiting for him to speak, again.

His eyes search mine, hesitant, and a droplet of anxiety falls from him, mingling with the luxurious scent of sandalwood.

When he finally speaks, his lips move over mine with his words. "Marry me?" he breathes.

My heart melts, filling me with glee and the ache of having hurt him. But I'm strong enough to answer him, this time.

"Yes," I whisper against his lips.

Nolan lets out a breath and relaxes against me. He crushes his mouth to mine, and we melt. His hands on the sides of my face pull me in deeper, and heat spreads through me. My spine tingles as his hand slides to the back of my neck, and his thumb caresses my ear lobe.

He pulls back, just far enough to gaze into my eyes, and the world falls away. Nothing beyond him exists.

He chuckles, filling me with music.

Epilogue
Ness

The last days of the glowflies' time in Rettland approach. Soon, they'll disperse. Having spent several months here, already, they feel the season changing.

Nolan stands before me, dressed in his finest clothes. Black trousers and a dark blue tunic cling to him, but his eyes hold my attention. They burn with excitement and love, stirring me to a fever pitch.

His mane of curls hangs loose about his face, and I want so badly to bury my hands in it. Dangling from his grasp, the red ribbon which bound our right hands together during the ceremony flutters.

But Liam and Sari have gone, now, as has the minister, a descendent of the man who married Nolan's parents.

Finally alone in the little grove of birch trees, with hundreds of glowflies floating through the trees above us and gentle waves lapping at the cliffside below us, Nolan lifts a hand to my neck. The ribbon tickles my chest, falling inside the neckline of my dark blue gown. It sends my heart fluttering, begging for his hands to rip the dress away and touch the places the ribbon grazes.

The intensity in his eyes pulls me in, and my hands find his waist, sliding beneath his tunic to touch tan skin and hard muscle. His heart skips a few beats in my ears, and I smile.

He lowers his lips to mine, grasping my hip with his free hand. I moan softly against his lips, and the kiss deepens. My skin burns for his touch, and my body aches to join with him.

I slide his shirt upward, relishing the feel of his body beneath my hands. The garment falls to the ground, forgotten in an instant. My lips find his neck, dropping delicate kisses from his jaw to his collarbone to his chest.

But his hands are moving, tugging my dress up and over my head. He tosses it aside, letting it fall where it may, and then his hands are on me.

My bare skin burns beneath his touch, and he nibbles softly at my ear. Nolan grasps my buttocks, pulling me against him. He kisses my neck, and my hand winds into his hair, desperate to keep his lips on my skin.

When it becomes too much, I unfasten his trousers and push them down. They fall to the ground, as eager to free him as I am, and he steps clear of them.

One of his hands traces my spine, sending delicate shivers through me and calling a deep moan from my lips. Lowering himself to his knees, Nolan kisses all the way down from my neck to my stomach, and raw electricity quivers through me.

He ties the red ribbon around my waist, an old Pack tradition calling on the Netherrealm for the blessing of fertility. The bow tickles my skin but is soon forgotten.

His lips find my stomach again, and he works his way lower. With his hands on my backside, his tongue dances over me, tasting all that I have to offer in this moment. My knees quickly weaken, and he pulls me down to kneel before him.

He sits back, and I settle atop his lap, taking him in. My body burns with the union. Nolan buries his face against my neck, and groans deeply, clutching my hips tightly. We move together, each desperate for more.

His teeth clamp down upon my shoulder, and I cry out with delight. A small growl slips past his lips, and he lays me back on soft moss. Thousands of glowflies twinkle above him, but I see only his magnificent, dark eyes.

My hand slides down his chest, over his stomach, dipping lower. Teasing, I stroke him and watch the ecstasy play across his face.

Nolan leans down to kiss me, stealing my breath away once more, and plunges inside me.

And the fever takes us.

Thank you!

For buying this book. For reading it all the way through. For being an awesome reader who reads.

If you liked it, please leave a review on Amazon, Goodreads, Barnes & Noble, your own blog... Anywhere, really. Reviews are the lifeblood of authors, helping books get noticed in the almighty eyes of search engine algorithms.

Other Books by this Author
Soul Bearer

The return of dragons? Slow burn romance? A part-Orc, underdog of a heroine? Yes, please.

Amazon: mybook.to/SoulBearerElexisBell

The Gem of Meruna

Oppression and a magical gem that can defeat a dictator? Slow burn romance? Yes, please.

Amazon: mybook.to/TheGemOfMeruna

Annabelle

Vigilante justice thriller set in a western? Weaponized parasol? Yes, please.

Amazon: mybook.to/AnnabelleElexisBell

World for the Broken

Slow burn romance in a dark, post-apocalyptic world? No holds barred, no punches pulled? Yes, please.

Amazon: mybook.to/WorldForTheBroken

About the Author

Elexis Bell is a quiet nerd with too many hobbies, including everything from gaming to shower-singing and even archery, weather permitting. She specializes in sarcasm and writing stories that make people feel. She's made a home for herself with her husband, their dog, and a small army of cats.

She writes dark, gritty stories, sprinkling gut-wrenching emotions over high fantasy romance, thrillers, post-apocalyptic romance, and science fiction.

For further information, follow her on Instagram, Twitter, or Facebook, or check out her blog on her website. There, you can sign up for her newsletter to stay up to date on all future book releases, giveaways, and on-going projects.

www.elexisbell.com